New Beginnings
in the
Little Irish
Village

BOOKS BY MICHELLE VERNAL

Michelle Vernal

New Beginnings
in the
Little Irish
Village

Bookouture

Published by Bookouture in 2023

An imprint of Storyfire Ltd.
Carmelite House
50 Victoria Embankment
London EC4Y 0DZ

www.bookouture.com

ISBN: 978-1-83790-393-1
eBook ISBN: 978-1-83790-392-4

For the best Mum and Dad-in-law a girl could wish for, Pam and Bob Vernal

TWO WEEKS UNTIL ST PATRICK'S DAY

May the Irish hills caress you.
May her lakes and rivers bless you.
May the luck of the Irish enfold you.
May the blessings of Saint Patrick behold you.
May there always be work for your hands to do.
May your purse always hold a coin or two.
May the sun always shine warm on your
    windowpane.
May a rainbow be certain to follow each rain.
May the hand of a friend always be near you.
And may God fill your heart with gladness to
    cheer you.

— IRISH BLESSING FOR ST
PATRICK'S DAY

1

Thirty-two-year-old Imogen Kelly confidently steered her little
red sports car around the winding Wild Atlantic Way coastal
road. She wasn't so confident about coming home to sleepy little
Emerald Bay, the village where she'd grown up, however. Well,
more to the point, Benmore House, where she was headed on
business. The big house was a grand spectacle from the roadside built to preside haughtily over the village and Emerald
Bay's fishing harbour, but by revisiting it, she knew she was
playing with fire. But as her mam, Nora Kelly, would lean over
the bar of the Shamrock Inn, the pub she ran with her husband,
Liam, and tell anyone who cared to listen: of her five daughters,
her second born had always pushed the boundaries.

Personally, Imogen preferred to think of herself as a typical
Libran who tested the limits. She might have the same chestnut
eyes and hair (although regular hair appointments had added
blonde and caramel highlights to the mix) as her mam, older
sister, Shannon, and middle sister, Hannah, but this character-
istic was behind her flair for design. She was an air sign and
wasn't frightened to try new things and embrace different
concepts. It had seen her enter the world of interior design and

begin running her own company. Imogen was proud of Imagine Interiors, and she'd built up a reputation amongst Dublin's affluential elite for inspirational and sympathetic design.

Of course, straddling the cusp of Scorpio meant she loved hard, and it was all well and good being passionate until your heart broke.

Imogen had always been a quick learner, resolving never to let her heart be shattered in two again. The best way to protect something so fragile was to construct a hard, shiny shell around it, and these days she kept a firm hold on the relationship reins too. Or, she had until Nevin Delaney had happened along.

She wished the daily horoscope she subscribed to would give her a clue about what would happen there. Nev was the first man to get under her skin since she'd left Emerald Bay for the bright lights and expensive home makeovers of Dublin and beyond. It wasn't sitting well going away like this after the heated exchange they'd had last night.

Imogen's fingers gripped the steering wheel. She'd sort things out between them later, she promised herself. For now, though, her mind turned to her sisters, who found her fascination with astrology amusing, but she was quick to point out they exhibited all the traits typical to their signs too.

Take Ava and Grace, for instance. They were the youngest of the Kelly girls, twins born in May under what else? Gemini. The symbol of twins. If that wasn't fortuitous, Imogen didn't know what was. They shared the star sign with their mam, and the trio were typical Geminis in so much as they could talk to a brick wall if there was no one else on hand, humour was used as a crutch and, annoyingly, they thought they knew a little about everything – or, in their mam's case, a lot. The three of them were apt to be spontaneous too, and frustratingly, or adorably, erratic, whichever way you wanted to look at it.

Shannon was a Virgo who was practical and diligent. Her

big sister always wanted to help others, which suited her role as the Galway region's public health nurse.

Hannah, the Aquarius in their family, was a humanitarian on a crusade to save the bees and feed the world. This was the latest in a long line of drives because their middle sister was on a quest to make the world better.

As for their dad, Liam, and nan, Kitty, who were both born in March, they were Aries. Their symbol was the ram, and sure, weren't the pair of them forever butting heads against things? Not literally, of course, but a more determined mammy and son you'd be lucky to meet. And as for a filter when it came to sharing what was on their mind – it was non-existent. Yes, definite Aries, the pair of them.

Imogen's fingers loosened their grip on the steering wheel, enjoying the catchy beat of Justin Bieber and Ariana Grande filling the coupe. That Imogen was a closet Belieber was a secret only her sisters were privy to. Nev hadn't a clue that when she was alone in her car, she liked nothing better than to sing her heart out to Ariana's part in her duet with Justin. His playlist brought home the twenty-seven-year age gap between them. It wasn't something she gave much thought to, believing age was just a number, until he began humming along to songs her mam and dad listened to. That, in turn, would lead her to dwell on what her parents would have to say when they finally met Nev. Lately, he'd been pressing for an invitation to do just that. It was what they'd fought about last night, as well as how his daughters seemed determined to drive a wedge between them. The fact she was only a few years older than them had not been well received.

The top was up on her car today, thanks to the chilly early spring wind blowing off the Atlantic, and Imogen glanced at the ocean on her right-hand side, seeing frothy white tops riding in to shore. She shivered, knowing how cold that water would be and suddenly longed for the balmy weather of her recent

Mustique getaway with Nev and the bliss of being stretched out on a sun lounger poolside, her phone switched off and a cocktail in hand.

Sometimes Imogen felt like she'd been born in the wrong country because she was much more at home in warmer climes – give her a maxi dress and sandals over woollies and jeans any day.

She eyed her brown wrists peeking out from under the cuffs of her classic silk blouse. The colour was proof of a holiday that was becoming a distant memory, but in an ode to it, she'd topped up the honeyed colour she'd come home with by religiously applying self-tanner each morning.

Mustique had been a much-needed break. A romantic reset for her and Nev away from the stresses and strains of his obnoxious offspring. He had three daughters she'd nicknamed Deb the Diva, Smelly Bella (short for Isobel, and she didn't smell, but it was all Imogen had been able to come up with) and Needy Noelle.

In Imogen's opinion, the sisters were all muddling into their twenties, therefore grown-ups who shouldn't be as demanding of their father's attention as they were. She'd swear they took turns ringing Nev when they knew he was out with her to screech their latest dramas down the phone. Dramas only Nev could sort. The role of evil stepmother in waiting for three grown-up young women wasn't what she'd signed up for.

She shook thoughts of the gruesome threesome away.

'Focus on things you're grateful for, like Shannon does with that journal of hers,' she murmured out loud.

The idea of committing her thoughts to paper when the varnish of life in Dublin was losing its lustre had proved a nifty trick because there was always something, no matter how small, to be grateful for. She'd had to scrape the barrel once or twice, like the time her gratitude log consisted of one entry: the pretty colour painted on her toenails. But, still and all, it had to count for something.

The first thing that sprang to mind today was the near miss with the coffee drip on the bottom of her cup when she'd stopped at her favourite organic cafe in Athlone for a smoothie bowl. Silk marked, so it was a blessing she had spotted this before it dripped on her blouse. She'd dabbed it dry with a serviette.

The blouse, tailored trousers and too-high pumps she was dressed in weren't a random choice on her part. On the contrary, they'd been carefully chosen for today's appointment at Benmore House. Imogen's edge over her competitors was her chameleon-like ability to present herself in a way that made potential clients confident she understood what they wanted and that she understood them. Say, for instance, their house was Georgian with classic features, or a grand dwelling that harked back to days of old, like Benmore House; then she'd opt for a classic, timeless look as she'd done today. On the flip side, if she were pitching for an edgy apartment filled with modern art, her fitted leather jacket, ripped jeans, rock 'n' roll band logo T-shirt and chunky boots would get an airing. Oh, and she'd go for mussed hair, the polar opposite of the sleek bun she was currently sporting.

A rabbit was bounding off the roadside. It disappeared into the waving golden-brown grasses. Signs of spring were everywhere. Imogen had seen an abundance of fat pink and white blossoms driving through some of the smaller towns. They were a little early, thanks to the last month being mild. So, too, were the tiny lambs gambolling about on spindly legs in the fields she'd not long passed.

Imogen frowned, peering into the distance. Something was moving across the road up ahead. Ducks! She slowed her speed instinctively, checking her rear-view mirror as the mantra their dad had drummed into them when they first learned to drive played like a tape recording in her head: 'It's them or us. Never stop suddenly unless you've checked the road is clear behind.'

The stretch of curving road was empty behind her and, satisfied it was safe to do so, she pulled onto the verge and came to a stop, giving the ducks right of way.

It was a veritable duck family outing, she thought, sitting up tall in her bucket seat to peer over the dashboard. She smiled, watching mammy duck bustling her downy yellow entourage of one, two, three, four, five, six fluffy babies along. Daddy duck, marked by his green-and-blue plumage, was bringing up the rear. They were in no hurry either, stopping halfway to admire the view and for Mammy to admonish one of her babies, who was cheeping back at her.

Imogen checked her phone in the hands-free holder, knowing she was pushing it to arrive at Benmore House at the arranged time. She was still a half an hour or so away and expected in a quarter of an hour. The roadworks outside Athlone were responsible for her tardiness. Day-tripping ducks, she didn't need.

'Come on, come on,' she muttered, her jaw clenching impatiently.

On cue, the family stopped to admire the view. By the time they moseyed off the road and into the blanket bog beyond, Imogen was grinding her teeth. She hated being late.

She'd just turned the key in the ignition to fire the engine up when she saw a splash of yellow on the rocky outcrop that led down to the beach from whence the ducks had come. A lone duckling was straggling out onto the road, and her heart sank as she angled her neck to see whether its family had noticed they were one short, but no, they were waddling on their merry way, cross-country. She turned the engine off, her conscience unwilling to leave it to fend for itself, and with a sigh, got out of her car.

A salty breeze cut through her, and, at that moment, a blue Hilux rounded the bend hurtling straight for the duckling.

Imogen forgot all about her dad's dire warning of 'us or them' as she stepped out into the middle of the road, waving her arms frantically at the vehicle to stop.

2

'What do you think you're doing?' A scruffy fella wearing a cap leaned out the window of the Hilux and bellowed a few yards from where Imogen was standing. He was clearly rattled.

He wasn't the only one. Christ on a bike, was that Bon Jovi blaring from that workhorse he was driving?

'The baby duck,' Imogen said, pointing to where the chick was cheeping around her feet. Her legs were shaking, and her heart was pounding, but she refused to show this heathen how shaken she was by the screech of brakes. 'You would have hit it if I hadn't stopped you.'

'For feck's sake,' he spluttered. 'I nearly hit you!' He took off the baseball-style cap and angrily ran his fingers through dark hair that sat a tad too long on his collar.

'No, you didn't. Sure, lookit,' Imogen said, ignoring the smell of burning rubber as she added, 'You're miles away, and if you weren't speeding, you wouldn't have had to brake so hard.'

'I was driving at the speed limit, for your information, but I didn't expect to see some mad woman dressed to the nines doing the fecking Macarena in the middle of the road when I came round the corner.'

Imogen was regaining her equilibrium and had no intention of arguing the toss with this Jon Bon Jovi wannabe. 'Well, don't just sit there reliving the eighties. Help me get the poor little thing off the road. Its family's over there.' She waved her hand in the direction of the field but made no move to scoop up the chick.

'Pick it up. It's a duckling, not a ferret. It won't bite,' he shouted over the top of his engine.

'I'm not frightened of it, but you can't just go round picking up baby ducklings.'

'Why not?'

'I don't know. I just know it's wrong. Have you a box or something I could scoop it into?'

'Listen, I'm running late here. Couldn't you give it a gentle nudge in the right direction?'

Imogen fixed him with her haughtiest glare. 'This is life and death we're talking about here, and I will not kick the baby duck off the road so you can get to wherever it is you're going.'

'You're not going to get out of the way, are you?'

'No. Not until this little one is safe and sound.' Imogen would not have it on her conscience that she'd left a tiny defenceless chick to take its chances on the open road. Not when there were eejits like your man about. She was gratified when he ducked his head back inside his vehicle before reversing a few metres and nosing the Hilux in behind her coupe.

The big blue beast dwarfed her poor little red car, and she'd have said your man there was suffering from the small man's disease were it not for two things. One, her dad, a big burly fella himself, drove a similar vehicle. And two, as he got out slamming the door shut behind him, she could see he was topping six foot.

She watched as he went around the flatbed and lifted the canvas cover to produce a cardboard box.

'Perfect,' Imogen said, pleased that they'd soon be going their separate ways.

He pulled a wad of sandpaper from it, tossing it through the driver's window onto the seat.

Imogen held her hand out for the empty box, and he passed it to her. She looked at him properly then and, surprised, saw recognition flitter across his face. However, she didn't know why she was surprised. You were only ever a few dozen steps away from someone you knew in this part of the country. Nevertheless, she raised an eyebrow and asked, 'Do I know you?'

'Imogen Kelly, right? Your mam and dad run the Shamrock Inn in Emerald Bay. I didn't recognise you with your hair pulled back like so.'

'That's me.' She studied his face closely before her eyes travelled down his flannel shirt and battered jeans. On his feet were a well-worn pair of work boots. He needed a shave, too, she thought as her gaze returned to his face. There was something familiar about him, all right. He grinned, and the penny dropped as a cheeky glint lit eyes as dark as his hair.

'Ryan O'Malley,' she announced, triumphant at having placed him. 'The bra-strap pinger!'

'For the record, it wasn't me who pinged your strap. I've four sisters who'd have murdered me if I got about the place doing that. It was Declan Horan who did the pinging.'

Imogen narrowed her eyes. 'But I saw you.'

'And Declan, right? Think about it.'

She thought hard, trying to conjure up the long-ago school playground scenes. When she did, she realised he was right. Declan had been standing next to Ryan on all the pinging occasions, but he was such a goody two shoes – unlike Ryan, who was always getting in trouble – so she'd just assumed Ryan was the culprit.

'You whirled around and bopped me on the nose, ruining my tough guy image.'

Imogen's voice bubbled despite herself. 'Ah well, serves you right for getting about with a gombeen like Declan in the first place. He'd never get away with that sort of carry-on these days. Do you still see him?'

'No, he moved to Galway.'

'And you're still here in Emerald Bay.'

'It's my home.' There was a touch of defensiveness in his tone.

Imogen shook her head. There were plenty of reasons to leave Emerald Bay, but she'd not be getting into those, not with the chirping reminding her she'd a rescue mission to complete.

'Listen, you don't happen to have a piece of bread in there, do you?' She nodded in the direction of his truck.

'I've my tomato sandwiches.' He looked at her suspiciously. 'Are you hungry? Because I'm warning you now, they're prone to going soggy.'

'No, not for me! If you can spare a piece of crust, I'll put it in the box, and the wee babby here should hop in of its own accord.'

Ryan shook his head, and she heard growls of, 'I don't fecking well believe this,' as he walked back to his vehicle and returned with a torn piece of crust after a few seconds. 'That do you?'

'Grand.' Imogen dropped the crust into the box and squatted down, balancing on the heels of her Gianvito Rossi pumps. Then, tipping the box on one side so the open end was in front of the duckling, she began making kissy noises between crooning, 'Come on now, you're safe with me.'

The little bird cheeped and obligingly hopped inside the box. Imogen gently righted it, smiling as it attacked the bread.

'Thanks a million for your help,' she said, dismissing Ryan. Then, carrying the box carefully over to the field, she stepped off the tar seal onto the wet, uneven earth, hoping the hems of her trousers wouldn't get dirty. A split second later, it was more than the hem of her pants she was worried about as she swayed precariously forward. Her back heel had become lodged in the damp soil. It was touch and go as to whether she'd stay upright, with gravity making a determined effort to win. But Imogen was equally determined and managed to steady herself without dropping the box.

She hoped Ryan hadn't witnessed her undignified display. He shouldn't have, because there was no reason for him to hang about any longer, and he'd said he had somewhere to be. A moment later the snort of laughter behind her saw her twist around.

'It's not funny.'

'Sure, if the shoe were on the other foot, you'd be laughing. No pun intended.'

'Ha bloody ha.' He was right though, she'd have been sniggering with the best of them had the situation been reversed. She freed her foot and took a tentative step, but this time both shoes sank, pinning her to the spot.

'Here,' Ryan said, appearing alongside her. 'Give the box to me.'

She handed it over and, unable to go anywhere, stood watching him stride across the uneven turf until he stopped and crouched down. He stood again and held the empty box out for her to see. She gave him a thumbs up as he closed the distance between them.

'Here,' he said gruffly, 'take my arm.'

Realising she had little choice unless she wanted to remain here like a human scarecrow, Imogen gripped his forearm tightly until she'd managed to pull herself free.

'I don't know why you'd want to be wearing the likes of those shoes in rural Ireland in the first place,' Ryan said, shaking his hair, which needed a cut.

Imogen took umbrage at his sanctimonious tone. It was on the tip of her tongue to tell him that the black heels, now coated in mud, happened to be a favourite of the Princess of Wales, so he could stick that in his pipe and smoke it. Instead, she sniffed and said, 'We're not all corduroy trousers and welly boots girls. Some of us happen to like fashion.'

His smirk only irritated her more, and she quickly released his arm, stepping back onto solid ground again.

'Well, I'm off. You're not the only one with somewhere to be.' And with that, she stalked back to her car, revving the engine and leaving him standing in a cloud of exhaust fumes.

3

Benmore House was in Imogen's line of sight now, rearing up from the hilltop on which it was perched to serve as an Anglo-Irish monument to the past. Over to her right, the waters of Emerald Bay harbour glittered a deep, mysterious green befitting its name. The bobbing array of red and blue fishing boats made a pretty montage, and overhead seagulls circled, squawking their indignance at the catch being unloaded from the Egans' boat not being shared with them.

Imogen raised a hand and waved in the fishermen's direction, not bothering to see if it was returned as she began to slow for the turn-off to Benmore. She had no argument with Rory, the father to the three Egan lads, the youngest of whom was Shane. It was him and his brothers she'd no time for. Not after the way they'd banded together in mutual surliness toward the Kelly family after Ava broke things off with Shane.

She could be as fierce as the next person when it came to her family, but petty was the word that sprang to mind over their behaviour.

It was a word she associated with village life in general. As far as she was concerned, Ava had made the right decision when she'd broken things off with that fishy-arse eejit to spread her wings with a move to London. It would have been heart-breaking to see her bright, beautiful sister shackled to Emerald Bay with a heathen like Shane before she'd seen anything of the world outside their village.

The coupe's wheels spun on the gravel as she veered off the main stretch of road, following the sweeping driveway to the house. That would give the Brothers Egan something to gossip about, she thought, imagining them trying to figure out what snooty Imogen – as she knew they thought of her – was up to, visiting the big house. What they didn't know, what nobody in Emerald Bay knew, was that she wasn't a stranger to Benmore.

One long-ago summer, a new world had opened its door to her here. And then, just as she was about to step through it, the door had slammed shut in her face.

As she pulled to a halt and wrenched the handbrake up, the radio announcer interrupted the music with a time check that told her she was thirty minutes late for her appointment with Sigrid Leslie. Her shoes were muddied, and her sleek updo had begun to break free. She cursed the stiff breeze blowing in off the sea as she'd rescued the baby duck. This was not how she'd visualised her return to Benmore House, but she'd have to do.

The well-tended lawns stretched wide on either side of the drive, offering a panoramic view of the bay, the colourful village and the surrounding brown, gold and green countryside.

Imogen knew that tucked away behind Benmore, a warm pile of brown stones built sometime in the nineteenth century, was a carefully clipped garden with secret places to sit hidden from the house. They were secret places where she'd fallen in love and opened her heart. She blinked hard as the memories rolled in quicker than a rogue spring tide. Her throat tightened and her pulse quickened while her palms, wrapped around the steering wheel, were suddenly clammy. What had she been thinking, agreeing to take this job? She hadn't been, was the simple answer. She'd been a fool.

Sigrid Leslie's telephone call had come out of the blue shortly after Christmas as Imogen worked on ideas for a high-end Killiney property. She had converted the second bedroom in her inner-city apartment into a home office and nearly fell off her ergonomic yet beautiful tan leather chair when she heard the voice with its precise vowels introduce herself. Sigrid was the elegant and much younger Swedish wife of Matthew Leslie, the eldest of the now passed Mr and Mrs Leslie Senior's two children and, therefore, owner of Benmore House.

The woman's English was better than hers, Imogen idly thought, trying to pay attention to what she was saying. When she mentioned Matthew Leslie's younger brother, Lachlan, Imogen's body stiffened as she gleaned the reason for Sigrid's call. She'd stood pressing the phone so tightly to her ear it hurt; the confident, always immaculate career woman had vanished, and in her place sat the young woman riddled with one thousand and one insecurities, staring blankly at the cityscape outside her window. How could the mention of Lachlan's name all these years later still hold so much power over her? She'd picked up her stress ball, squeezing the life out of it, somehow managing to focus on the rest of the conversation.

There was to be a late summer wedding held on the grounds of Benmore House. Sigrid's brother-in-law, Lachlan, was marrying his English fiancée in what was to be an intimate affair at the house where he'd grown up. Imogen had wondered how intimate could be equated with a house the size of Benmore as Sigrid went on to say that the guest rooms hadn't been decorated since her husband's mother had resided at the house, and were now in desperate need of a makeover.

'A dear friend, Lady Sarah Hatton...' There'd been a pause then, as she waited for a word of acknowledgement from Imogen.

'I remember Lady Sarah and her beautiful home in Enniskerry well,' she'd dutifully trotted out. 'It was a joy and a privilege to help in its restoration.' She also knew for a fact *Lady* Sarah had bought her title and the job had been a nightmare, given the planning permission required before any alterations could begin.

'Yes, quite. Sarah recommended you, and it felt serendipitous when she told me of your connection to Emerald Bay. I was so impressed on my last visit to Abbemoore House by how you managed to stay true to the Baroque style yet brought in just enough of a hint of Rococo to rein it back. So many of my friends' houses feel as if they should be selling tickets to tourists at their front door. It wasn't in the least ostentatious, and I could see straight away you understood how to use proportion and scale.'

Jesus wept! The woman sounded like she'd picked up the *Interior Designers Handbook*. Imogen had been about to reply, 'Thanks a million.' But chose to adopt a slightly plummy tone as she replied with a simple thank you.

'Sarah told me of your connection to Emerald Bay.'

'Yes, my family own the Shamrock Inn in the village.'

Sigrid skated right over this. The fact that she was the daughter of a publican was of no interest to her. 'So, you're familiar with Benmore House.'

'Yes, I am.' Imogen closed her eyes, recalling her awe at the faded opulence of Benmore when Lachlan had shown her around the first time. Her sixteen-year-old self had been smitten with the feast of furnishings harking back to a bygone time.

Sigrid wanted her to draw up a plan for cosmetic tweaks to the four upstairs guestrooms, and to oversee a bathroom renovation. There was only one bathroom on that floor, and it was seriously dated. She had already engaged a local builder to undertake the work, but Sigrid and her husband Matthew had decided they wanted Imogen on site to ensure that things ran smoothly when work began.

The Swedish woman's unflappable demeanour had wavered at this point as she pinned the reason for the short notice on her brother-in-law. She'd confided he was apt to spontaneous, spur-of-the-moment decisions, irrespective of the spin they might put others in.

No love lost there then, Imogen thought, having first-hand experience of how Lachlan Leslie, the spoiled baby born when his mother was closer to fifty than forty, thought only of himself. So why did the mention of his name still cause her heart to race?

Her automatic response as she threatened to pop the stress ball was to decline the contract.

'Mrs Leslie, I'm afraid I'm fully booked, and it would be impossible to oversee such a project personally. I'm sorry.'

'Call me Sigrid, and I'm afraid I simply can't take no for an answer.'

As it transpired, she didn't have to because she'd made Imogen an eyewatering proposal. And, when push came to shove, Imogen was a businesswoman with a mortgage to pay who'd not cut her nose off to spite her face, as Nan would say.

Besides, she told herself sternly, her brief summer romance with Lachlan was ancient history. Why should she let it interfere with her common sense? Because he was her first love, that was why. She'd moved on, of course, she had, but you never forgot the sweetness of falling in love at sixteen.

In the end, she'd agreed to rearrange her calendar. Since then, though, she'd wondered if her decision to accept the Leslies' proposal had come down to the financial rewards, or was it because she couldn't resist prodding at a wound that had never completely healed, despite what she told herself.

The virtual interior design world was a blessing. Once she'd got the red tape of planning permission out the way, Zoom meetings had ensued with the general style, colours, furnishings and layout all agreed without the need for Imogen to leave Dublin. She'd drawn up the plans, taking into account lighting, wall finishes and the necessary plumbing fixtures for the bathroom.

But the Leslies weren't paying her an exorbitant sum to navigate the red tape involved with renovating a historic house like Benmore or to sit behind her computer for the project's entirety. All too soon the time had rolled around for her to pack her case in readiness for her two-and-a-half-week stay in Emerald Bay. Her mam and dad were delighted she'd be back under their roof for the duration, but this trip was going to be all work, not pleasure.

And now here she was, back at Benmore House.

4

Once upon a time, there would have been a cast of characters tucked away behind the scenes keeping the cogs of Benmore House turning, Imogen thought. A butler, housekeeper, maids, groomsman, a lady's maid. The cast of *Downton Abbey* sprang to mind. Of course, the lady of the house would never have been the one to answer the door, but times had changed, and today, Sigrid Leslie opened the door wide as she greeted her with a simple, 'Imogen. How nice to meet you at last in person.'

Imogen surreptitiously checked Sigrid out. Her verdict was the same as it had been after their initial Zoom meeting. The Swedish woman was glacial. She guessed her to be around ten years older than herself, although it was hard to guess anyone's age these days. That she was a perfectionist had swiftly become apparent in their numerous online meetings. Mind, given what she and her husband were paying, she could be as particular as she liked. From experience, Imogen knew it could be quite different meeting somebody in the flesh to conversing with them through a computer screen, but her employer's perfect smile didn't quite reach her ice-blue eyes in person either.

'Hello and a thousand apologies, Sigrid, for being late.'

As Sigrid leaned in to air-kiss her cheeks, Imogen detected Chanel No. 19 and decided the distinct green, soft musk fragrance suited her. The air-kissing was a skill she'd honed by practising on her flatmate in the days before her business had boomed and she'd been able to put the deposit together for her apartment. Oh, the bliss of no longer opening the fridge to find her almond milk container emptied, or to go to brush her teeth only to find the toothpaste rolled up and squeezed dry! The first time she'd attempted the greeting on a client, she'd all but head-butted her. Not her finest hour, but all was well that ended well because she'd got the job.

Once the ritual was over, Sigrid invited her inside, enquiring about her journey.

Imogen hesitated, then angled her foot to show her muddied spike heel. 'I had to make an unexpected pit stop on my way here, which is why I'm running late, and I would have changed my shoes, but they're all buried down the bottom of my suitcase and I didn't want to keep you waiting any longer. It, er, it couldn't be avoided.' She was burbling, but she didn't want to be responsible for marking the gleaming parquet floor she could see spanning the entrance either.

If Sigrid was curious about what had happened, she didn't show it as she waved her hand dismissively. 'I understand. Things happen. Our builder was supposed to be here too, but he's also running late.' She pursed her lips. 'And if you wouldn't mind slipping your shoes off – we have the floor waxed and polished every spring, and it's only just been done. Besides, we're very relaxed here at Benmore. Matthew and I like to keep things casual.'

'Of course. It's not a problem.' Imogen knew her own smile didn't quite reach her eyes as she cursed her cross-country exploits, knowing her feet would freeze on the hard wooden floors. One thing she'd learned about the big houses of Ireland was that they were usually freezing. And as far as keeping things casual went, the woman was wearing a cream suit, also Chanel – Imogen knew her labels. She was hardly slopping about the place in Ugg boots either, she thought, registering her matching pumps. The mind boggled as to what her idea of being dressed to the nines would be. However, as the sole director of Imagine Interiors, Imogen's policy was what the client wants, the client gets. So she slipped the heels off.

No! Too late, she saw her left big toe, with its poppy polish, poking through the sheer knee-high socks she favoured under trousers. These were another little-known secret that Imogen preferred to keep to herself. She groaned silently as Sigrid averted her eyes from the toe, being too well bred to mention it as she ushed Imogen inside, closing the door behind them.

Imogen immediately found herself standing in a space that harked back to a different era and took a moment to absorb the ambience. Sometimes she fancied the walls in these old houses spoke to her.

'I thought you might enjoy light refreshments after your drive.' Sigrid was already padding past the grand staircase to the hallway beyond.

A cuppa was music to Imogen's ears. She was gasping and, now she thought about it, peckish too. But first, she needed the loo. It had been a long drive. 'Lovely, thank you, but could I use your bathroom first?'

'Of course.'

She was about to move toward the stairs, knowing the bathroom was tucked away next door to the morning room on the left. But then she hesitated, remembering that, so far as Sigrid knew, she'd never been inside Benmore.

'It's just over there on the left at the bottom of the stairs,' the older woman directed.

Imogen thanked her before setting off in that direction, feeling decidedly short in her stockinged feet. The floor was lethal, she thought, feeling her feet sliding on the boards. But at least her toe gave her grip, although she could hardly count that as something to be grateful for. Then again, she was grateful to make it to the bathroom without doing the splits.

As she washed her hands, Imogen glanced into the mirror, cringing at her bird's nest hairdo before unpinning it and letting it fall, which was an improvement. Then, pushing the door open, she found Sigrid fiddling with a vase of flowers on a stand at the foot of the staircase.

She slid the yellow rose she held in her hand back into the vase and stepped back to admire her handiwork before acknowledging Imogen with a, 'Shall we?'

Imogen nodded, following her hostess around the staircase to the hallway running the length of what she knew to be the ballroom.

'Lachlan and Victoria's reception is to be held in here.' Sigrid pushed open the double doors to reveal the dance hall.

Victoria... Imogen sounded the name out in her head, wondering what the girl who'd finally convinced Lachlan to settle down was like. As she stared at the expanse of polished floor, she felt herself spinning back to the day Lachlan had taught her to waltz on those very boards. The warmth of his hand through her thin T-shirt as he led her about the floor, counting the steps out loud. How many times had she stood on his toes? His shoulders shook each time, but he'd encouraged her to keep going because she'd soon get the hang of it. He was right. Suddenly, the steps had slotted into place, and as they glided about the room, she'd felt like a princess.

'I suppose it will be nice for the ballroom to be used again.' Sigrid's voice brought her back to the present as she pulled the doors shut, and they walked to the end of the hall, turning left.

The drawing room had been Imogen's favourite space in the house. It was while sitting with Lachlan in the love seat, one of two by the bay window that looked out over the acreage, that two things had become clear to her. The first was she was in love with Lachlan Leslie, and the second was that one day she'd work with beautiful spaces like this.

The room hadn't changed.

The bay window flooded it with natural light, and the plush drapes formed a frame to the land belonging to the estate. The love seat was still there, and she longed to sit in it, tucking her legs alongside her.

The decor was busy, as befit the period, with oak tables Imogen identified as eighteenth-century displaying silver candelabras. The panelled walls were painted a pale pink and adorned with gilt-framed artworks. Two colourful wooden duck decoys caught her attention on an occasional table. The wooden American folk-art carvings were not only sought after but highly valuable.

Sigrid tracked her gaze. 'My husband came across those at an auction and had to have them. He never misses the opening of the duck season on the first of September. I'm not a fan, personally.'

Imogen was unsure whether she meant the decoys or duck hunting. 'It's a beautiful room.'

'Thank you.' Sigrid ushered her toward the two-seater Jacquard-covered sofa. 'Please. Have a seat.'

Imogen did so, turning her back on the window and her memories.

'It's the way the light in here is never the same. That is what makes it special. Don't you agree?'

Imogen murmured acknowledgement as Sigrid sat opposite her in one of the armchairs. The two women were separated by a modern glass table upon which sat a cake dusted in icing sugar on a china stand. Two side plates with cake forks and a knife and server were also set out in readiness.

She was right, Imogen thought, trying not to drool at the sight of the cake. It was the light.

Sigrid picked up the bell on the table, giving it a purposeful shake before talking about the whirl that was the Stockholm society scene they'd left behind for the summer. 'It's a breath of fresh air to return to Benmore. We stay until October and then spend a month in Dublin before returning to Stockholm.'

Imogen half expected a young maid to appear in a black dress, white apron and mob cap any second, but the rattle of teacups brought forth an older, stout woman dressed in a cardigan, blouse and skirt. On her feet, she wore sensible shoes that wouldn't make a sound padding about the various rooms. Servants should be seen but not heard, ran through Imogen's head as she tucked her big toe out of sight and smiled her appreciation as the woman, the Leslies' housekeeper, presumably, set the tray down.

She'd seen her before, Imogen realised, and it came to her where. At the Bus Stop, Emerald Bay's corner shop. The village was around a ten-minute drive from Benmore and the housekeeper had been chatting to Mrs Gallagher in accented English on a few occasions when Imogen had called in.

'Thank you, Francesca. I can see to things from here,' Sigrid said as the woman nodded to her and then Imogen, no hint of recognition on her face as she exited silently. Once she was out of earshot, Sigrid leaned toward Imogen conspiratorially. 'Francesca is a treasure.' She began setting out the delicate cups and saucers. 'How do you like your tea?'

'Oh, with a splash of milk, thank you.'

Sigrid saw to the tea, adding a slice of lemon to hers. Then she slid the cup and saucer across the table to Imogen, asking, 'Can I tempt you with a slice of lemon cake?'

Imogen bit back, 'I thought you'd never ask,' to respond politely, 'Yes, please. It looks wonderful.' She picked up her cup and took a sip, scalding her mouth.

'Francesca's lemon cake is my guilty pleasure. It's made with ricotta, and the recipe was passed down to her by her mamma.'

'Those are always the best recipes,' Imogen said. 'My nan, Kitty Kelly, is a wonderful baker. She makes the best apple cake. Thank you.' She put her cup back on the saucer, accepted the side plate, and forked off a mouthful of the cake to sample. 'Mm. Divine.'

'I shall let Francesca know you said so.' Sigrid looked pleased as she began to tell her about her daughters. 'Mila has a talent for art while Juni is our academic. The girls attend boarding school in Dublin.'

There was a wistfulness in her tone as she spoke of them. She missed them. Imogen would have hated being sent away from her mam and dad each school term, but the world the Leslies inhabited, splitting their time between Stockholm, Dublin, and Emerald Bay, was different to the one the Kelly family moved in.

When she'd dabbed her mouth with a napkin and finished her tea, Sigrid stood smoothing her skirt and suggested she show her around.

'I'd like that,' Imogen said, also standing, hoping Francesca wouldn't curse her for leaving a pile of crumbs behind on the rug. She traipsed after Sigrid, aware of distant hammering and nearly walked into the back of her Swedish hostess as she came to an unexpected standstill.

'The builder is here.' Sigrid frowned, turning around to face Imogen. 'I hope Matthew's not disturbed by the noise. He's working in his study.' She stood with her ear cocked to one side, listening out.

At the mention of 'study', a shudder rippled through Imogen as she was reminded of a secret Maeve Doolin, who'd resided in Emerald Bay her whole life, had revealed at Christmas. It was situated beside the morning room in the west wing, and Imogen hoped Sigrid wouldn't insist on tapping on the door to introduce her to her husband. She didn't think she'd be able to keep her expression neutral if she stepped inside that room.

Maeve's story had been the talk of the village in the weeks after Christmas, so Mam said. What happened to her had only widened the gap between the Leslie family and the residents of Emerald Bay. Imogen doubted village tattle ever reached Sigrid or her husband's ears, though.

Satisfied the work going on upstairs wasn't causing a problem, Sigrid bared her perfect, small white teeth and gave a stiff smile. 'I'll show you the library. Perhaps the west wing can wait for another day. As I said, my husband is working.'

'Of course, and I'd love to see the library.' It was then that Imogen slipped up. 'Do you still have the signed first edition of Yeats's "Wild Swans at Coole"?'

She didn't realise what she'd said until Sigrid's head snapped up and pinned her with a questioning gaze.

Oh, feck, she thought.

5

'How do you know about the Yeats?' Sigrid queried with a raised eyebrow.

The surprise was evident in her voice; yes, Imogen fancied she could detect a hint of suspicion there too. Maybe that was just down to her guilty conscience, though. Either way, her mouth had run away with her. She was indeed her mam's daughter. She'd even got all hot and bothered like Nora Kelly was apt to do, too, since she'd reached a certain time of life.

There'd been a window of opportunity where Imogen could have dropped the information she was already acquainted with Benmore House into her conversation with Sigrid. That she'd had a short-lived romance with her client's brother-in-law half her lifetime ago was no big deal. Yes, all right, he was her first love, but everyone had one of those.

Lachlan had the run of the place for a week that summer with his parents away and a housekeeper charged with keeping a wary eye on him. Together, they'd roamed the manor house rooms as he introduced her to his world. Then, when his parents had returned, they'd hidden from view in the gardens.

For reasons she didn't understand, Imogen had stayed quiet
when talking to Sigrid in the months leading up to her coming
to the house in person, and the time to mention her previous
visits had been and gone. Now she'd come across as sneaky if
she were to suddenly drop it in the conversation that she and
Lachlan were already acquainted.

'Oh, er, I went through a moody Yeats phase when I briefly
fancied myself as a poet at high school.' She shrugged in a *didn't
we all* manner. 'Perhaps my English teacher was aware of a first
edition here at Benmore and mentioned it. I really can't
remember now.'

Her suitably vague response appeared to satisfy Sigrid, who
led her into a timber-panelled, ceilinged room that smelled of
leather. Through the window, a ray of light bathed the wood-
work in a warm glow. Hardback books, gold lettering on their
spines, lined one wall while a tapestry dominated the other.
The floor on which she stood was covered by a large Persian rug
which was a respite from the chilly boards, and a world globe,
along with a cluster of eclectic antiques, were displayed upon
an expansive desk. Several armchairs were scattered about,
inviting you to sink into them and while away a few hours with
a good book. It was a beautiful room.

'As it happens, we do still have it. It's quite valuable. Would
you like to take a look? I'm a lover of poetry myself.'

Imogen's heart began banging against her chest. That book
was what had started it all. 'Yes, thank you. I'd like that very
much.'

While Sigrid ran a finger along the shelves looking for the
book, Imogen was already losing herself in memories of an
unseasonably warm day not long after school had broken up for
the summer holidays. She'd turned sixteen a few days earlier,
and now her hand went to her neck to toy with the delicate
silver heart pendant on the necklace her parents had given her

to mark the occasion. She wore it religiously like a talisman, only taking it off at night.

That day had enticed all the village kids to seek respite from the heat in the sparkling waters of Emerald Bay, which transformed from green to blue when the sun shone.

Imogen had been stretched out on her beach towel, wearing sunglasses that kept sliding down her nose, slippery with sunscreen. Hannah, Grace and Ava were splashing around in the shallows with their friends. Britney Spears was blaring courtesy of Obvious Orla's boom box, mingling with the shrieks of laughter coming from both the water and drifting down from the ruins of Kilticaneel Castle, where the younger kids liked to play. She pretended to be absorbed in the battered book of poetry she was holding, thinking reading Yeats gave her an air of intellectual aloofness.

Just that morning, she'd overheard Nan telling Dad carting around poetry didn't mean Imogen would be off to Trinity as soon as she'd finished her schooling. 'It's a phase, is all, son. Sure, look at yourself at that age, stomping about Emerald Bay with your Doc Marten boots on. You'd my lipstick smeared across your mouth and more hairspray in that hair of yours than Nessie Doyle stocks in her salon. A tornado wouldn't have budged a hair on your head,' she'd muttered, unaware Imogen was earwigging.

Dad had asked her to please stop bringing his short-lived Goth stage up, to which she'd replied the memory was seared on her brain, and he was lucky all he had to contend with where Imogen was concerned was Yeats.

Imogen's afternoon at the beach hadn't got off to a good start when Declan Horan had blocked her sunshine to ask if he could spread his towel next to hers. There was no point encouraging him, she thought, saying sorry but her sister Shannon had asked her to reserve a spot next to her. Declan had mooched off to try his luck with Kitty Foyle instead. He'd have a much better chance with the ladies if he'd leave his spots alone, Imogen thought.

So, there she'd been in her yellow bikini with Yeats for company when a stir had whipped around the sandy inlet. Imogen peered over the top of her glasses seeking the cause of it: a barefoot, bare-chested lad clambering over the rocks with a towel slung over his shoulder. He was berry brown, which instantly set him apart from the pasty white chests turning pink presently on display. And his arrival reminded Imogen of one of those old Westerns Grandad, God rest his soul, had loved, where a stranger rides into town. The newcomer, she could see even from a distance, was good-looking. And she wasn't the only one to have noticed, judging by the number of girls striking poses on their towels or pretending they were stars of a James Bond film exiting the water.

You didn't get many tourists here in Emerald Bay, where there was no holiday park like there was on the outskirts of Kilticaneel, the closest town. Perhaps he was someone's grandson, come to stay for a few days. Imogen pondered the possibilities, pretending not to watch as he began picking his way across the hot sand. She buried her nose in her book as he got closer and on this occasion didn't say a word when he flicked his towel out next to hers.

Shannon, waiting for Nan to finish packing a picnic for them, could find her own spot, Imogen thought. Oh, how she wished Fi was here. She missed her best friend desperately when she spent her two weeks in Kerry at her cousins each summer. It was like her right arm was missing or, at the very least, her partner in crime. Either way, she'd be texting her about this close encounter when she got home. Annoyingly, there was no reception on the beach, and this was the most exciting thing to have happened so far during these holidays!

Imogen concentrated on being cool, calm and collected, but

it was hard when all her nerve endings were tingling. She wished she were a more confident girl like Obvious Orla over there, covered in fake tan and running down the beach with her red swimsuit wedged up her arse like she was about to rescue some eejit from the ocean.

'What's that you're reading?' the stranger asked, looking over at her as he sat down.

'Yeats.' Imogen was relieved it hadn't come out as a squeak. She wasn't used to feeling shy.

'We have a first edition of his up at the house. My father's always banging on about it.' His voice had the carefully constructed vowels of someone schooled privately.

'Up at the house?'

'Benmore. I'm Lachlan Leslie.'

Imogen was glad of her sunglasses as her eyes widened. The Leslie family were rarely seen in the village, holding themselves aloof from the locals and thus creating an awestruck distrust.

'What are you doing here?' she blurted, feeling like a culchie as soon as the words left her mouth.

'I was bored.' He shrugged. 'Aren't you going to tell me your name?'

'Imogen.'

He looked a little like one of the Jonas brothers; she loved Joe Jonas. She'd had a heated discussion with Shannon last night over who was sexier. JT, aka Justin Timberlake, her sister's favourite, gazing down from the wall above her bed, or Joe Jonas, tacked to the ceiling above Imogen's. There was no competition so far as Imogen was concerned.

She listened as Lachlan told her he'd been left to his own devices for the week with his parents away visiting friends.

'You've got a brother, though, haven't you?'

'He's a lot older than me and spends all his time in Dublin these days.'

Aside from the housekeeper charged with keeping him fed

and watered, he'd been rattling around the enormous home for two days. He was supposed to be putting his nose to the grindstone, studying, after a lacklustre year at school, but he wasn't academically minded, and she'd sympathised, hearing how his parents didn't get that.

'So' – he shrugged – 'here I am.'

'Here you are,' she echoed.

Shannon and her pal Freya appeared just then. Sarongs knotted low around their waists, which would have been more at home in Hawaii than on an Irish beach.

'You said you'd save us a spot,' Shannon said, checking out the interloper. She had a picnic basket in her hand, but Imogen was no longer hungry.

'Feck off, Shannon,' Imogen mouthed, relieved when Freya, quicker on the uptake, read the scene correctly and tugged her elder sister away.

'Have you been in yet?'

'No.'

'I dare you to.'

Imogen could never resist a dare, and she forgot all about being shy. 'I will if you will.'

'You're on.' Lachlan grinned, getting to his feet. He held his hand out to help her up.

Obvious Orla, jiggling by the water's edge, getting the attention of every hormonal lad on the beach except the one she was hoping to attract, glared at Imogen as she ran shrieking into the waves with Lachlan. Orla was oblivious to poor Declan, who'd got so excited watching her bosoms vying for freedom he'd swallowed water and was coughing and spluttering about the place. A fecking useless lifeguard she'd make, Imogen thought in the split second before the cold water washed over her.

Later as they dried off on their towels, Lachlan had invited her to the house. 'I'll show you the Yeats first edition,' he said.

'I don't want to get in trouble with your housekeeper. Not if you're supposed to be studying.'

'She won't notice. When the parents are away, the mice will play.'

'What do you mean?'

'She'll be watching daytime TV instead of whatever she normally does. She and I have an unspoken understanding.'

'Oh.'

'Are you coming then?'

'OK.'

As they left the beach, she felt as if one hundred pairs of eyes were boring into her back.

Imogen blinked as Sigrid pulled the book from the shelf, sending up a puff of dust before passing it to her, she recalled Lachlan doing the same thing. A bolt of electricity had shot through her as his hand lingered on hers. At nineteen, he'd been three years older than her, and she remembered thinking he was very worldly.

'Thank you,' she said, aware Sigrid was watching, waiting to see her reaction as she opened the book carefully. She made all the right noises to show her appreciation over the signed name-plate before passing it back.

Sigrid slotted it into place and then glanced at her wrist-watch. 'We should head upstairs so you can meet the builder and get on your way. I imagine it's been a long day with the drive down.'

Imogen's eyes creased. 'Yes, and my parents will be eager to see me.'

'Quite.'

They climbed the sweep of staircase and Imogen did her best to ignore the beady-eyed gazes from the ancestral portraits peering down on all those who ventured upstairs.

The hammering grew louder as they reached the top of the stairs. The doors to the guestrooms were open, and Imogen

observed dust covers over the furnishings in preparation for
work to begin. She'd never been in any of these rooms, but as
she walked around them, there was a sensation of knowing the
spaces intimately. The virtual design programme she used was
to thank for this. She'd already spent many hours poring over
them. The smell in each room was faintly musty, and she
longed to stride over to the windows and open them wide. A
room's scent was something an online experience couldn't
convey.

Sigrid waited while Imogen made a few notes, and then,
after she'd surveyed the last room on the landing, they reached
the source of the disruption. The bathroom door was open, but
still Sigrid knocked sharply. Imogen hoped the poor builder
didn't get a fright and bang his thumb with the hammer. She
hung back, half expecting to hear expletives. None were forth-
coming, though, as Sigrid told him she'd like to introduce the
interior designer who'd be overseeing the project, including the
bathroom fixtures and fittings.

Imogen groaned inwardly as Ryan O'Malley, with a light
sheen of sweat glistening on his chest visible through the open
top button of his ancient flannel shirt, stepped out of the bathroom. His hair was so dark it almost had a bluish tinge under the
light, and he needed a trim, she thought primly. A shave
wouldn't go amiss, either. The combined effect gave him a
swarthy look. She'd been so caught up in rescuing the duckling
earlier that she'd barely noticed he was wearing shorts despite
the inclement weather, or that his legs were leanly muscled
with the sort of tan that comes from long hours spent working
outside. A tool belt was slung low around his hips in case there
was any doubt he was a builder. For his part, he clocked who
the designer was, and a cheeky grin spread across his face.

'Imogen, twice in one day.'

'You two know each other then?'

'Yes, Imogen and I go way back.'

Imogen offered up a weak smile.

Of all the builders in all the towns, or whatever Bogart's famous line was in *Casablanca*, Ryan O'Malley had to be working on her project. Well, even though he denied being the high school bra-pinger, he'd get what for if he attempted any funny business this time around.

6

'Imogen Kate Kelly, your father's been worrying himself sick! He was about to go out looking for you, so he was. He's been driving me mad, giving me traffic report updates every half hour. You know how he worries when you drive down from Dublin.'

'Mam, I told you I wouldn't be home until at least three o'clock, and it's only four now. Despite what Dad thinks, I'm a perfectly able driver. Tell him I'll be home in ten minutes.'

'An hour's a long time in a parent's life. God willing, one day you'll find that out for yourself,' Nora muttered before singing out, 'She's grand, Liam. She'll be home shortly.'

Imogen heard her dad's voice in the background. 'Tell her, Nora, if she'd listened to me and bought a yellow sports car, I wouldn't go on like so.'

Nora began to repeat just that, and Imogen cut her off. 'I heard him, Mam.' She was well aware of her father's preference for yellow vehicles because of their visibility on the road. He drove a Hilux not dissimilar to Ryan O'Malley's, only Liam's was an obscene pee colour, and he might have talked Shannon into driving a bumblebee on wheels, but she'd not be seen dead in one. 'Cop yourself on, Mam; a yellow sports car isn't the same as a red one.' Mam had made no secret about how much she enjoyed putting a headscarf on and going for a blast with Imogen, the top down on her sporty little coupe. She said it made her feel like a film star.

'I suppose you've got a point.'

'Will we have the fish pie for dinner?' It was time for a change of subject, and Imogen's tummy rumbled at the prospect. It was a tradition established since she and her sisters had all finally moved out. Apart from Shannon, who'd moved back in at Christmas. Whenever any of her offspring returned to the family fold, Nora Kelly would make them their favourite dinner to welcome them home. While Imogen didn't like the smell of fish, she adored her mam's creamy calorific fish pie. Or Nan's, for that matter. She wasn't fussy about who made it, just as long as there was a generous serving on her plate.

'We will.'

'Grand.' Her hand was already reaching for the keys dangling in the ignition, eager to put distance between herself and Benmore House. The lure of the familiar sights and sounds of life at the Shamrock Inn was calling. Tomorrow morning, when she was expected back at the house, would roll around soon enough. Then, remembering Shannon's Persian cat, Napoleon, who was residing in the family quarters above the pub these days, she added, 'Mam, I'll be more like twenty minutes because I'll have to call into Heneghan's Pharmacy and pick up some of those antihistamine tablets. You can tell Shannon she'll be footing the bill.'

Thanks to Napoleon, there was no way she'd be risking a repeat of the swollen eyes she'd suffered at Christmas. She was allergic to cats and had barely been able to see, so puffy were her poor eyes, let alone show her face outside her bedroom until the antihistamines had kicked in. If they were in America, she could have sued.

'Ah, now, Imogen, don't be giving out about Napoleon. He's a grand little fluffy fellow so long as he sticks to a dry biscuit diet. Your father was after slipping him some titbits under the table the other day, and we had to evacuate the kitchen half an hour later. We've got used to having him roaming about the place now, and the regulars love him. Oh, and did I tell you Shannon's after telling us he's an extremely rare sort of a cat because of his tortoiseshell colouring?'

'No, Mam, you didn't.' Imogen laughed even as she told her to remember she was her child, taking automatic precedence over a flat-faced, farty feline, even if he was a rare breed. She could afford to giggle, given she'd not have to share a room with Shannon, who insisted on letting Napoleon sleep on her bed. No way, José! With the twins and Hannah away, she'd be claiming their space as her own.

'Mam, my phone is about to go flat. I'll see you soon.' The screen died, and she started the car swerving deftly around Ryan's vehicle to zip down the driveway and out onto the main road. It wasn't long until she was whizzing past the row of post-card-pretty thatched cottages with clusters of daffodils bobbing their heads as if in greeting alongside the front paths. The cottages were holiday lets now, apart from Maeve Doolin's house, the cutest of them all.

Shannon had travelled with Maeve and her new fella, James, who was Maeve's grandson, to his home in Boston. Maeve, wishing to spend time with her extended family, had generously insisted on paying Shannon's fare, saying it was of comfort to her to have a nurse sitting alongside her on the plane. They all knew she was eager to help Shannon and James's blossoming romance bloom. Her sister had only been able to secure a couple of weeks holiday, but she'd been lucky to get that at short notice, especially with the health service always banging on about being understaffed. She'd come home, but Maeve had stayed on, and for the time being Shannon's romance with James was being conducted long-distance.

Imogen had reached the outskirts of the village when she saw Enda Dunne's collie, Shep, sitting forlornly on the side of the road. The black-and-white dog was getting on in years, and it wasn't like him to not be with Enda or, if Enda was supping at the Shamrock Inn, sitting outside Dermot Molloy's Quality Meats waiting for his master's return. She frowned, hoping the old boy wasn't hurt, then pulled in to the kerb, opening her car door to call Shep over.

He didn't move from his spot, so Imogen got out of the car to check he was all right. She had only taken two steps when, busy looking at Shep, her ankle went as she failed to see the pothole. Her arms flailed, and it was touch and go as to whether she'd stay upright, but in the end, gravity won.

'Ouch!' she yelped as she landed in a crumpled heap on the road.

Shep barked and trotted over to her. He nuzzled her hand. There was nothing wrong with him then! She carefully moved her ankle from left to right and checked whether she'd broken it. It hurt, but it was probably just twisted. That was something.

'This is your fault, you know,' she admonished the dog, whose tongue was lolling as he panted alongside her.

He whined, fixing woeful eyes on her, and she ruffled his coat.

'All right, all right. It's not you. It's these stupid shoes. I know.' She bit her lip; she couldn't sit here until dark so there was nothing for it but to haul herself upright. Imogen gingerly hobbled around to her car's passenger door, ouching all the way.

'Come on, you.' She opened the door and patted the seat in an invitation to the dog. 'I can't leave you behind now, can I? Besides, if I know your dad, he'll be where I'm after heading anyway. He's a thing for my nan, don't you know – not to mention a pint.'

A woof told her Shep did know, and he wagged his tail before jumping on to the seat. Imogen closed the car door, slid into the driver's side, and turned the key in the ignition, thinking not only would she need to pick up antihistamines from Heneghan's, but she could also do with a roll of bandage to strap her ankle too. There was a click but no roar of the engine springing into life, and with an ever-deepening frown, she jiggled the key back and forth before trying again and again.

Nothing happened.

Imogen didn't know much about cars, but she knew she'd flatten the battery if she continued trying to get it to start it when it wasn't going to.

'Feck!'

Shep woofed his agreement.

Her eyes flitted to her mobile, intending to ring her dad to ask him to pick her up. Then, remembering it was flat, she raised her eyes heavenward. 'You're not on my side today, are you?'

There was no lightning bolt in reply, and she looked to Shep. 'I can't walk the rest of the way into the village on this ankle. I suppose we'll have to flag someone down.'

'Ruff,' Shep replied.

Imogen swung her legs out of the car once more and, leaning on the door frame for support, scanned the horizon, but instead of a car heading down the road toward her, she spied Mr Kenny. He was a beacon in the high visibility jacket his son had bought him as he drove his motorised scooter down the middle of the road at surprising speed.

She waved out as he approached, and he braked so hard she thought he might fly over the top of the handles. Her heart was in her mouth as he lurched forward but mercifully stayed in his seat.

'Hello there, Imogen. Have you broken down?'

'I have, Mr Kenny.' She began filling him on her tale of woe by saying she'd seen Shep sitting on his own and found it odd.

'I'd agree with you there. It's odd, right enough.'

Shep had moved over to the driver's seat and barked his greeting to Mr Kenny.

'Hello there, boy.'

'So, I pulled over, and when I got out of the car to check on him, I fell over. It was thanks to that pothole right there.' She jabbed her finger in its direction.

Mr Kenny's wily blue eyes travelled from the pothole to Imogen's shoes. 'I'd say those stilts you've strapped to your feet are as much to blame as the pothole.'

Imogen was beginning to fall out of love with her Gianvito Rossi pumps. 'Either way, I think I've sprained my ankle.'

''Tis twice the size of your other one.'

'Yes. Well, anyway, there's nothing wrong with Shep, which is a blessing. I was going to drive him down to the Shamrock Inn because Enda's probably there, but' – she shrugged – 'as I said, my car won't start, and my phone's dead, so I can't ring my dad and ask him to pick us up. You wouldn't have a phone I could use, would you?' She looked at Mr Kenny hopefully.

'Sure, and what would I want with a yoke like that?'

'That's a no, then?'

''Tis. I've my son telephoning me every five minutes when I'm at home to see if his auld da's still breathing as it is. The pub's where I go to get some peace.'

'Fair play to you. Am I right in thinking it's the pub you're after heading to now, then?'

'I am, yes.'

'Would you ask my dad to fetch me?'

'Imogen Kelly, I can't very well leave a damsel in distress on the side of the road. What sort of a heathen would that make me? Mrs Kenny would turn in her grave if she thought I'd left you here to fend for yourself.'

Imogen managed to flash her teeth despite her throbbing

ankle. The main road into the village of Emerald Bay might be quiet, but it was hardly a kidnapper's hotspot.

To her alarm, the elderly gent patted the seat behind him. 'There's plenty of room on the back here, girl. Climb aboard, so. Your stallion awaits.'

Jesus wept! There was no way she was climbing on the back of that thing. She'd be taking her life in her hands because Mr Kenny was a law unto himself. So far as he was concerned, the road rules didn't apply to him. As such, she grasped hold of the handiest excuse. 'I can't leave Shep here on his own, Mr Kenny. It wouldn't be fair now.'

'Sure, 'tis not a bother. Shep there can run alongside the scooter. It will do that collie good to get some exercise. He's looking very round about the middle. It's all that sitting about outside Dermot Molloy's butchers cadging the free sausages that's done that. C'mon with you now. I'll not be taking no for an answer.'

There was nothing for it, Imogen thought, pulling Shep from the car and informing him he was to run alongside the scooter. Then, locking up, she pocketed her keys, hopped over to the scooter and cocked a leg, hoisting herself onto the back of her ride. 'Mr Kenny, you won't go too fast, will you?'

'You'll be safe as houses with me, Imogen. Hold on tight now.'

She put her hands around his middle and her grip tightened, hearing the engine rev. Imogen shot back as he put the pedal to the metal, grateful she was holding on with a death-like grip, or she'd have gone sailing off the back. It was just as well her sisters weren't about to see this, she thought, making sure Shep was keeping up with them.

For an old dog, he seemed energetic enough. The rate he was going, Imogen reckoned he'd give the horses at the Irish Grand National a run for their money.

Beep, beep.

Mr Kenny returned the greeting, sounding the car horn speaker, courtesy of his son.

Imogen, who'd squeezed her eyes shut, opened them in time to see Ryan O'Malley overtaking them with an enormous grin across his face.

Imogen's middle finger twitched, and she'd have given him a rude sign if she wasn't terrified of letting go of Mr Kenny.

So it was that Imogen found herself being chauffeur-driven down the main street of Emerald Bay on a motorised scooter. The bunting fluttered overhead, and the doors of the colourful shops opened as villagers stepped outside to watch the spectacle.

Her face was the colour of a ripe plum as Mr Kenny sounded the horn once more.

Imogen decided this was not one of life's Instagram moments, but she'd laugh about it one day.

Not just yet, though.

7

The village drums had been beating because by the time
Imogen and Mr Kenny hooned past Mermaids at the top of the
village and made a pit stop at Heneghan's Pharmacy before
reaching the Shamrock Inn, the word was out.

Imogen Kelly was riding pillion on Mr Kenny's motorised
scooter with Shep the collie dog chasing up the rear.

The shop owners and their customers had piled onto the
pavement to watch the spectacle passing down Main Street.

Imogen understood how the Pope must feel during the
papal tour when the crowds came out to greet him. She
wondered if she was expected to wave.

'Welcome home, Imogen!' Eileen Carroll, the owner of the
Knitter's Nook and the village gossip, sang out. 'Is it a wedding
or a birth that's brought you back to Emerald Bay?'

'Work, Eileen,' Imogen called back. As if any village
wedding or new baby would have escaped Eileen's quivering
antennae. There was more chance of Hannah giving up her
worthy causes and becoming part of the greed-driven corporate
world she despised than that happening.

Her mam and dad had been forewarned she was on her

way and were waiting outside the Shamrock Inn, a bemused expression on both their faces at a sight they'd never thought they'd see. They'd be wanting an explanation as to what was going on, Imogen thought, relieved when the scooter came to a halt. Shep caught them up, panting lustily after his run and began lapping up the scratch behind the ears Liam was giving him.

'Thanks a million for the ride, Mr Kenny. How're you, Mam, Dad?' Imogen clambered off the back of the scooter with as much decorum as she could muster, wincing as she placed her foot with the bad ankle down. She was given a meaty-armed squeeze by her father and a cuddle from her mam, and when she was released, she said, 'If Enda's in there, tell him his dog could do with a bowl of water.' She'd seen Shep's lead still attached to the telegraph pole as they passed the butchers where Enda parked him each afternoon when he visited the Shamrock Inn. The dog must have freed himself and gone walkabout for whatever reason.

'Hold on.' Liam held up his hand, and his blustery tone made him look even more barrel-like than usual. 'How about you tell us what's going on first.'

It wasn't a question but rather a demand.

'And what are you after doing to that foot of yours? I'll never know why you can't wear shoes that won't see you breaking your neck. It's not the catwalks of Paris you're after strutting down daily, Imogen. I mean, look at these,' Nora raised her trouser leg to show off her sensible loafers and launched into a monologue of the merits of leather uppers for support.

Imogen looked at her father and raised her brows. Nora was always apt to burble when worried about one of her girls, and Liam was a professional in stopping her mid-flow.

'Nora, you'd best be putting that slender ankle away, or you'll have pulses racing about the village. Isn't that right, Ned?'

Mr Kenny had replaced his scooter with his walking stick,

leaning heavily on it as catching Liam's wink, he said, 'Nora Kelly, my poor heart's not able for any more excitement today.'

Nora hastily dropped her trouser leg, not wanting Ned Kenny keeling over on her conscience.

Imogen smiled despite her throbbing ankle. She was keen to get inside, wanting to take the weight off her foot and take the tablets purchased from the pharmacy.

Mr Kenny had taken door-to-door shopping to the next level after she'd tapped him on the shoulder as they sped along to ask if they could call in at the pharmacy. She'd thought they would make the turn on two wheels so sharply did he angle the handlebars to the right.

Mrs Tattersall, who happened to be leaving the chemist at the same time, wasn't impressed at nearly being mowed down and held the door to the chemist's open begrudgingly. Mr Kenny nudged the scooter inside, ignoring her pursed lips mutterings about him being as bad as the Kilticaneel hooligans who tore through the village.

'Thanking you, Edna,' Mr Kenny interrupted. 'And how's Jim keeping these days?'

Imogen thought she might be retirement age by the time the woman stopped harping on about her husband's bad knees and quack doctors. It was a blessing to see one of the local teenagers drop a chocolate bar wrapper which set Edna Tattersall storming off to deliver a sermon on littering.

The lovelorn pharmacy shop assistant, Nuala, had stared at Niall Heneghan, Emerald Bay's widowed pharmacist, as though Jesus himself was informing Imogen that the anti-inflammatory he'd recommended for her pain was safe to take with an antihistamine.

Imogen had listened, thinking that Mr Heneghan might be an educated man, but he was a fool regarding what was right under his nose. As Nuala rang up the various tablets and a bandage roll, Imogen asked about the supermodel cardboard cut-out in the front window advertising a new perfume the last time she'd been home. A lacklustre hay fever display had replaced it.

'Oh, when the promotion was over, we took pity on Paddy and let him take Bridget home with him.'

'Bridget?' Imogen asked, knowing Paddy, who spent his days worse for wear from the drink, had got it into his head that the life-size cut-out was his lady love.

'That's what he called her.'

The mind boggled, she'd thought, as Mr Kelly, with much beeping on the scooter's part, had reversed expertly back out the door.

Now she soaked in the familiar green exterior of the Shamrock Inn. By the looks of things, her dad had given it a fresh lick of paint, as he was apt to do at the advent of spring. Meanwhile, her mam's green fingers had been tending the window boxes upstairs. It was only March, but the boxes already held a profusion of pink and purple petunia, while two hanging baskets framed the cheery red door her parents were blocking in a riot of red and blue lobelia.

'Well?' Nora Kelly, hands on hips, was waiting for an explanation as to why Imogen had been chauffeur-driven home on the back of Mr Kenny's motorised scooter.

'Mam, Dad, can we get inside first and then I'll fill you in? My ankle hurts.'

'Come on then.' Nora turned and bustled back inside the pub, holding the door open for Mr Kenny while Imogen and Liam gave him the right of way.

'There's a pint on the house for you, Ned, as a thank you for rescuing my daughter,' Liam said, and Imogen leaned on her dad's arm for support.

'Sure, I feel like I'm walking you down the aisle,' Liam said as she hobbled into the pub alongside him. 'Take your time there, Imogen, because I've a feeling this is the closest I'm going to get to that for the foreseeable future where any of you girls are concerned.'

'It's not like it was in your day, Dad.'

'No. It's not.' Nora Kelly tossed back over her shoulder. 'You're all after cohabiting together before you've got a ring on your finger. It's still living in sin, you know.'

'You've got to try before you buy, Mam.'

Nora made a snorting sound. 'There's a chance you'd not be here if I'd done that. Sure, if I'd known your father was incapable of putting his dirty socks in the laundry basket, I might still be footloose and fancy-free.' She bustled through to the family quarters, and Imogen caught the words 'put the kettle on' before the door closed behind her.

It was tongue-in-cheek. Imogen knew her mam and dad loved the bones off one another, as did her nan and late granddad, with whom they'd grown up at the Shamrock Inn. She fancied it was for this reason that she and her sisters had set the bar high regarding the men in their lives. They'd a lot to live up to.

'Hello there, Hannah. How're those bees of yours treating you?' Enda Dunne was propping up the bar in his usual spot, toying with a Guinness beer mat and hoping for a glance of Kitty Kelly.

'I'm Imogen, Mr Dunne. I'm an interior designer.' She couldn't resist a quick hair flick as she tried to reassemble her pride.

Enda Dunne carried blithely on. 'There's been two bee stings already since those hives went in the beer garden.'

The words 'bee stings' were said with the same gravity you might reserve for fatality, Imogen thought, shaking her head. 'What's this about hives out the back?' She looked up at her dad. 'You told Hannah to forget it when she was on about it at Christmas.' Her sister had tried to talk her into making beehives an addition to the rooftop garden which came with her top-floor apartment, but she'd given her a flat-out no.

'She's a determined one, your sister. She gets it from your mother. We knew we'd not get a moment's peace until we did our bit for Ireland's bee population.'

'But Dad, you can't have punters getting stung when they're trying to enjoy their pints in sunshine.'

'That was Lorcan's fault.'

'Lorcan McGrath.'

'One and the same. He was wearing a snazzy orange shirt, hoping to impress the ladies from your mammy's Menopausal and Hot Monday meeting. There are one or two widows in the mix, and Mona Murphy's after giving her husband the heave-ho. The bees thought Lorcan was a giant flower sitting there so.'

'They got him here and here.' Enda pointed to his chin and cheek. 'It wasn't pretty, but Kitty came to the rescue with the vinegar, good woman that she is.'

Christ on a bike! Lorcan McGrath, a farmer who'd been on a quest to find a lady love for as long as Imogen could remember, had a face like a bulldog chewing a wasp as it was.

'We'll get honey, you know. I can tell you that sweetened the deal. I'm after watching YouTube videos on beekeeping. Sure, it will be a doddle.'

'I don't know why you're looking so chuffed with yourself about the honey. Mam would smack your knuckles with the teaspoon if she caught you hoeing into it. How much weight are you after losing since Christmas?' To Imogen's eye, he'd be lucky if it was a pound, especially with Nan sabotaging her mam's efforts to follow the doctor's orders and lose a stone or two every chance she got.

Liam mumbled something incomprehensible, and Imogen remembered Shep. 'Enda, Shep's outside. He must have got loose from outside the butcher's because I found him sitting on the roadside at the end of the village. He could do with a drink

as he's after running into the village behind Mr Kenny's
scooter.'

Ned Kenny was settling himself on the green leather-
topped stool he favoured at the bar and eyeing the tap of his
favourite ale.

'I'll get you that drink in a jiffy, Ned. Just let me get Imogen
settled out the back. And Enda, I'll bring you a bowl of water
for the dog,' They paused to hear what Enda had to say about
Shep.

'Ah well now, that will be on account of that minx Chanel.
She lives up that way. She's got Shep dancing to a merry tune,
so she has. He's smitten with her.'

'Chanel?' Liam and Imogen chimed.

'The Brodys' cocker spaniel.'

'So, there's life in the old dog yet,' Mr Kenny said, chuckling
away.

Imogen's mouth curved weakly at the joke. Oh yes, she was
home, she thought, scanning the pub and seeing a smattering of
familiar faces. The decor, straight out of a Pinterest board for
traditional Irish country pubs, hadn't changed one iota since her
grandparents' day. There was something very comforting,
though, in knowing you could go away and spread your wings,
then return home from time to time to find everything as it was
when you left. It gave Imogen a sense that everything would be
all right where Nev was concerned. Sure, if Hannah could talk
Mam and Dad around to the idea of beehives down the back of
the beer garden, then she'd be able to convince them the age gap
between her and Nev didn't matter.

Kitty Kelly was stirring the filling for the fish pie on the stovetop when Imogen limped into the kitchen on her father's arm. Her nan turned and beamed at her granddaughter, her wide smile lighting up her blue eyes like her son's. Liam had inherited his mam's gingery colouring, although Kitty's was fading to a sandy hue these days. The twins had inherited the paternal side of the family's colouring, while Shannon, Imogen and Hannah took after their mam with dark eyes and hair.

Kitty told Nora to put her elbow into mashing the potatoes for the fish pie topping. Then she let the wooden spoon rest against the side of the pot, wiped her hands on her pinny and held her arms out toward Imogen. A Nan hug was better than a sweet cup of tea or chocolate. She instantly felt better.

'How're you, Nan?' she asked, letting go of her father's arm and sinking into an embrace that smelled of freshly baked bread and, yes, fish, but she didn't mind one little bit, squeezing the little lady back.

'I'm grand, but your mam's after telling me you've been in the wars. Son, don't just stand there like a useless lump – fetch the poor child a chair.'

Imogen lapped up the sympathy, and once Liam had pulled out a seat from the kitchen table, she allowed Kitty to help her to sit down. Then she lifted her injured foot onto the chair where Grace always sat when she was home.

'The first thing you want to be doing is getting those ridiculous shoes off your poor feet,' Kitty tutted, sliding Imogen's pump off. 'Mark my words, Imogen. You'll be dealing with bunions by the time you're my age if you keep tottering about like so. And don't get me started on the back problems. If He' – she raised her eyes heavenward – 'had intended you to get around in those, you wouldn't have been born with flat feet!' Then, satisfied she'd said her piece, she tootled off, returning a moment later with a cushion from the television lounge, which she eased under her granddaughter's foot.

'Thanks, Nan.' It was a relief to have her foot elevated, and she caught the bag of peas Nora tossed over with a sense of déjà vu. She'd spent a portion of her Christmas visit lying about with frozen peas for company. Oh, but they felt good on her ankle. She opened the Heneghan's Pharmacy bag and placed the tablets and bandage roll on the table. 'Mam, can I have a glass of water, please?'

Nora obliged while Imogen fiddled with the tablets.

Liam loitered in the doorway as her mother put the water on the table in front of her daughter. Then waited, the spuds forgotten, for an explanation of what had happened.

Imogen swallowed the pills with a drink and then said, 'I saw Shep on the side of the road at the top of the village on my way home. You know he's always with Enda or outside Dermot Molloy's waiting for him.'

There was a murmur of agreement.

'I was worried, so I pulled over to check on him and was too busy calling him over to watch where I was going. I didn't see the pothole in the road until it was too late.'

'And you went down like a sack of spuds,' Kitty finished.

'I wouldn't have put it quite like that, Nan, but I did go over on my ankle. As for Shep, he was fine. I mean, he's just after running a half marathon here to the Shamrock. Don't forget his water, Dad. He'll be thirsty.'

'I won't.' Liam dutifully rummaged in the cupboard for a suitable bowl, listening as Imogen filled them in on the rest of her story.

'Well, it was lucky that Mr Kenny came along on his scooter when he did,' Kitty clucked.

That was debatable, given her carefully cultivated image was in tatters thanks to her tandem ride into the village. And why did Mr Smart-Arse, Ryan O'Malley, have to drive past and see her? 'Hmm,' was her non-committal reply.

'Will you tell her, or will I?' Liam looked pleased with himself.

'Tell me what?' Imogen was all ears.

'No point asking Nora, Liam. You know your mouth always runs away with you,' Kitty said with a solemn shake of her head.

'That's not true, Mam.'

'Is it not? I recall a certain son not too far from me right this very minute who promised he wouldn't breathe a word about me deciding to enter my Barmbrack into the Great Emerald Bay Bake-Off last St Paddy's. I told you Eileen Carroll is more competitive than those tennis-playing Williams sisters when it comes to the fruit loaf. And what do you know? She buys all the sultanas and raisins from here to Galway. So, I'll not be breathing a word to you about what I'm planning on entering this year.'

'Jaysus, Mam, you'll be bringing that one up at me wake.'

'Not if I get there before you, son.'

Imogen cleared her throat noisily. 'Would one of you just tell me whatever it is?'

'Hannah, Grace and Ava are coming home for St Paddy's! Of course with you and Shannon here, I'll have all my girls together.' Nora beamed. 'Why don't you invite your young man down? It's high time you introduced him to us.'

Imogen, unable to help herself, had winced at her mam's turn of phrase: 'young' man. She mustered up a bright smile. 'Grand, Mam.'

'That's settled then.' Nora looked pleased.

Imogen hadn't been aware it was up for debate in the first place. Christ on a bike, what would Nev make of Emerald Bay's celebrations with its rag-tag parade down Main Street featuring, amongst other dodgy floats, Lorcan McGrath on his tractor? She remembered the last 17 March she'd spent in the village and had to ask, 'Carmel Brady's Colleens aren't going to be leading the parade again, are they?' The Silver Spoon tearoom's owner taught Irish dance – although what her qualifications were to do so were questionable, because future Riverdancers her pupils were not. Carmel, who prided herself on being inclusive in her classes, taught all age groups. Imogen blinked, but the sight of the merry band of middle-aged dancers in their frilly costumes with dimpled knees and two left feet was scorched on her eyeballs.

'Sure, it's one of the most anticipated highlights of the parade,' Nora said.

'The craic's mighty when the Colleens take to the street,' Liam added.

God save us, Imogen thought.

'Liam, don't forget Ned's pint,' Nora reminded her husband, moving things along.

'It's all up here.' Liam tapped the side of his head and held his hand out toward Imogen. 'Keys.'

Imogen dug her hand into her pocket and passed them over.

'I'll take the jumper leads and see if Dermot can spare his young apprentice for half an hour to give me a hand. We'll soon get that car of yours started.'

'Thanks, Dad. But what if it isn't the battery?'

'Then I'll ring the garage over in Kilticaneel and get an idea of what we're looking at.' Liam carrying the water, edged carefully to the connecting door. 'Nora, would you keep an eye on the bar once I've sorted Ned and Enda?'

Nora nodded, and Liam disappeared back through to the pub.

'How's life treating you up there in the big smoke, Imogen?' Kitty asked.

'Nan, you make it sound like you've not heard from me in months. I FaceTime you all every couple of days.' Nan had never got the hang of it, and Imogen usually wound up with a bird's-eye view up her nostrils.

Kitty slid a plate of the good biscuits Nora kept hidden away from Liam toward her. 'And don't be thinking about doing the calorie counting like your mammy here. You're skin and bone, so you are. You girls are always so busy. It's a good job you pop your heads in here now and again so I can feed you back up. I'm looking forward to seeing your sisters too.'

Imogen knew better than to argue with her, and she took a chocolate biscuit, crunching into it. She was supposed to take the anti-inflammatory with food anyway, and as her nose tingled with a threatened sneeze, she cast a wary eye around the kitchen. There was no furry face peeking out at her anywhere. 'Where's the cat?'

'Napoleon's asleep on Shannon's bed. He enjoys a siesta in the afternoon sun,' Nora supplied.

A safe distance away for the time being, then, Imogen thought, relaxing.

Kitty scraped the pie filling into a dish, and Nora spooned dollops of mashed spud on top before doing something artful with a fork to give it swirly peaks. Then she picked the plate up and popped it in the oven while Kitty stacked the pots by the sink.

They rubbed along well together, her mam and Nan, Imogen thought, watching them fondly.

'Shannon will be home from work soon. She'll be able to bandage that ankle of yours for you. Will you tell me what Benmore House is like inside later? I'm dying to hear all about it,' Nora said before she followed after her husband.

'I will, Mam.'

Kitty made them both a cup of tea and, sitting down opposite Imogen, she cut straight to the chase. 'So, we'll finally meet this Nev of yours.'

The biscuit turned to sawdust in her mouth. 'Oh, Nan.' She flicked her hand dismissively, not meeting her wily gaze. 'Nev's in property development, and he's currently working on a big project. I don't know if he'll be able to spare a weekend away, and it is short notice.'

'Any fella who's worth his salt would find time to meet his girlfriend's family, Imogen,' Kitty said, watching her grand-daughter over the rim of her teacup.

What could she say to that? Imogen knew it was true, but it wasn't Nev who was reluctant to show his face here in Emerald Bay. The pressure for Nev to meet her family was coming from both sides. She couldn't very well fess up that she was petrified of her parent's reaction to his age. Not to him or them. Her dad was a big softie, but he could be fierce regarding his girls. Nor could she blame Nan for being curious about him, not with her history of calling things off before they got serious. At just over seven months, Imogen was heading for a relationship record. It was easy to keep her life separate from her family in Dublin but nigh impossible here in Emerald Bay.

'You know your mam and dad are beginning to wonder if you're ashamed of them. Him with his high-flying job and all.'

'Nan!' Imogen's eyes shot up from where she was examining a knot in the table's scrubbed wood top. 'Of course, I'm not ashamed of them!' The very thought of her parents thinking that was upsetting. She knew she put on airs and graces like others did lipstick, but it wasn't who she was deep down. It was a coat of armour. And hand on heart, she'd never been ashamed of where she came from. Embarrassed on the odd occasion, definitely, like when she was fifteen, and her dad had appeared at the nightclub over there in Kilticaneel and hauled her and Fi out. Or, worse, Mam giving her the birds and the bees chat. But those were normal teenage things.

Kitty put her tea down. 'I didn't say you were. I said they were beginning to wonder.'

'Imo!'

Shannon's sudden appearance was a welcome one, Imogen thought, relieved to get Nan off the topic of Nev.

'What have you done to your foot?' Shannon asked, dumping her carpet bag full of medical supplies on the table before giving her sister a hello hug. She released her and frowned. 'You're not looking your usual fashion model self, unless wild and woolly is in this season.'

Imogen put a hand to her hair which was a bit of a bird's nest. 'It's my ankle, not my foot, and a trip on the back of a motorised scooter driven by Ireland's answer to Lewis Hamilton will do that to a girl's hair.'

Shannon's eyebrows shot up.

'There's tea in the pot, Shannon,' Kitty said.

'I'll join you both in a minute – just let me get out of my uniform. You've got some explaining to do, Imo.'

9

Imogen had drilled Shannon for the latest about her and James as her sister wound the bandage tightly around her ankle. The dreamy expression in Shannon's eyes as she cut off Imogen's circulation told her everything she needed to know. Shannon Kelly was head over heels in love, and Liam was quick to interject into their conversation once he'd put the phone down on the mechanic who'd towed Imogen's car back to the garage in Kilticaneel, James Cabot was a keeper.

Imogen listened as Shannon, safety pinning the bandage, told her his mam was doing as well as expected, adding that cancer was a bastard. Nobody argued as she went on to say Maeve was making the most of every moment with her new family.

Satisfied with her handiwork, Shannon straightened and gathered knives and forks from the drawer under the kitchen worktop to set the table. Liam sat down alongside Imogen and told her the mechanic said she'd be without her car for the next few days, at least while he got to the bottom of what he suspected was an electrical problem.

Imogen tapped her fingernails on the table, pondering what to do because she needed a car to get to Benmore House.

'Does he have a courtesy car I could use, Dad?'

'He does.'

Problem solved, she thought, relieved it had been a simple fix.

'Only it's on loan to Derbhilla Roche at the moment because she was after giving that lad of hers a driving lesson when Sergeant Badger – you know how he all but covers his Garda vehicle in camouflage to catch the speeders on the country lanes?'

Imogen nodded. She did know first-hand.

'Well, he saw them bunny hopping along there and noticed they'd no L plates displayed, so he flicked his siren on to get them to pull over. Of course, the poor lad was spooked. He hit accelerate instead of the brake, and they wound up in Lorcan McGrath's paddock. No one was hurt, though, that's the main thing, but the poor sheep got a terrible fright, and then Lorcan was after getting stung twice by the bees—'

Imogen cut her father off, having heard enough. 'How will I get to Benmore House? I couldn't borrow your truck, could I?'

'Well, normally I'd say yes, but I've got an appointment with the chiropractor in Kilticaneel for my back tomorrow.'

'It's not bending your knees when you're changing the barrels has done that,' Nora tutted, catching the end of the conversation as she swept through from the bar.

'Don't look at me,' Shannon said, seeing Imogen do precisely that. 'I need mine for my rounds.'

'Don't fret on it now,' Nora said as she and Kitty began to dish up steaming plates of fish pie with a side serving of buttered cabbage. 'We'll sort something out.'

The conversation around the table turned to Benmore House once they were all seated. Imogen, between forkfuls, described the opulent grandeur of the house, which in parts was beginning to fade, and explained what she'd been tasked with doing. Kitty and Nora were lapping it up. Both women were intrigued to learn what the house was like behind closed doors.

'Well now, that's news so: Lachlan Leslie getting married in the gardens,' Nora said, forgetting her weight-loss programme as she reached for a buttered bread roll. 'I love a wedding, me.'

'Bully for him,' Liam muttered, spearing a shrimp. He'd no time for what the house on the hill or its part-time inhabitants symbolised. 'I wouldn't hold your breath for an invitation, Nora.'

'I won't be, but it would be nice to catch a glimpse of the bride. I wonder if they'll do a drive through the village?'

Shannon was nonplussed over Imogen's latest interior undertaking, knowing what had happened to Maeve Doolin at the house. Although at the mention of Lachlan Leslie, her gaze flicked toward her sister. 'You were friendly with him way back, weren't you?'

Imogen tensed, her fork poised halfway to her mouth. *Here we go.*

'I didn't know that,' Nora said, speaking with her mouth full. Her brown eyes widened at this bit of information.

'You played that card close to your chest.' Kitty looked toward Imogen.

Liam muttered something incomprehensible where the only words Imogen caught were 'arrogant and arse'.

'Thanks a million,' she lobbed across the table at Shannon.

'What? I was just saying.'

The expectant eyes of her family were upon her, so, with a sigh, she said, 'I met him at the bay, and we hung out for a few weeks in the summer holidays when I was sixteen. I didn't tell you because there was nothing to tell – and even if there was, I was a teenager; therefore, I didn't tell you anything.' But, of course, there was plenty to tell. He'd broken her heart, and his mother, the old witch, had made her feel inferior and not worthy of her son. It was a feeling she'd fought hard to shake for the longest while.

'Sounds about right,' Liam said. 'It was like getting blood out of a stone trying to find out what you girls were up to when you were that age. You turned me grey before my time, the lot of you.'

'You're sandy, not grey,' Nora stated loyally, having swallowed her food. 'Like Bryan Adams.'

'A cuddly Bryan Adams.' Shannon smirked.

'With a penchant for his mam's cooking,' Kitty added, before saying, 'You always were a secret squirrel, Imogen.'

Imogen snorted. 'Chance would have been a fine thing! Everybody knows everybody's business in Emerald Bay.' She scraped up the remains of the creamy sauce, having already resolved to run her finger around the pot for any leftovers before it went into the sink.

'What was she like? Your Swiss one. She strikes me as a cool customer,' Nora asked curiously.

'Swedish, Mam. And Sigrid's one of those dream clients who makes my work easy because she lets me get on with my job.'

'But is she nice?' Nora persisted.

'And did she offer you a cup of tea?' Kitty enquired. This was of vital importance in Kitty's world. In her opinion, a host who didn't offer their guest a brew was not worth bothering about, never mind Imogen was at Benmore House on business.

'She's pleasant, but I'm there to work, not exchange meaningful heart-to-hearts with her, and yes, I got tea and a slice of lemon cake.'

'I should think so, too,' Kitty sniffed. 'Eat up. I've bread pudding for afters.'

'God Almighty, Shannon! Would you slow down? Nobody's going to take the plate off you,' Liam remarked.

'She'd be around my age, wouldn't she, Imogen?' Nora asked.

'A few years younger, Mam. I don't think she'd be fifty. Their two girls are only in their early teens.'

'Women are having children later and later in life, Imogen. It's what keeps me going where you girls are concerned.'

Imogen and Shannon rolled their eyes at their mam's martyrish tone.

Nora allowed herself a few seconds to feel sorry for herself for her lack of grandchildren before asking, 'Did you notice her getting red in the face and fanning herself?'

'No. Why?' Imogen wished her mam would get to the point.

'Only, I thought you could mention my Menopausal and Hot group to her. Tell the poor woman she doesn't have to suffer in silence in that big house if she's after having hot flashes.'

'I don't think she's suffering, Mam. Your woman was as cool as a cucumber.' But then, she remembered who else had been at Benmore House. 'Oh, and I tell you who's doing the building work. Ryan O'Malley.'

Shannon snorted. 'The bra-pinger? You punched him in the nose at high school, didn't you?'

'I did – only he's after telling me today he was falsely accused. But yes, that Ryan O'Malley.'

'Aileen mentioned their Ryan was working on a renovation up at Benmore. He's from good stock and a good boy, looking after his mam and dad the way he has,' Nora said. Liam nodded his agreement. 'The O'Malleys have had a hard time of it lately,' she said to Imogen.

'Why? What happened?' Imogen was curious.

'Poor Don had a stroke,' Nora supplied.

'He's had to make lifestyle changes,' said Liam, reaching for a bread roll.

Nora slapped his hand away. 'Speaking of which, you'll not

be having that and a serving of your mam's bread pudding. So, what's it to be?'

Liam put the roll back in the breadbasket.

Imogen listened to her mam inform her father of the benefits of the Mediterranean diet before lamenting what a good son Ryan was, packing his life up in London like so to take over his dad's building business. It had been a weight off poor Don and Aileen's minds.

Her assumption that he'd never left Emerald Bay made Imogen flush. She felt awful. He must think her a right up-herself madam. How many other sons would drop everything as he had? she wondered. She might be on the fence about whether he was guilty as charged when it came to the bra ping-ing, but she admired his selflessness, and he went up in her estimation.

'I'm after having a brainwave.'

'I thought you looked strange, son,' Kitty said, eyes twinkling as Liam pulled a face at her.

'Imogen, you just said yourself Ryan O'Malley's doing the building work up at Benmore. Why don't you give him a call after dinner and see if he can't pick you up on his way through in the morning?'

It made sense, but Imogen was reluctant. 'I don't know how to get hold of him, Dad.' It was a poor excuse, and she knew it.

'Sure, I've got the O'Malleys' number,' Nora said, pleased to help. 'Aileen's in my Menopausal and Hot group, even though she's technically well past all that. It's the get-together she enjoys.'

'It's the wine you lot enjoy,' Liam stated.

That was that then, Imogen thought, knowing she'd have to go cap in hand and ring Ryan O'Malley after dinner.

The conversation moved swiftly to St Patrick's Day and the fete, while the pudding was enjoyed.

'We'll be a full house that weekend with all you girls home,' Nora said to no one in particular.

'Is the Laura Ashley suite booked?' Imogen asked. She was still miffed her mam hadn't let her see to the redecorating of the guest rooms, but then Nora insisted Imogen's flair for decor had been passed down from her. That was debatable, she'd thought, inspecting the Cape Cod seaside-themed bedrooms and the floral abomination at the end of the hall overlooking Main Street.

The Kellys were well used to sharing their family quarters with the guests who'd come to stay in the rooms above the Shamrock Inn. James had stayed with them over Christmas, affording him and Shannon plenty of time to realise they were made for one another.

'It is. We've a gentleman not far from where James lives coming to stay.' Nora ignored the Laura Ashley jibe as she saw the time and got out of her seat. She began clearing the dishes off the table. Chloe, who manned the pub while the Kellys had a dinner break, would be moseying home soon, and she and Liam would take over.

'I'd help with the washing up, Mam, but I can't stand for long on my ankle,' Imogen apologised.

Shannon said something about bringing in a bar stool so she could perch at the sink, and Imogen poked her tongue out at her sister's back. She was desperate to hobble upstairs and ring Nev.

'Would you like to watch *Fair City* with me, Imogen?' Kitty asked.

'No, thank you, Nan. I've got phone calls to make.'

'Are you after ringing your fella to tell him about the party?' Nora asked, a stack of dirty plates in her hands. She put them down on the worktop and wiped her hands on a tea towel.

'I'll see if he can make it, Mam, and I need to ring Ryan O'Malley, too'

Nora retrieved her phone book from the drawer that was

home to everything from scissors, pens, and a few random spools of cotton. Tearing off a piece of paper from the notepad by the landline they kept predominantly for the business these days, she jotted down a phone number.

Shannon, hearing her mam reference Nev, raised an eyebrow in her sister's direction. Imogen had shared a photograph of herself and her new beau with her sisters at Christmas. Having seen Nev with her own two eyes, Shannon understood her sister's reluctance to introduce him to the family.

'Here we are. You'll get hold of Ryan at that number.' Nora pressed the paper into her daughter's palm. 'And don't be worrying about the dishes. Off you go now. Shannon can manage.'

This time it was Shannon who poked her tongue out as Imogen excused herself and hobbled upstairs.

10

———

Imogen closed the door of the room she'd commandeered, having tried out the three beds like she was Goldilocks before deciding Ava's was just right. It was the bed she'd slept in at Christmas, but she'd wanted reassurance she wasn't missing out. Ava, who was mad about Napoleon the cat, wouldn't mind bunking in with Shannon again when she and Grace came home for a long weekend.

The beach vibe her mam had run with in here had a relaxing aesthetic, she decided. Her verdict was that if she were a paying guest, given the nightly rate, she'd be happy enough with it. Dad had carted her bags up and deposited them at the foot of the bed. They were waiting to be unpacked, but first, she needed to check her phone. She'd left it charging on the bedside table because even though she was a grown woman in her thirties, she didn't dare break her parents' rule about no phones at the dinner table.

A yawn threatened as she unplugged it from the charger. It had been a big day, and stifling it, Imogen pulled the spare pillow out from under her head and placed it at the bottom of the bed to rest her ankle on, getting comfortable before she scanned the phone screen greedily. She was desperate to see if she'd missed any calls from Nev and was relieved when she saw his number displayed. He'd rung forty-five minutes ago and not left a message, but the fact he'd rung was a good sign that he was as eager to kiss and make up as she was.

She was about to ring him back when she hesitated and decided it would be prudent to organise tomorrow's ride to Benmore first. She fished the O'Malleys' landline number Mam had scribbled down out of her pocket and, unfolding it, tapped the digits out. She placed her spare hand on her tummy as it rang, groaning softly. She'd eaten way too much, but it had been a delicious break from her usual low-carb, organic foods diet. There was no point in being disciplined when she was home because Nan would never let her hear the end of it if she hinted at using almond milk or adding a sprinkle of chia seeds or the like to her porridge. Sometimes Imogen wondered what would happen if she ate what she liked and fired her trainer, sadist that she was. Would Nev still want to be with her if she didn't add a certain sparkle when her arm was linked through his at the various events they attended in Dublin? She was saved from having to probe that thought deeper by the phone being picked up.

'Aileen O'Malley speaking.'

'Hello, Mrs O'Malley, it's Imogen Kelly calling. Would Ryan be about, please?'

'Oh, hello there, Imogen. Your mam told us at our meeting last Monday that you were back in Emerald Bay for a few weeks. How are you settling in?'

Imogen suspected more time was spent gossiping over their family lives at these Menopausal & Hot get-togethers of her mam's than mulling over remedies for the night sweats.

'Grand, thank you, Mrs O'Malley. There's nothing like Mam and Nan's home cooking.'

Aileen O'Malley gave a tinkling laugh. 'Our Ryan says the

same. So, Nora was saying you're home to get Benmore ready for the big wedding too?'

'Yes, I am.' Imogen remembered what Mam had said earlier. 'Mrs O'Malley?'

'Aileen, dear.'

'Aileen. I was very sorry to hear about Mr O'Malley being unwell.'

Aileen's voice caught. 'Thank you, dear. It's not been easy for any of us, least of all Don. But we've got each other, and the children have been wonderful. Ryan's seeing to his dad, but he won't be long, if you'd like me to ask him to call you back?'

'That would be grand, thank you, er, Aileen.'

'Give me a tick to lay my hands on a pen. It's a mysterious thing, Imogen, how there's never one about when you need it.'

'I know what you mean.' Imogen laughed. For that very reason, she kept a box of ballpoints in her desk drawer at home.

The woman was back a moment later. 'Right, I'm good to go.'

Imogen recited her mobile phone number and, saying her goodbyes, ended the call. She stared up at the ceiling. What was Ryan helping his dad with? she wondered. It must be incredibly difficult to see your parent go from being fit, able and independent to needing care like so. She bit her lip, deliberating on how they'd cope if something like that happened to their dad. The answer was a simple one. They'd manage because they were family, and that's what you did.

Hoping Ryan wouldn't be too long calling her back because she was desperate to ring Nev, Imogen was distracted from any further thoughts by a mewling and scrabbling at the door.

'Get away with you,' she called, which only intensified the carry-on outside the door. She hauled herself off the bed and began unpacking which wasn't easy on one foot, all the while trying to ignore Napoleon's increasing desperation to come in. She'd just hung up a trouser suit when it went silent. Her eyes narrowed, and she tilted her head to one side, listening out, but could hear nothing apart from the sounds of Nan shouting at the television below. This was what it must feel like to be under siege, Imogen thought, hopping over to the door, unable to resist a peek out the door to see if the coast was clear.

A flurry of tortoiseshell fur flew inside the room, and Imogen shrieked as Napoleon leapt on her bed and, lifting a paw, began to wash. He gave her a look she read as, 'You're fighting a losing battle, sister. I always win in the end.' Her nose itched, and she sneezed violently twice and, gasping for air in between, caught a whiff of something eyewatering. She hobbled to the top of the stairs and bellowed, 'Shannon! Get that cat of yours out of my room.'

Shannon's dark head appeared at the bottom of the stairs. 'What are you shouting about?'

'Napoleon tricked me into opening my bedroom door, and now he's sitting on my bed like he owns the place, and he's after letting off. It's disgusting.'

Shannon's mouth trembled.

'It's not funny. Do something about it.'

She disappeared and reappeared a split second later, armed with a can of peach air freshener as she stampeded up the stairs.

Imogen stood aside as her sister swept into her bedroom and scooped up her cat. Holding him tight, she marched down the hall to her room, popping him in there and closing the door.

'You should have told him he was a naughty boy,' Imogen said as her sister returned and began to spray the freshener about the bedroom. 'Jesus wept, Shannon. I'll smell like James from the Giant Peach story.'

'It's better than smelling like rotten fish, isn't it?'

'You're going to have to do something about that cat. He's a menace.'

'He only wants to get to know you is all.'

'Well, the feeling's not mutual.'

Her phone began ringing from over on the bed and, shutting the door on her sister, she stalked over to answer it.

'Hello, Imogen speaking.'

'Hi, Imogen, Mam said you rang.'

The air freshener caught in her throat, and she erupted into a violent coughing fit. 'Sorry,' she gasped, limping over to the window and flinging it open wide. The laneway it overlooked was empty, and she breathed in the fresh air in great big gulps.

'Are you OK?'

'Fine,' Imogen rasped. 'Shannon's cat sneaked into my room and did something unspeakable, and then Shannon sprayed half a can of air freshener in here. I'm hanging out the window now so I won't die of peach air freshener poisoning. Oh, and I've twisted my ankle.'

Ryan was laughing.

'It's not funny.'

'It is from where I'm sitting. I can ring you back if you want to go and get a glass of water.'

'No, you're grand.'

'Did you enjoy your ride into town earlier? That was a class act.'

She bit her lip, having almost forgotten about her motorised chariot, thinking Ryan hadn't changed from their schooldays, as she caught the mirth in his tone. He was still a smart arse. She didn't want to get caught up telling the story of what had happened for the umpteenth time either. 'It was a tad brisk, given that breeze, but otherwise, so far as Uber experiences go, it was grand, thanks. I'll be leaving my review on Trip Advisor shortly under the heading Unique Experiences in Emerald Bay.'

'I hope Ned didn't charge you!' Ryan said, properly laughing now.

To her surprise, Imogen realised she was smiling. 'No, you'll be glad to know he didn't.'

'Good, because I wouldn't put it past him to register himself as an Uber driver if he cottoned on it could be a good way to earn his beer money.'

Laughter bubbled at the idea of the one and only Uber driver in Emerald Bay picking up his punters on his motorised scooter.

Remembering why she'd rung, Imogen said, 'You've probably guessed my car's after breaking down, and it's going to be out of action for a few days, so I wondered if I could catch a ride to Benmore House in the morning with you?'

'You know you'll get tongues wagging in the village, don't you?'

'What do you mean?'

'Well, riding on the back of Ned Kenny's scooter one day and being picked up by a local builder the next. Before you know it, you'll be thumbing a ride on Lorcan McGrath's tractor!'

Imogen convulsed. 'That, I can promise you, will never happen. Can you help me out?'

'Of course, it's not a bother. I'll pick you up at about eight?'

'Thanks a million. I'll wait for you out the front of the pub.' Saying goodbye, she hung up. 'Sorted,' she said out loud. 'Now you've got to fix things between you and Nev.' She took a deep breath and rang his number.

It went to voicemail. She left a breezy message asking him to give her a call back when he could, then hung up and tossed the phone down on the bed next to her.

It was an anti-climax, and she wasn't sure what to do with herself. She didn't want to hang out here all evening and planned to pop through to the pub to see who was about for a chat. Then, remembering her case, she set to finishing her unpacking. By the time she'd hung the last of her clothes up, enjoying all the extra wardrobe space having the room to herself afforded, her ankle was aching and her phone signalled an incoming FaceTime call.

She hastily peered in the mirror, wiping her eyeliner where it had smudged, moistening her lips and fluffing her hair before sitting on the edge of the bed. She was grateful to take the weight off her foot. 'Hello, you,' she answered as Nev's familiar face filled the screen. The background was nondescript, signalling he was in a hotel room.

'I'm sorry, Bunny, I'm missing you already.' His expression was earnest as he smoothed back his thick thatch of silvered hair. 'I've been in back-to-back meetings all day, and all I could think about was you.'

'Me too. I hated leaving Dublin with things hanging like that between us.'

'You're at the Shamrock Inn, then?'

'Yes.' She angled the phone to give him a look at her bedroom. 'Although it's been quite a day.' But she didn't want to get into all of that. It was time to clear the air, and there was only one way she could do that. 'St Paddy's is a big deal in Emerald Bay, and my sisters are all coming home for the weekend. Mam and Dad are after inviting you to come and stay.' Her body was tense. 'I'd like you to, too.'

Nev, who'd raised a red wine to his mouth, lowered the glass. 'I'm supposed to be heading to Dusseldorf that weekend, but I'll get Prue to reschedule it for the following weekend. I wouldn't miss the chance to meet the couple who made my beautiful girlfriend.'

A warm glow settled over her, and all the tension left her body. She'd chosen Nev, and her dad would have to accept that. That was all there was to it. Sure, lookit, the man could win over hard-nosed financiers worldwide, convincing them to invest. Liam Kelly would be a walk in the park by comparison. 'I wish you were here now.'

'Me too. What would we be doing if I was?' He gave her that half-lidded look.

Imogen knew, given she was in her bedroom at her family home, it wasn't likely they'd be doing anything more than holding hands. Nor was she in the mood for being a FaceTime femme fatale, but she didn't want him getting sulky just as they'd made up. So, she gave him the pouty come-to-bed look she knew he loved and began to tell him what he wanted to hear.

When she'd finished, and he'd picked up his wine again, she asked, 'And what about your girls, Nev?' She knew he carried a lot of guilt over his divorce from their mother, and to be fair, it was his fault. He'd been the one who'd had an affair. She knew his girls flung this in his face regularly, blaming the sins of their father for their failings regarding their relationships.

'I'm going to speak to them, I promise. As soon as I get home from London. You're right: they're old enough to sort out their problems without Dad intervening.'

Imogen exhaled. It was a big step for him to put his foot down, proving he was as serious about her as she was about him. 'Thank you.'

'I love you, Imogen. You're my number one girl.'

She could see it in his eyes. He meant it, and she was putty in his hands. 'I love you too.' At least, she thought she did. Her only prior experience of being in love had been the legs-turning-to-jelly, heart-racing kind. Nev didn't make her feel like Lachlan had, but that kind of love was for kids. He was the first man she'd come close to opening her heart to since it had been trampled on all those years ago; sixteen was a tender age to learn that life wasn't a fairy tale. Besides, Nev ticked all the boxes, and so far as Imogen was concerned, there was a lot to be said for box-ticking.

'Things will be different when you get back to Dublin, I

promise. Use this time away to think about moving in with me when you get back, Imogen.'

'I will.'

Nev had said all the right things. Imogen felt much better when she disconnected the call. Moving in with him was a natural progression of their relationship. She could rent her apartment out, which meant it didn't just make romantic sense but financial sense too. Always one to take things a step further, she lay on the bed a while longer, expecting to drift off into a wedding day fantasy where she envisaged life as Mrs Nev Delaney, but then it took a turn, and it was Lachlan Leslie standing next to her at the altar.

Imogen swiftly pulled the plug on the image and sat up, unaware of where that daydream had come from. The best place for her was the pub, where she decided there was bound to be craic of some sort happening.

One thing was sure, she thought, shuffling from the room: she couldn't be trusted on her own.

11

Imogen shivered, beginning to wish she'd pulled a jacket on over her silk jumpsuit. She glanced at her wristwatch, thinking she should have known better. In Ireland, you needed to dress for four seasons in one day. Ryan was due in four minutes to pick her up, and she hoped he was punctual because her ankle was already aching, and she wasn't used to wearing flat shoes either. Having decided it was better to err on the side of caution and be a few minutes early rather than the other way around, she'd been standing outside the pub for a good three minutes.

The day hadn't kicked off to the best start because she'd overslept, and Shannon had taken forever in the bathroom. As a result, her make-up was slapdash, and her hair piled high in a wobbly topknot. She'd planned on skipping breakfast, but Nan had other ideas, sitting her down for a bowl of porridge before she'd let her out the door.

Paddy McNamara was weaving his way down the footpath of Main Street toward her even though it was barely eight o'clock in the morning. A spark of sympathy flared at the sight of him. It was no wonder the tourists gave him a wide berth. He did look like he was up to no good with that tatty old mac of his.

She could see the bottleneck of whatever tipple he'd got his hands on protruding from his pocket.

'How're you, Paddy?' she asked as he drew nearer.

He stopped, swaying as he dazzled her with his gappy, yellow-toothed grin. 'Nora Kelly. You'd give the Rose of Tralee a run for her money on this fine morning, so you would.'

Imogen managed not to grimace at the fumes coming off him, smiling instead. 'I'm Imogen, Paddy. Nora's daughter.'

'Imogen,' he corrected himself. 'This year's Rose of Tralee.'

'That's kind of you to say, Paddy. You're out and about early.'

'Ah, well now, that's down to Bridget, that is.'

He was so serious it was comical, Imogen thought, as the cardboard supermodel on display in the window of Heneghan's Pharmacy over Christmas and now ensconced in Paddy's cottage sprang to mind. She played along with him. 'What's happened?'

'She booted me out, so she did. We're after having words, so I decided to go down to the park and pick her a bunch of flowers to see if I can't smooth things over.'

There was no point telling him that picking flowers in the park was prohibited, she decided. 'That sounds like a good plan, Paddy, but why don't you get yourself something for breakfast first? The Silver Spoon will be opening up about now.' Imogen knew Carmel Brady liked to catch the tradespeople passing through from Kilticaneel of a morning. She opened her phone wallet and pulled out one of the notes tucked away, pressing it on Paddy.

'You've got a heart that will see you at those pearly gates when your time comes, Shannon. Tell your mammy I said so.'

Imogen's eyes twinkled as he said the wrong name, not bothering to correct him, and he turned back, staggering in the direction he'd come from, singing 'Bridget O'Malley' mournfully.

Out of the corner of her eye, Imogen saw Mrs Tattersall emerging from the Bus Stop across the way. Risking a glance over, she saw the village bite was bumping her trolley bag behind her with a face like a pickled gherkin.

It was a bad move and she instantly regretted her nosiness when Mrs Tattersall called across the street to her. 'The Gallaghers have only gone and put the price of bread up again.'

Imogen hoped to get away with a sympathetic smile, but it wasn't her lucky morning.

'And the price of milk would make your eyes bleed. But sure, what am I to do? Mr Tattersall likes a milky cup of tea with his toast in the morning. Not much in this world gives that man pleasure these days, what with his knees paining him so. And I'll not have him deprived of his breakfast because those two there are lining their pockets.'

Mother of God. She could do without her moaning on, Imogen thought, taking note of the headscarf she never left home without, along with her brown coat. No wonder the only pleasure the long-suffering Mr Tattersall got was tea and toast.

'And would you tell your Shannon, I'm beginning to think that a leprechaun trained the doctor she works for. Those tablets he's after getting Mr Tattersall to trial haven't made a blind difference to his poor old knees.'

'I'll pass it on, Mrs Tattersall,' Imogen replied, thinking she'd do no such thing. She let out a puff of air, relieved to see Ryan's Hilux heading down the street. She needed a double shot espresso to deal with the likes of Mrs Tattersall first thing in the morning, and there was no chance of that in Emerald Bay, she thought, waving out.

The road was empty, and Ryan veered across the centre line to pull over, facing the wrong way outside the Shamrock Inn. Imogen bit down on her bottom lip, trying not to laugh at the apocalyptic expression on Mrs Tattersall's face. She hobbled around to the passenger door, which Ryan had leaned over to open for her and hauled herself onto the seat.

Ryan was giving the older woman a cheeky grin and wave.

'You know you're for it now, don't you? She'll be on the phone to Sergeant Badger as soon as she gets in her front door.'

He grinned, flicking his hair out of his eyes. 'It won't be the first time.'

Imogen placed her laptop case in the footwell and buckled in. Meanwhile, Ryan, having checked the coast was clear, gunned the engine, pulled away from the kerb and swung the truck over to the left-hand side of the road with a little more gusto than was necessary. Imogen didn't dare look back over her shoulder but guessed the older woman would be shaking her fist.

'Thanks for picking me up.'

'No big deal. I'm coming this way anyway. How's the ankle today?'

'A little better, thanks.'

'You want to try and keep the weight off it as much as possible.'

'Hmm.'

They lapsed into silence, passing by the slew of pastel-coloured shops on either side of Main Street. The only sign of life was inside the Silver Spoon, as she'd not long told Paddy. She peered around Ryan, trying to see if Paddy was in there, but they'd already passed by the tearoom and were level with Freya's art gallery and bespoke jewellers. Freya, Shannon's best friend, had painted the shop a bold blue which suited its name, Mermaids.

Freya had joined them in the pub last night, and Imogen picked up on her seeming a little quiet. She'd asked Shannon about this when Freya went up to the bar.

'It's Oisin who's getting her down, arty-farty eejit that he is.'

Imogen hadn't met Freya's fella, but she'd heard her gushing about him at Christmas before she'd hotfooted it over to West-port, where he was staying for the festive period. She'd gleaned enough from Shannon's body language each time Freya dropped Oisin's name into the conversation – which, from memory, was frequently – to know her sister had him pegged as a waste of space.

'He was supposed to be in Emerald Bay this weekend to help Freya select the paintings he wants to sell at the Paddy's Day market. Instead, he'll wind up leaving it to her to organise everything. That's how he rolls.'

'Why isn't he coming?' Imogen asked, making sure Freya was still out of earshot and thinking perhaps Shannon was being too harsh.

'For the usual reason: a better offer. Freeloading arse.' Shannon's mouth had done that puckered thing it always did when she disapproved of something.

'Wow! You really don't like him, do you?'

'No.' Shannon's reply was clipped as she sipped on her OJ.

She might have blue hair and dress like she should be dancing around a stone table in a paddock, but Freya was far too nice to be putting up with this Oisin gombeen, Imogen thought as Freya sat back down.

As the Hilux rounded the bend leaving the village behind them, Imogen remembered what she'd learned about Ryan's family the night before. She opened her mouth, and they both spoke at the same time.

'Sorry, you go first,' Imogen spoke up.

'Any word on your car?'

'Not yet. The mechanic who collected it last night thought it might be electrical, which means expensive. But hopefully you won't have to cart me back and forth for longer than a few days.'

'I don't mind.' He held her gaze for a moment.

There it was, Imogen thought, the mischievous gleam in his

eyes she remembered so well from their schooldays. Were his eyes brown or black? She wondered why she was contemplating his eye colour in the first place and was the first to look away.

'What were you going to say?'

Imogen wasn't sure how to word what she wanted to say, so she kept it simple. 'Just that Mam told me what happened to your dad. I'm very sorry.'

Ryan's grip tightened on the steering wheel. 'He's not dead.'

Her cheeks pinkened at his harsh tone. She wasn't used to being flustered, and she found herself giving a bumbling apology.

'I, er, I know. I'm sorry that came out wrong. I should have chosen my words more carefully. I meant to say I was sorry to hear you've all had a tough time.'

'Feck!' Ryan banged the steering wheel with both hands, and Imogen jumped. She could see the muscle in the side of his neck working then he exhaled slowly. 'You're right. It is tough, but that doesn't give me the right to be offhand with you. I knew what you meant. Sorry.'

'It's OK.'

He took his eyes off the road to see if she meant it.

'It's OK,' Imogen said a second time with a small smile.

His shoulders relaxed, and his earlier good humour was restored as, turning the dial on the radio up, he said, 'Great song.'

Imogen fought back a bubble of laughter forming in her throat to no avail.

'What?' Ryan looked amused.

'Guns N' Roses?'

'You can't beat an eighties power ballad.'

This time Imogen did laugh. 'If I catch you playing the air guitar, I'll have to find another ride.'

'I'll bear that in mind. What are you into?'

There was no way she was confessing to being a Belieber –

she'd never hear the end of it. Instead, she gave a vague hand wave and said, 'Oh, this and that,' then looked to the harbour. There was no sign of the Egans' boats this morning. They'd still be out at sea, she supposed. Then, turning her head back in Ryan's direction, she asked, 'Do you have a girlfriend?'

Imogen was as surprised by the question as Ryan. Where had that come from? she wondered, feeling like she'd eaten a hot chilli. 'You can tell me to mind my own business. I was making small talk, is all.' When she was in Dublin, she'd no trouble maintaining her sophisticated facade, but five minutes back in Emerald Bay and she was behaving like a Blurt-it-out Breda.

'Er, not at the moment.' There was no sound other than Axl hitting the high notes, and then Ryan spoke up again. 'I'm guessing you know I returned to Emerald Bay earlier this year after Dad's stroke?'

Imogen nodded. 'My mam did mention it. You know what this place is like. You buy a new pair of shoes, and the whole village knows about it.'

Ryan's laugh was ironic. 'You're not far wrong there. Anyway, Dad's not supposed to have any stress, and there's always stress when you run a business. That's why I wound up things in London, where I'd lived for the last five years.'

'Including your relationship?' In for a penny, in for a pound or however the saying went, Imogen thought.

Ryan nodded. 'She was a city girl. Emerald Bay wouldn't have worked for her, and I couldn't expect her to give up her life.'

She tried to hear whether there was a resentful 'too' hanging unsaid in the air but couldn't pick anything up. 'I'm a city girl. I don't know if I could live here again.'

'I think you *think* you're a city girl.'

Imogen bristled and fixed him in her line of sight. 'What do you mean by that?'

He shrugged. 'Forget I said anything.'

They lapsed into silence, and Imogen stewed over what he'd said because he'd hit a nerve.

Ryan O'Malley didn't know her. He didn't know anything about her. They hadn't seen each other in years, for one thing, and for another, how dare he make assumptions about who she was.

It was a relief when he indicated and turned off onto the stretch of driveway leading to Benmore House.

12

Sigrid's nipped-in dress was impossibly glamorous for a day spent rattling around home, even if home was Benmore House, Imogen thought. Hadn't the woman heard of leisurewear? She explained why her ankle was bandaged while Ryan began carting building gear in. She'd limped up the front steps ignoring his offer of an arm to lean on because his city-girl comment still rankled. She finished her explanation as to how she'd hurt herself, leaving out her piggyback ride to the village on Mr Kenny's scooter.

Sigrid, her blonde head tilted to one side, passed no comment as she informed her that she and Mr Leslie were leaving for Galway shortly. 'Matthew's cousin is having a dinner party.' Her nose wrinkled, giving a clue as to what she thought of the cousin.

Imogen had seen the couple's Range Rover parked outside the front entrance with cases in its open boot when she and Ryan had pulled up. She'd thought perhaps Matthew Leslie was heading away on business. Sigrid's reaction to her husband's cousin made her more human, and she was tempted to reply that they all had 'that' cousin or, in her case, 'those' cousins, but the woman was too difficult to read and she didn't want to overstep the employer/employee line, so she said nothing.

Matthew Leslie appeared then, and if he were to strike a pose, he could have been mistaken for a model in an old Burberry advert. The laptop bag over his shoulder was the only prop ruining his country-gent look. She wondered if he had a separate wardrobe for Stockholm and Dublin. His phone was jammed to his ear, and he talked rapidly into it as he strode toward them.

'Matthew's work is tricky with the different time zones,' Sigrid explained, looking peeved nonetheless.

Imogen knew from running her own business that the smartphone could be a blessing and a curse. Always being contactable the biggest curse of all. She thought of Nev and how her whole body would tense when they were out for dinner and his phone would bleep. Why was an incoming text or call always of more importance than the person whose company you were presently in? she wondered.

Matthew barked instructions down the phone, then, holding it out in front of him, glared at it before ending the call with a shake of his head. 'The man's an idiot,' he muttered under his breath, and then his expression cleared seeing Imogen standing beside his wife.

'Sorry about that.' He cemented a smile in place. 'Good morning. We've yet to meet.' The phone was slipped into his pocket, and he held his hand out in greeting. 'I'm Matthew Leslie, and you must be—'

'Imogen Kelly. It's lovely to meet you, Mr Leslie.'

'Matthew, please, otherwise I shall have to call you Ms Kelly.'

Imogen's smile was professional. He was very smooth. A slick businessman in every respect. She recognised the ability to

charm and strike like a snake in him because she'd seen it in
Nev when it came to wheeling and dealing.

This was the first time she'd been close to Matthew Leslie,
having only ever seen him from a distance. Shannon said with
his ginger, sandy colouring, he reminded her of how Prince
Harry would look in a few years, and she agreed. He wasn't her
type, but from the circles she mixed with in Dublin, she knew
power was as attractive to some women as conventional good
looks like those of his younger brother.

'Sigrid has been singing your praises.'

Imogen nodded toward Sigrid, and the corners of her mouth
turned upward in appreciation.

'Matthew, before we go, I need a moment to run through
what's happening today with Imogen.'

'Of course, I've one more call to return before we get on the
road. I'll see you in the car, Sigrid. Good to meet you, Imogen.'

Imogen felt dismissed, watching Matthew Leslie stride
toward the front door. She doubted he ever dawdled anywhere.
Coming back from a return trip to his Hilux, Ryan stepped
aside to let him pass. He called out a cheery, 'Morning, squire.'
That made Imogen's lips twitch, but Matthew's phone was
ringing once more, and Ryan received a dip of the head in
return as the older man answered his call.

Ryan caught her eye as he crossed to the foot of the steps
and gave her a wink which she ignored as she fetched her iPad
and began scrolling through the pertinent points of the coming
week's schedule. She was all business herself as she explained
that the decorating crew based in Kilticaneel should be here by
ten o'clock at the latest to begin stripping the dated floral paper
lining the walls of the guestrooms.

Imogen wasn't likely to be rushed off her feet today, which
was a blessing given her ankle. Aside from checking what had
happened to the bed linen which should have been delivered
two days ago, she was surplus to requirements. However, she

needed to work on other projects, which she could do from the comfort of her bedroom back at the Shamrock Inn.

Once she'd finished, Sigrid gave her a satisfied nod before striding over to the enormous mirror which made the expansive foyer seem even larger. She checked her hair and make-up before telling Imogen she and her husband would be back late afternoon tomorrow. 'You have my number, of course.'

'Of course, but everything's in hand here.' She smiled reassuringly. 'Enjoy your break.'

Again, there was that nose wrinkling, implying the night away was to be endured rather than enjoyed. Then Sigrid picked up her handbag off the entry table and adjusted the leather strap over the crook of her arm, displaying the distinctive gold H informing fashionistas it was a Hermès. 'Lachlan and Victoria are coming to stay this weekend,' she said. 'They're bringing their wedding planner and will arrive late Friday evening. The happy couple will stay in Lachlan's old room and I thought Jean-Paul could take the end guestroom. I assume you have no plans to begin work on it before then?'

Imogen shook her head weakly. 'Not before then.'

'Good.' Sigrid turned to join her husband.

Imogen could hear the rumble of the Range Rover's engine and a door slamming before the vehicle crunched over the gravel. Upstairs, the strains of some punchy old rock song drifted down toward her. She was aware of none of this as she put her fingers to the base of her neck, feeling her pulse throb over Sigrid's words still echoing in her head.

Lachlan Leslie, the boy who broke her heart, was coming home to Emerald Bay. She needed to talk to the only person who really knew about what had happened between her and him: Fi.

The orangery was as good a place as any to make a private call, she decided, calling out a good morning to Francesca, who was dusting in the drawing room as she hobbled past.

It was a gorgeous space and she took a moment to appreciate her surroundings as she sat down on a wicker chair and leaned back into the cushion. She could smell the citrusy aroma of the tangerine trees in the rustic Italian pots clustered about. Her eyes travelled beyond the arched windows spanning the room's length that brought the outside inside. 'You're not here to wax lyrical all day, Imogen,' she muttered, thrusting her hand in her pocket for her phone.

A few seconds later, she heard a familiar voice. 'Imo!'

She could hear the smile in her old friend's voice. 'Hi, Fi. How is the Dally clan?'

'Aside from living in a madhouse, we're all good. Now then, when are you coming to see us?'

Imogen felt a twinge of guilt. Fi had always been there for her, but their lives had taken different trajectories these last five years, and she hadn't been as good a friend as she ought to have been.

'Euan's keeping well?' She was avoiding answering her friend's question.

'Working too hard, but you know how it goes. And don't be trying to sidetrack me. Lottie and Ben would love a visit from their Aunty Imo. FaceTiming doesn't count, and I desperately need some civilised company. C'mon now. I know you're back in Emerald Bay, sure, Galway's only around the corner.'

That was an exaggeration if ever she'd heard one, but Fi had a point. Emerald Bay was a hang of a lot closer to where her friend lived than Dublin.

'What's it like being back at Benmore House? Is it weird like you thought it would be?'

Imogen nodded, and then, realising Fi couldn't see her, she said it was.

'Well, it's got to be a good thing. You can draw the line under your Shakespearean tragedy once and for all.'

'Fi!' She'd always been a straight shooter, Imogen thought.

Fiona was unrepentant. 'It's true, Imo, you turned a straight-forward summer romance into your version of *Romeo and Juliet*. We've all had our hearts broken, but we move on and forget. And don't even think of saying the "C" word.'

'Can I spell it?'

'Go on.'

'C-L-O-S-U-R-E. I never got any.'

'It's in the past, Imo. Finish your work at Benmore and forget about first loves and whatnot. Concentrate on Nev. He makes you happy, doesn't he?'

'Mm.' Imogen was beginning to wish she hadn't rung now, even if part of her could hear the sense in Fi's words.

'Charlotte Evelyn Dally, give that back to your brother this minute!'

A scuffling sounded.

'Imo, two seconds.'

'Sure.' She watched a white butterfly flitting outside as her friend sorted out the tussle between siblings. She wasn't mater-nal. Some women were, some weren't, and it was just as well she wasn't because Nev had no desire for any more children. He'd been straight up with her about this from the start. It would be better to go their separate ways if Imogen found this a problem before they both got in too deep.

Imogen had told him she'd worked too hard to build her business to take her foot off the gas and become a mother. The world was overpopulated as it was, and she had no intention of adding to that 8.05 billion figure by procreating. They'd both looked pleased with themselves then at being on the same wave-length as they clinked glasses over the table, and Nev said, 'To us.'

'To us,' she'd echoed back.

There was more to it than that, of course. Women thought they could have it all these days, career, family, the works, but it hadn't worked that way for Fi or any of her Dublin girlfriends. They might be tiny, but babies upended your world no matter how adamant you were that they would fit in with your life and not the other way around. She'd seen it time and time again.

Take Fi as a prime example. Her best friend had had a brilliant life in Galway as a young solicitor for the city's most prominent firm. She was on a fast track to partnership, and then she met Euan, an engineer. Things had happened very quickly after that because one minute Imogen was listening to her friend gushing down the phone about the fabulous new fella she'd met and the next she was holding up Fi's train as she trotted down the aisle behind her. And then she'd found herself standing up at the font in her official godmother capacity while baby Charlotte was baptised.

She'd felt an instant connection with the little person whom she'd vowed to support and love. That they'd understand one another was a given because Lottie was a Libran too.

Imogen was an excellent godmother. She never forgot birthdays, and she always kept a notebook with her. It was her Lottie Book, and she used it to jot down pearls of wisdom to guide her god-daughter through those treacherous teenage years in due course. But when it came to the hands-on being a mam stuff, well, that was better left to Fi.

Fi had juggled motherhood and her career initially, but when baby Ben came along one year after Lottie, she didn't return to work at the end of her maternity leave.

'But what about your career?' Imogen had been horrified. 'Things don't stand still, Fi. You won't be able to pick up where you left off in a few years when you decide you've had enough of being at home. And what about that house you and Euan were talking about? The one with the big garden for Lottie and Ben to play in? You won't be able to afford the repayments on that if you drop down to a single income.'

Fi's response had surprised her. 'Euan's doing well at work, and the park's not far from our house. I can take the children to play there. We don't need a big house. We just need each other.'

Imogen wasn't giving in, though. 'But you've worked hard to get to where you were.'

'Imo, the thing is, I don't care whether Mr Self-Important's merger goes through or Mrs Up-My-Own-Arse buys the company out anymore. That's not a good attitude to take into the office with me every day. Besides, the option to return part-time is being kept open for me if I do decide being home with the children all day isn't for me, or if money gets tight.'

Fi's voice brought Imogen back to the call at hand. 'Phew, that's sorted. So?'

Imogen realised she wanted an answer to her earlier question. 'How about Thursday? Does that work for you?' She ran through what she'd tell Sigrid. She'd arranged to drop in on the furniture restorers to check on progress, and while she was there she'd check out a local gallery with a collection of paintings that might provide the perfect finishing touches for the guestrooms.

A heart-to-heart with Fi would have to wait until then.

'Perfect. You can come along to our music and movement session, and we can have lunch out afterwards. There's a new cafe that supposedly does the most divine choux pastries. We'll have a calorie blowout!'

'I can't wait,' Imogen replied weakly, wondering if she'd be expected to sing along to 'If You're Happy and You Know It Clap Your Hands' or the like.

13

Imogen's phone bleeped the arrival of a text as she attempted a complicated parallel parking manoeuvre near Fiona's end of terrace house. The parallel park was her speciality, and before she'd met Nev when she'd toyed with the idea of online dating, she'd wondered whether it should feature in her list of attributes. Her dad was to thank for teaching her this important life skill, although poor Hannah had never mastered the art and often had to drive around for hours to find a parking place.

Once she was satisfied her car was safely sandwiched between the two vehicles, she checked her messages. A secretive smile teased the corners of her lips, seeing it was from Nev. He messaged her two to three times a day, and she would Face-Time him after dinner, just as they did when he was away on business – as he so often was. Still and all, her job could take her away from the city they called home too.

The text was on the saucy side. Nev had a libido that didn't stop. She'd no complaints when she was in the mood, but there were times when she'd have been happy with a cuppa and a cuddle – something he didn't understand. He was a man used to getting his own way in the bedroom and the boardroom. On this occasion though, had she been in Dublin, this message might have seen her downing tools and paying him an impromptu visit at his office. It wouldn't be the first time the blinds had been drawn and the door locked.

One evening, he'd had her in stitches as they sat in a restaurant with the raucous atmosphere and cobbled lanes of Temple Bar spread below them. Smelly Bella, his middle daughter, had accidentally been on the receiving end of one of his suggestive texts and demanded Daddy pay for counselling. A naughty rendezvous wasn't on today's agenda, however. Nope, today she was off to a music group for toddlers and had dressed for the occasion in her Sweaty Betty activewear. Imogen figured if she could make it through a box-fit class in her current outfit, she could handle an outing with a baby and a toddler.

It was a relief to have her car back again and to no longer be hobbling about. Her ankle was much better, she thought, reaching down onto the passenger seat floor for the steering wheel lock. She slotted it into place because you had to be careful about joyriders as the owner of a sporty little coupe, and Fi and Euan didn't live in the most salubrious part of Galway city. Her eyes flitted to the red-brick house they called their starter home. 'More like a stuck home,' she mused out loud, getting out of the car and making for the front door.

She pressed the doorbell, hearing it chime inside. A thudding and a piercing scream followed. Imogen heard Fi's muffled voice as she gave what sounded like orders followed by footsteps. Then, with a grubby-faced Ben hanging off her hip, her friend flung the door open. Her face transformed from harried to happy as a huge smile spread across her face at the sight of Imogen.

'Thank feck you're here. One of those mornings, you know?'

She didn't know, but since Fi had what looked like a blob of plum jam stuck to her shirt, which was on inside out, and she was rocking bed hair – and not the artfully contrived kind – she could guess how her morning had gone.

'Can I get off, Mammy?' A petulant voice drifted from the front room.

'Not until you've finished doing your poo.' Fiona rolled her eyes. 'Potty training.' She held the door open wider, and Imogen stepped inside, pausing to plant a kiss on Ben's head, which, cradle cap aside, was the cleanest part of him, leaving behind a lipstick print. She did the same to Fi's cheek before poking her head around the front room door where her god-daughter was squatting over a potty. Her head was angled between her legs, inspecting the contents.

'Hello, Lottie!' *Dear God, the smell!*

The little girl's head shot up. 'Aunty Imo, look!' The pride and wonder at the potty's contents shone on her face.

Imogen sensed Fi giggling behind her. 'Er, well done, Lottie. That's brilliant.' She'd grown since her last visit. Height wasn't something you could gauge over the phone, and with her hair in bunches like that she could see Fi in her. The last time she'd seen Lottie, she'd thought she was going to take after Euan. 'You're getting so big.'

'It's because you eat your vegetables, isn't it, Lottie McDotty?'

Lottie gave her mother a sceptical look that made Imogen laugh. 'I know who she picked that look up from. Like mother, like daughter.'

Fi dimpled. 'I know. It's scary sometimes. I caught her wagging her finger and asking Ben if she was talking to a brick wall yesterday.'

Imogen snorted.

'Do the Peppa Pig noise again, Aunty Imo,' Charlotte lisped.

She obliged, finding Ben being thrust at her and thinking he was a bonny little fellow, feeling his weight as she held him out at arm's length.

'He won't bite, Imo. He's got no teeth, for one thing. Watch him for me, will you, while I sort this one here out.' Fiona turned her attention to her daughter. 'You're a clever girl, Lottie. Well done. Shall we go and wipe your bottom.' She whisked her and the potty off to the bathroom. 'Or would you, Godmother, like the honour?'

'No. You're grand.' What had she let herself in for? She thought, hoisting Ben onto her hip and opening a window to let some air in. Then she sat down and bounced the little boy about on her lap. He promptly threw up a milky liquid on both of them.

Mother and daughter returned a few minutes later, and Lottie clambered onto the sofa, wrapped her chubby arms around Imogen's neck in a hello hug, nearly strangling her in the process.

'Welcome to my world,' Fiona said, holding her hands out for Ben. 'Go and sponge yourself off.'

14

The community centre hall echoed with the chatter of mothers and fathers and the squeals of littlies charging about. The odd shyer child huddled into their parent, sucking their thumb, and Imogen wondered if it was their first visit. Or maybe they were just tired.

'How're you, Fi?' A woman wiping her little one's face with a wet wipe asked as Imogen followed her friend's lead and sat down cross-legged on the wooden floor. When was the last time she'd sat on the floor with her legs crossed like so? School, she concluded.

'Oh, you know what it's like.' Fiona grinned.

'I do.'

The two women smiled at one another in a weary, exasperated way. Was this some secret mammy code? Imogen wondered, feeling a little left-out.

Fiona had put her on Lottie duty, and she was presently engaged in peekaboo with a little boy whose trousers looked suspiciously full. Her nose twitched. Yes, suspiciously full indeed, but before she'd time to dwell on this her attention was grabbed by a woman who marched into the hall dressed in a vibrant yellow pair of dungarees, with silver hair hanging in two plaits.

'Christ on a bike! What the feck is your woman there wearing? She looks like your Laa-Laa Teletubby one. That, or a geriatric Pippi Longstocking,' Imogen muttered, receiving an elbow in the ribs from Fiona. However, her friend was trying not to laugh as they looked at the woman taking centre stage.

Parents began calling their children back to the fold.

'Hello there,' the star of the show said. 'I see we have a few new faces here with us today. Welcome, welcome all. I'm Kerry, and this here is Katie.' From behind her back, she produced a rag doll. 'Say hi, Katie.' She waggled the doll and went on to perform a ventriloquist act that had the children mesmerised but would have had a certain Britain's Got Talent judge wincing.

'It's fecking Chucky!' Imogen received a second elbow in the ribs.

'Here at Kerry and Katie's Play with Music group, we're all about the children, aren't we, Katie?'

Katie nodded, and there was a smattering of applause.

All about the five quid donation at the door, Imogen thought, managing to keep this to herself as Lottie ran over and plopped down in the crook between her crossed legs.

She jiggled the little girl about, making her giggle, and the sound made her smile.

'Now, whose turn is it this week to hold Katie?'

Hands shot up in the air, and then Kerry, via Katie, asked each parent to tell her what their child had achieved that week.

'Theo made it through a grocery shop without a tantrum.'

'Gemma stayed in her bed all night.'

'Lizzie ate all her golden vegetable medley.'

'Ben rolled over,' Fiona said proudly.

She reached Imogen. 'Er.'

'The potty,' Fiona whispered.

'Lottie did a poo in the potty.'

And on it went.

Imogen's competitive streak flared when Katie was handed to a curly-haired bruiser of a toddler called Rufus, who'd managed to aim his pee-pee stick, as his mam called it, in the toilet bowl. Fiona had grabbed her hand before she could put it up and claim favouritism on the two K's part.

'Don't you dare,' she hissed.

'But a poo in the potty's a much bigger achievement than aiming a pee-pee stick.'

'You might not say that if you'd spent weeks mopping up wee.'

Fi had a point there, Imogen conceded, settling down.

Kerry then pushed play on her stereo, and the group burst into a song about stealing a cookie from the cookie jar. Imogen didn't know the words, but she joined in with the actions as enthusiastically as any parent in the room. Nobody could be as enthusiastic as Kerry, though, and the tunes were very catchy because as the following number began to play, she realised she'd a silly smile on her face watching Lottie join in. Her favourite song was about a jack-in-the-box, where they all had to pretend to be a jack-in-the-box popping up.

To her surprise, the half hour session whizzed by, and she found herself shuffling around to form a circle to take a corner of the parachute Kerry had produced. They wafted it up and down, singing it was 'parachute time'. The toddlers waddled about underneath while the babies crawled, enjoying their freedom. Fiona had to pull her back from shuffling out to join them.

Five minutes later, after her friend had arranged her social calendar for the week – who knew being a mam entailed so many get-togethers – they wandered down the street.

'Admit it, you enjoyed yourself,' Fiona said as she pushed the double buggy along.

'OK. It was sort of fun.'

'Sort of fun!' Fiona snorted. 'I haven't seen you breaking out the moves like that since the parish committee organised a disco to raise funds for the new church pew cushions.'

Imogen's grin was sheepish. She was surprised by how much she'd enjoyed the session. The fun the littlies were having was infectious, and the look of wonder on their faces as they played under the parachute was magic.

'Where's this cafe then? I need sustenance after that.'

'Just up around the bend there.'

They sat down to an enormous cream puff each and a mug of coffee. The cafe had a French theme, and a tempting array of patisserie treats in the cabinet. The Irish girl behind the counter greeted them with an enthusiastic bonjour, and Imogen made a mental note to tell her mam where the gaff was. Nora Kelly was a Francophile, if ever there was one. She'd be in her apple cart here.

Ben was asleep in the buggy while Lottie, kneeling at the table, jammed her finger in the middle of the chocolate éclair Imogen had treated her to.

'How's the grand makeover at Benmore House going?' Fiona asked.

Imogen tapped her lip, signalling Fiona had icing sugar there, and she wiped it off.

'It's going well. Sigrid—'

'Ooh, Sigrid, is it?'

'Sigrid,' Imogen continued, 'is leaving me more or less to my own devices. You know how much I hate clients who hover and dither.'

'Mm.'

'Oh, and you'll never guess who I'm working with?'

'Who?'

'Ryan O'Malley.'

'Not Ryan O'Malley from school. The bra-pinger.'

'The one and the same, although he's after telling me it wasn't him.'

'He was quite a cutie from memory, with those dark Celtic eyes, and he was always sweet on you.'

'No, he wasn't.'

'He was, too, but you were too moony over Lachlan Leslie to notice. And then we all finished school and went our separate ways.'

'Well, even if he was, that was years ago.'

'Is he still cute?'

Imogen shrugged, 'I haven't thought about it. I know he's got this annoying habit of singing random lines of songs.' She'd discovered this over the last few days. It was bad enough listening to all that long-haired, permed angst he insisted on playing, but now and then, he'd burst into song, making her jump. Her nerves were shredded. Nor did he care who was around to hear him attempting to hit the falsetto notes as if he were wearing skin-tight leather trousers.

'What do you mean?' Fiona questioned.

'Say like, Bon Jovi's "Living on a Prayer" was on the radio.'

'OK. Unga, unga, unga, unga.'

A few heads turned their way.

'What was that?'

'You know the opening bit of the song.'

'Jaysus.' Imogen shook her head. 'Well, the song's playing away, and suddenly he'll let rip with three random lines.' She picked up her cream puff and took a big bite, squirting cream out either side.

'What, that's it?'

'Yeah.'

'Cop yourself on, Imo! Annoying habits are leaving your boxer shorts on the bathroom floor for your wife to pick up or not closing drawers whenever you open them. Let me tell you, that's fecking annoying.'

Imogen laughed and told her friend about the duckling rescue, her car breaking down and the resulting twisted ankle. Then she waited patiently for Fiona to get a grip of herself after she snorted a spray of cream across the table when she got to the part where Mr Kenny had given her a ride home on the back of his motorised scooter. Once she'd stopped gasping for air and clutching her stomach, Imogen said, 'I had to cadge a ride to and from Benmore with Ryan for a few days, but my car and ankle are as good as new now. Well, almost.' She flexed her foot, still feeling a twinge in her ankle, and decided it was only good manners to pick up some beer or chocolates to thank him for running her about. She'd do that on the way home, she decided, before elaborating on Mr O'Malley Senior's stroke. 'Ryan came home and took over his dad's building business so he could take things easier.'

Fiona tilted her head to one side, and her expression was sympathetic. 'It shows great strength of character to make a sacrifice like he's done in coming home to help his family. Not everyone would.'

Imogen thought of Maeve Doolin and how her son barely saw his mother. He was caught up in his life with his wife and children in England. Although Shannon had told her he'd taken to ringing his mother daily since James had arrived on the scene. 'He's probably scared of being disinherited,' Shannon had added. She'd no time for Fergus Doolin.

'You're right.'

'What's that saying about never being more than six feet away from a rat in London?' Fiona said. 'Well, in Emerald Bay, you're never more than a centimetre from someone you went to school with.'

It was exactly like that, Imogen thought.

· · ·

Later, as Imogen drove along the wild swirl of coast road leading her home toward Emerald Bay, she pondered over her afternoon with Fiona and the kids. She'd gone to Galway brimming with intentions of confiding in her friend how Lachlan's impending arrival at Benmore House this weekend had her in a spin. Imogen also needed her friend's advice on Nev's visit to Emerald Bay for St Patrick's Day. Or, more to the point, how to handle her father when he copped on to the age gap between them.

Instead, she and Fi had reminisced about their schooldays, giggling over shared memories. It was fun.

They'd also spent an excessive amount of time discussing Ryan O'Malley.

What on earth was that all about?

15

Beer and chocolates, Imogen decided as she indicated to turn off Main Street. But instead of parking behind the pub and doing a danger run past the beehives in the beer garden, she did a U-turn. It was just as well that neither Sergeant Badger nor Mrs Tattersall was anywhere in sight, she thought, pulling up outside the Bus Stop corner shop.

'Hello there, Mrs Gallagher,' she sang out as she perused the shelves.

Brenda Gallagher looked up from the open magazine in front of her and pushed the reading glasses with their thick black frames back up to the bridge of her nose. 'I heard you were home, Imogen. How're you keeping?'

'Grand, thanks. How're you and Mr Gallagher?'

Brenda rolled her eyes. 'Himself is upstairs, in bed. Tis only the hay fever he's suffering with, but he's convinced it's the flu. It's the same this time every year, so.'

'Man flu.' Imogen smiled.

'It's a terrible affliction indeed. Now then, can I point you in the direction of what you're after?'

'No, thank you,' Imogen replied, knowing the canny grocer

would only steer her toward the dearest box of chocolates in stock. She moved off to inspect the confectionary aisle.

The door jingled, and Imogen heard Nessie Doyle greeting the shopkeeper as she plucked a box of Quality Street off the shelf. Her eyes watered at the price, and she wished she'd had the foresight to stop in Galway. Unfortunately, the six-pack of lager Imogen picked up next wasn't much better.

Jesus wept, she thought, heading for the counter. Mam was right. The Gallaghers whispered about plans for a world cruise once they retired, would no doubt be funded from the pockets of Emerald Bay's villagers. Before she reached her destination, however, Nessie Doyle, the woman responsible for more bowl haircuts when she was a child than Imogen cared to remember, stepped into her path.

Nessie was armed with a packet of chocolate biscuits and a jar of coffee, looking like she meant business. 'For the clients,' she said, tracking Imogen's gaze. 'We like to go the extra mile at Nessie's Hair Salon and offer our clientele a choccie biccie and cup of Nescafé.'

The salon name was as uninspiring as the cuts she delivered, Imogen thought, remembering the glass of bubbles and Belgium chocolates she'd been offered at her last appointment in Dublin.

'How're you, Imogen?' Nessie enquired. 'It was Christmas the last time we saw you, wasn't it?'

Imogen nodded, forcing a smile as she clocked Nessie's latest 'do'. The streaks of colour and spikes reminded her of a peacock that had inadvertently strutted into an electric fence.

Nessie eyed Imogen's hair. 'I'm glad I caught you. I noticed your hair streaming behind you the other day when you were catching a ride with Mr Kenny. It's the baylage you're sporting there, isn't it?'

'I'm sorry?' Imogen blinked. Had the woman just compared

her hair to cow fodder? *Charming*, she thought, wishing she wasn't blocking her path.

'The baylage,' Nessie repeated. 'With the Caramello ends.'

'Oh.' A giggle rose in Imogen's throat, but she swallowed it down in case Nessie had her scissors on her. 'You mean the bal-ay-age,' she replied slowly.

''Tis what I said.' Nessie's lips pursed.

'I specialise in the dip and dye, and those ends look more Milky Bar than Caramello. I'm fully booked for the next three months, Imogen, but seeing as you're a local, I'll squeeze you in. And you might want to put in a good word with her ladyship up the road there for me too. Tell her I've got a ten per cent special offer for new customers.'

Imogen could only imagine what Nessie would do to Sigrid's groomed flaxen locks if she got her hands on her. 'I will indeed,' she fibbed, eager to pay for her items and get going.

Mercifully, Nessie announced she'd forgotten teabags, leaving the way clear for her to place the goods she was carrying down on the counter.

Brenda rang them up, and Imogen begrudgingly handed over her card.

'Imogen Kelly, where would you be off to with those beers and chocolates? Sure, Valentine's Day has been and gone,' Eileen Carroll asked from where she was blocking the entrance and the daylight. The owner of the Knitter's Nook was wearing a hand-knitted cardigan over her sensible ensemble. As the proprietor of Emerald Bay's woollen shop, she was a wool devotee, often heard spouting the wonders of the natural fibre and its ability to keep you warm in winter and cool in summer.

Imogen debated picking up her purchases, tucking them under her arms, lowering her head and making a break for it like one of those American footballers heading for the goal line. Eileen was a big woman, though; undoubtedly Imogen would come off worst if she tried to take her on. No, better to stand her ground and deflect the conversation, she decided. 'You'd be right there, Mrs Carroll. I hope Mr Carroll was after giving you chocolates and roses.'

Eileen sniffed in a manner that suggested Mr Carroll had not showered his Valentine in gifts.

'My Cathal got me a lovely card with a cherub firing a bow and arrow through a love heart.' Brenda, who'd returned to her magazine, looked up and joined in the conversation.

'Mr Carroll and I don't go in for that sort of thing.'

Imogen, seeing a chink of light, edged toward the door, but Eileen glared at her like a Gardai officer in a cardy about to perform a lie detector test. 'Is someone poorly, Imogen? If that's the case, I don't know that the beer's a good idea. Flat lemonade's what the doctor ordered.'

'Nobody's sick, Mrs Carroll.' There was nothing for it. The woman had a bloodhound's nose for sniffing out the business of others, and like a dog with a bone, she'd not give in until she had her answer. 'I'm just dropping these around to the O'Malleys.'

'Terrible, terrible thing,' Eileen, Brenda and Nessie, who were all waiting to be served, clucked.

'Oh, this isn't for Mr O'Malley,' Imogen exclaimed as though she'd been injected with truth serum. 'They're for Ryan. A thank you for running me back and forth to Benmore House while my car was in the garage these last few days.' Were the lights exceptionally bright in here, or was it just her? she wondered.

The three women exchanged a knowing glance, and annoyance made Imogen's cheeks flame. 'Nev, my partner, is coming down next weekend for St Paddy's. I can't wait to see him. It's hard being away from each other,' she said, laying it on thick.

'That sounds serious,' Eileen said, her eyes lighting up. 'Is it the wedding bells we'll hear soon then, Imogen? Your nan's kept that one quiet.'

Imogen would give the trio something to gossip over, she

decided. 'You never know, Mrs Carroll. You never know.' Then, leaving the three women to digest the juicy titbit she'd dropped, she made a run for her car.

The O'Malleys' house was a bright, two-storey, yellow beacon a few streets behind Main Street, and Imogen pulled up outside. It was dinner time, and she could smell a barbeque in a nearby garden as she walked up the front path. The conservatory off to the side was a new addition, she noticed, waiting for someone to answer the door.

It was Mrs O'Malley who greeted her. She had a streak of flour on her cheek and an apron tied around her waist. Ryan took after his mam, Imogen thought, smiling at the weary-looking woman. They shared the same arresting, dark eyes, although these days, Mrs O'Malley's hair was more silver than the coal black of her son's.

'Hello, Mrs O'Malley, is Ryan about?'

The older woman looked blankly at Imogen for a moment, and then recognition dawned. 'Hello there, Imogen. Our Ryan said he's been giving you a lift to the big house on account of your ankle.' Her eyes moved past Imogen to her parked car. 'You're mobile again, though, I see.'

'Yes. That's why I'm calling. I wanted to drop these in for Ryan. They're a thank you for the rides to and from the house.' She lifted the cans and chocolates.

'I'll take those for you, love. You've just missed him. He's gone for a run, but you're welcome to come inside and wait for him to get back.'

Imogen handed the thank-you gifts over. 'I won't come in, thanks, Mrs O'Malley. I'll be expected home for dinner. If you could pass those on with a thank you from me.'

'I will do, but you didn't have to do this. Sure, Ryan would tell you the same thing if he was here.' Her smile gave her an apple-cheeked look.

Imogen shrugged, unsure what to say. Calling goodbye, she walked back to her car feeling oddly disappointed as she turned the key in the engine and headed home.

16

Imogen's stars that Friday morning had hinted at her feeling out of her depth today and that she should keep an eye out for a sign that good luck was heading her way. The daily horoscope was her first port of call once she opened her eyes. She'd digest it in bed until, catching sight of the time, she'd fling the sheets off in a panic. The very mention of good luck had her debating whether to nip across to the Bus Stop and purchase a lottery ticket. However, after shovelling down the porridge Nan wouldn't let her out the door without and then knocking back her coffee, a glance at the wall clock confirmed she didn't have time. No surprises there; she'd never been much of a morning person. Mam, in frustration, used to threaten to pour a bucket of cold water over her most mornings when she'd still lived at home.

'Don't be speeding now, Imogen.' Liam tried to look stern, rattling the newspaper he was reading as she scraped her chair back and slung her laptop case over her shoulder. 'How often do I have to tell you to pull the chair back and not drag it? And just because you drive a car that would be at home in the Italian Grand Prix doesn't mean you're allowed to have a lead foot on that accelerator. Are you listening to me, Imogen Kelly?'

'Yes, Dad, and I won't.' Napoleon brushed past her leg, and she felt the familiar eyewatering tingle signalling an epic sneeze was on its way. He was determined to win her over and had taken to leaving love tokens outside her bedroom door. This morning, the precocious cat had dragged one of Liam's socks down the hallway. So long as he left it at footwear and didn't venture into the realms of underwear, they'd be grand. 'Atishoo!' The little cat fled.

'If you set your alarm fifteen minutes earlier, then you'd not have to rush like so,' Nora tutted. 'You'll give yourself indigestion the way you gobble your breakfast.'

'Yes, Mam.' Imogen, glad to make her escape before Nan said her piece too, closed the back door behind her. She was instantly aware of a low humming. There was a buzzing about the two hives at the bottom of the garden signalling the bees were busy as their industrious noise carried in the silence of the morning. If she got stung, Hannah would be for it when she came home next weekend, Imogen vowed, keeping a wary eye out as she crossed the car park.

She made it to her car safely and was soon on her way. As she drove towards Benmore House, she barely noticed the foamy white crests on the waves in the harbour or the boats being buffeted about by the blustery wind. Nor was she aware of the confetti of blossoms falling like snow. Instead, she was churning over her horoscope's prediction that she'd feel out of her depth today. Not that this was breaking news; she'd felt like she was on tippy-toes down the deep end of a pool ever since she'd learned Lachlan would be in Emerald Bay for the weekend. Well, Benmore House, to be exact.

Imogen eyed her thumbnails. They looked stumpy compared to the rest of her manicure, and she was annoyed with herself. Nail-biting was a habit she'd broken years ago, but since being home, she'd chewed these two off and had her hand slapped away from her mouth by her nan last night. The memory of the foul-tasting deterrent Mam had coated her nails with, insistent she'd get the worms if she kept biting them like so, saw her grimace.

Ryan's Hilux was already parked up, and she slipped in alongside it.

Sigrid had mentioned she had friends coming over for lunch on Friday. There was no sign of her or Matthew Leslie as Imogen walked through the foyer, so she decided to head straight upstairs. Sigrid knew where to find her.

Imogen placed a hand on the smooth banister rail, hearing Ryan whistling away as she took to the stairs. The first guestroom door was open, and she stepped inside, surveying the stripped walls before unhooking her laptop case and setting it down on the bed covered with a protective sheet. The first thing on today's to-do list was to ring the decorating firm to check the painters would be returning on Monday as agreed.

Imogen's fourth phone conversation of the morning saw her nostrils flare as things got heated. She was on the phone with the carpet company, who'd rung to say the room measurements had been muddled. On hearing the company would be sending someone out to re-measure next Wednesday, Imogen had seen red. She could feel herself teetering on the edge of the slippery slope, knowing from experience that one tardy contractor could have a domino-like effect on a project. By the time the call was disconnected, the manager had assured her their contractors would be at the house first thing Monday morning. A throat cleared behind her, and she spun around to see Ryan. He held up his hands in mock self-defence. 'Remind me not to cross you. Sorry, I wasn't listening in, but I caught the tail end.'

Still riled, Imogen bit back, 'You can't let people walk all over you in business.'

'I won't argue with you there,' Ryan said in a mollifying tone as he thrust his hands in his tool belt.

She looked at him with one eyebrow raised in a 'what do you want?' fashion.

'Thanks for dropping around the beer and chocolates last night, but you didn't need to do that.'

Her claws went back in and amusement danced. 'Your mam said you'd say that.'

Ryan grinned. 'My mam knows me too well.' He disappeared down the hall, and a few seconds later, he called out, 'This one's for you.'

The remnants of her bad mood disappeared, and she laughed at the irony as 'Every Rose Has Its Thorn' by Poison began to drift toward her. He was a cheeky so-and-so, she thought.

Imogen wondered if Sigrid's guests minded being treated to Ryan's caterwauling as he clattered away inside the bathroom. But at least he was on task with completing the framing. She'd half expected Sigrid or Matthew to march upstairs and pull the plug on the portable stereo he carted upstairs each morning at some point, but the music didn't bother them, muted as it was between the floors. That, or they were closet fans of the rock power ballad.

Sigrid's ladies who lunch had arrived an hour and a half ago. The three women Imogen had observed as she gazed out the windows to see them emerging from a sleek, silver Mercedes Benz were more or less Sigrid-style clones. The only point of difference being none of them had her Agnetha from ABBA colouring. She guessed they were here for a lettuce leaf and liquid lunch, given they were all stick insects, and quickly turned away from the window lest she got caught staring.

Focus, Imogen, she told herself sternly, returning to the task.

She'd decided as soon as she'd surveyed the initial images of the guestrooms that armchairs, with rolled arms obviously, positioned by the windows for guests to sit and admire the parkland-like view, were a must. As luck would have it, she'd managed to source a set of four Edwardian, carved mahogany salon armchairs in need of recovering at an antique auction in Dublin. The chairs had since been delivered to a furniture restoration company she'd used in the past located in Galway, and the upholsterer was ready to start work on them. But Imogen was holding things up by being unusually indecisive over the fabric coverings.

She stared at the swatches of material she'd brought down from her go-to fabric store in Dublin. The shop conveniently had a branch in Galway, and once she made her mind up and sent through her choices, they'd courier the material to the upholsterer's workshop. Sigrid, who'd approved the overall colour palette for the bedrooms, had left the final choice of fabrics and hues to her, saying, 'It's your area of expertise, Imogen. I trust you to choose well.'

Usually, this was music to her ears. There was nothing worse than a colour-blind client insistent on running with an eyesore scheme and then happily telling all and sundry who their designer was. Not today, though. Today Imogen would love for someone else to march on in and point to the pale blue or lilac swatch and say, that's the one.

The knowledge Lachlan would be here for the weekend had turned her into a Can't-make-her-mind-up Caro, and even though closure was a wince-inducing turn of phrase, this word kept springing to mind. The more she stewed, the clearer it became. Where Lachlan was concerned, she needed to close the book on that chapter of her life. If she were honest with herself, it was why she'd said yes to this project in the first place. A part of her had hoped to see him and banish the ghost of her first love. It was high time, too, that the wounds festering from the late Mrs Leslie Senior's whiplike tongue healed.

It had cut deep to be told as a sixteen-year-old that she was not good enough and nor would she ever be. To have her self-esteem trampled on had been painful and an experience she'd do her best to ensure Lottie never had to endure. She wanted her god-daughter always to feel proud of who she was and what she did. But, most of all, Lottie should believe in herself. Imogen had noted this in her Lottie Book, knowing she needed to practice what she intended to preach.

Mrs Leslie was six feet under, and it was too late to prove her wrong, but this weekend was a chance to show Lachlan his mother had been mistaken in her assumptions about her.

The cloying scent of Chanel No. 19 filled the room, and Imogen's head snapped up from where she'd been staring, unseeing, at swatches to find Sigrid. Her cheeks were flushed, and her eyes were not as sharp as usual as she scanned the room.

'Hello, Imogen.' There was the slightest slur to her words. 'Where are the artworks?'

'I'm sorry?' Too late, Imogen remembered her white lie and hoped she'd made a smooth recovery as she replied, 'Oh, the artworks I went to see in Galway? Sorry, I've been debating the colour swatches, and I was a million miles away. No. They weren't right after all. I've heard the gallery in the village is excellent, so I thought I might call in there this evening on the way home, now the other pictures are off the table.'

'A shame.' Sigrid swayed like a spindly tree in the wind. 'And I like the lilac.' Her finger pointed to the swatch on the left.

Problem solved, Imogen thought.

'Would you come downstairs? I want to introduce you to some friends of mine. You never know who might need your skills in the future.'

'Of course, thank you.' Imogen thought the glacier was melting, taking stock of the Swedish iceberg's almost warm smile. Sigrid had been wining rather than dining with her friends since they arrived, by the looks of her. Still, word of mouth was how she smoothly transitioned from one job to the next. *Put your best foot forward,* Imogen told herself with a rueful glance at her footwear as she trailed after Sigrid. She couldn't wait to be back in her Gianvito Rossi's tomorrow, but in the meantime she focused on Sigrid's weaving steps, keeping a wary eye on her to ensure she made it back down the stairs in one piece.

Imogen sat down on the warm flagstone stairs outside the front door and tilted her face toward the sun. The wind had dropped a little, but still her hair whipped around her face. She tucked it firmly behind her ears and breathed in the fresh air. She needed it after smarming with Sigrid's friends, but if it meant work rolled her way, she was happy to play the game. Once she'd cleared her head, she intended to make the final call on the rest of the colours for the remaining bedroom chairs.

She could smell the sweet scent of cut grass, and in the distance, the gardener was pootling about on his ride-on mower. He was far enough away from the house for the sound to be a dull thrumming, and the cooing of pigeons in the eaves above her head overrode it.

She might have spent the last half hour schmoozing, but she hadn't been offered a glass of wine or piece of the quiche Lorraine set out in the orangery for lunch. Her stomach rumbled, angry at her lack of organisation in bringing a bite to eat with her. She supposed she could wander inside and ask Francesca to make her something but was reluctant to do so. The housekeeper's day was busy enough at the beck and call of the luncheon brigade.

Imogen heard footsteps and, shading her eyes, twisted

around to see who was coming, worried she was about to be caught lazing about on the job, but it was Ryan. Mr Leslie was no doubt laying low, having no wish to be accosted by a group of tiddly women. Besides, she'd every right to be out here. She was entitled to a break.

'Can I join you?' Ryan was holding a lunchbox and flask.

She felt a stab of envy. A cup of tea and a sandwich would hit the spot right now. 'Sure,' much as she'd have liked to tell him, *No. It's a big place go find your own spot in the sun.* Massaging her temples, she attempted to ward off a threatened headache. At least he'd left that portable stereo of his upstairs.

Ryan sat down, and she stared at his heavy work boots while he opened his lunchbox and wondered how he managed to be tanned given the time of year. Maybe he'd had a week abroad. He'd be right at home in Zakynthos, she thought rather meanly. Her dad had been reading a piece from the paper about how the lager louts were beginning to gather on the Greek island's notorious party strip already.

'I'm starving.'

Imogen made no comment, hearing the click as he opened his lunchbox.

'Can I tempt you?'

He was waggling an eco-wrapped package at her. Hannah would approve, she thought, guessing its contents. 'A tomato sandwich?'

'Yup.'

She'd turned him down the other day when one had been on offer but today asked, 'Does it have butter and lots of salt and pepper on it?'

'Sure does.'

'I don't want to steal your lunch.'

'Sure, I've plenty,' he said, pointing to the contents of his lunch box, which was as tempting as any Marks and Spencer picnic hamper.

He wouldn't miss one sambo, Imogen decided, taking it from him. 'Thanks.' She unwrapped the package. 'I wouldn't have had you down as the type of guy that uses these.' She waved the daisy-patterned beeswax wrap, all illusions of hard-drinking, lager lout vanishing.

'Birthday present from one of my sisters. It's good for the environment, she said, and I'm happy to do my bit.'

'My sister, Hannah, would love you.'

'She's a couple of years younger than you, right?'

'That's her, and then there are the twins.' She took a bite of the sandwich; there was something special about soggy tomato sandwiches. It was probably the way they reminded her of childhood picnics at the bay. All that was missing was the gritty taste of sand. She made short work of it and then filled him in on Hannah's crusades and the fact there were two beehives down the back of the beer garden at the Shamrock Inn, thanks to her sister twisting their parents' arm.

'Good for her,' Ryan said.

'I'll remind you that you said that when you get stung while supping your pint in the sunshine.' She watched as he held a pie up to his mouth and bit into the gold crust, sprinkling pastry flakes all over his shorts. 'That's not one of Dermot Molloy's bacon and egg pies, is it?' she asked, trying to keep the envy out of her tone.

'It is,' he mumbled through his mouthful before holding it out to her. 'Want a bite?'

She knew she shouldn't, but the pies from Dermot Molloy's Quality Meats were award-winning around these parts, and she snatched it off him. 'Thanks.' She decided she'd have to take a leaf out of his book and put together a packed lunch tomorrow, taking a generous bite before passing the pie back reluctantly. Jesus, Mary and Joseph, was that buttered brack he had in there too? she thought, eyeing what was left in his lunch box.

'I can un-sandwich the brack, if you like?' Ryan's eyes

danced in amusement as he polished off the rest of the pie. 'I'm getting full anyway.'

Imogen didn't believe him, but she accepted the brack, relishing the sweet fruitiness of the loaf. 'What star sign are you?' she mumbled through her mouthful.

'Leo.'

'The king of the jungle. An insufferable show-off,' she said boldly. Leo was also highly compatible with her star sign, Libra, but she'd not be mentioning that because she was very happy with her Gemini man.

'Thanks a million.'

Imogen grinned, praying she didn't have sticky sultana stuck in her teeth. It was then something plopped onto the top of her head, and, with a frown, she patted around to see what it was.

'Ugh!' she squealed as she touched the squidgy warm pigeon poop.

Ryan sent more crumbs flying. 'That's good luck, that is.'

She remembered her horoscope and frowned, never understanding the correlation between a bird crapping on your head and good luck.

'Here,' Ryan said, producing a crumpled packet of tissues from his pocket. She took them gratefully and cleaned it off as best she could. Then, getting to her feet, she thanked him for the sandwich and bite of pie before heading inside and striding toward the bathroom to ensure she was properly cleansed of the bird poop.

If Hannah ever embarked on a save the manky pigeon mission, she'd be on her own, she thought, pushing the door open.

Imogen's face lit up, seeing Nev's name appear on her screen as her phone rang, and she snatched it up, eager to hear his voice. 'Hey, you.' She rested the phone in the crook of her neck so she could carry on tidying away the swathes of fabric and paint test pots littering the floor. She was nearly finished for the day and was keen to get away lest Sigrid and her pals summon her to join them for an after-work tipple. The plan was to call in at Mermaids on her way home, as she'd mentioned to Sigrid. If she could find the perfect paintings at a local gallery, it would make for a good talking point amongst the Leslies and their guests. Not to mention how good it would be for Freya's business too.

'What are you doing?' Nev's voice was smoky.

'I'm on my hands and knees,' she replied in an equally throaty voice, pleased he couldn't see her roll her eyes.

There was a sharp intake of breath, and she pictured him sitting back in that enormous leather chair of his and loosening his tie, but she wasn't in the mood for game-playing. 'Tidying up,' she said in a matter-of-fact manner that would pour cold water on any ideas he might have been getting. 'I'm still at the house but about to head off. What are your plans this evening?'

If she thought her role as an interior designer required a certain amount of social networking, she had nothing on Nev. A night curled up in front of the TV was never an option.

'I've got the gala dinner at the Clayton in Ballsbridge tonight.'

Imogen detected a hint of sullenness in his tone, recalling how he'd wanted her to attend the evening with him. They'd fought about it initially because Nev wasn't used to people not fitting in around him. But, on the other hand, it made her alluring to him because he loved a challenge and found her independence exciting until it didn't suit him. Like tonight's dinner.

However, Imogen had put her foot down by refusing to finish early today as he'd suggested and drive back to Dublin for a long weekend. She'd be spending time with her family as planned, she'd informed him before suggesting he take one of his daughters to the dinner instead. She'd thought they'd be only too happy to take her place.

He snapped out of his mood with a 'Shit! Hold on, would you? I need to check. Prue picked up my suit from the drycleaners—'

There was a thunk, then silence, until she heard a door opening and muffled conversation. Nev wouldn't function if not for Prue, his long-suffering PA. He'd confided in her once that his ex-wife, Genevieve, had accused him of having an affair with her. Imogen had felt uncomfortable hearing this because it had crossed her mind to wonder whether anything had happened between himself and Prue, an attractive woman. Nev had squashed that idea by saying he thought of Prue like he would a trusty canine companion. Imogen had not been sure what to make of that.

'She has it all under control.' Nev came back on the line.

'I never doubted it. Who're you taking tonight?' Her money was on Needy Noelle.

'Noelle's free.'

Bingo. 'Grand. It all worked out then.'

Nev didn't reply to that. 'What are your plans? A leer up in the pub, is it?'

Did she detect the slightest of sneers? Imogen frowned and stared at a nail in the timber boards she was kneeling on. She decided to give him the benefit of the doubt but couldn't keep the defensive note out of her voice. 'I'll give Mam and Dad a hand behind the bar over the weekend. The craic's always good at the Shamrock of a Friday and Saturday night.'

'Listen, Prue's signalling my four forty-five is here. I'll have to go, darling. I'll miss you tonight.'

'I'll miss you too.'

'I love you, Bunny. I can't wait to see you next weekend,' Nev trotted out, using his pet name for her.

'Me too,' she fibbed, adding the expected, 'I love you too,' before ending the call.

A cough sounded behind her, and she swivelled to see Ryan. He was tapping his watch. 'It's getting on for five. You'll be off soon, won't you?'

'As soon as I've straightened this up.' Imogen swept her hand around the general mess, wondering how much of her conversation he'd been privy to.

'I'd say I've another good hour or so before I can pack up. I don't want to see this place for the next two days.'

Imogen made a non-committal sound as she stared at his biceps under the sleeves of his T-shirt. She guessed they were the result of hard work rather than the personal trainer private gym sessions Nev favoured.

'Will I be seeing you in the Shamrock tonight?' Ryan asked.

'Pardon?' She dragged her eyes away.

'Will I be seeing you in the pub tonight?' he repeated.

'Is the Pope a Catholic,' Imogen fired back, making him grin. 'Mam and Dad will set me to work behind the bar, no doubt.' It was only fair because she'd got off lightly at Christmas after her allergic reaction to Napoleon. She'd have to earn her keep this time around.

'I'll see you there then.' Ryan moved away.

'See you.' Imogen returned to her tidying, wondering why the sight of his muscled arms had got her hot under the collar. She was missing Nev, she concluded, and she was a woman at her sexual peak according to the magazine she'd read the last time she'd been to the hairdresser.

Five minutes later, with the tidy-up job done, she stood up and eyed her laptop case. An idea formed, and she slid the bag under the dust cover draped over the bed before she could talk herself out of it. Sigrid had said she was expecting Lachlan and his fiancée late this evening, although she seriously doubted Sigrid would be about to greet them – not after the amount of vino consumed in the orangery today. No doubt she'd be snoring by 6 p.m.

The bag containing her laptop and notes provided the perfect excuse to call by the house tomorrow morning to pick it up. Feeling pleased with herself, Imogen picked up her purse and closed the door before she could second guess what she was doing.

She padded downstairs and, passing through the foyer to the front door, heard peals of laughter emanating from the back of the house. *Yes, Sigrid would definitely be snoring by 6 p.m.*

She noticed the Mercedes was still parked in the drive, too, expecting it to remain there. If Sigrid's guests wished to return home, they would need to be collected and dropped off. Or perhaps Matthew Leslie would play taxi driver. The thought of three drunk women giggling in the back of his Range Rover while he sat behind the wheel with a dour expression amused her.

It had been a productive afternoon overall, she thought, slotting behind the wheel of her car with no further hiccups after her morning call with the carpet layers. As she sped off down the driveway and Benmore House got smaller in her rear-view mirror, her fingers tapped out the beat on the steering wheel to the latest Bieber song that happened to be playing. Her mood was a curious mix of excitement mingled with a dash of self-disgust at her underhandedness, leaving her laptop case behind. But the open vista of boggy moorland and ocean was a welcome distraction. She wondered what Nev would think of her home, passing by the familiar landmarks of the thatched row of cottages, Kilticaneel Castle and Emerald Bay's harbour before slowing her speed as she entered the village. He was such a city slicker who'd probably never donned a pair of wellies in his life; would he think her family a bunch of culchies?

Freya's sign twirling in the wind was a timely distraction from that unsettling train of thought and she pulled over outside Mermaids, pleased she'd caught her before she closed.

Eileen Carroll was standing outside her woollens shop passing the time with Rita Quigley, who owned the village's bookshop, Quigley's Quill. Upon seeing Imogen, Eileen pulled her cardigan closed and leaned in conspiratorially to Rita in a manner that suggested she was the topic of conversation.

Oh, how she'd like to flick the gossipy woman the birdy, Imogen thought, knowing she wouldn't dare. She'd never hear the end of it if she lost control of her middle finger. Life in a small village cultivated small minds, she thought crossly, quickly taking her family out of that equation as she pushed the door to Mermaids open. Freya, too, for that matter.

She felt even crosser recalling Ryan's words about her only thinking she belonged in the city.

What did he know? Because she certainly didn't belong here in Emerald Bay.

18

To her surprise, when Imogen pushed the door open and stepped inside the eclectic gallery-cum-jeweller's, she saw Shannon leaning against Freya's workbench. Aside from her and Freya, no one else was in the gallery. Her sister was still wearing her nurse's uniform and had a glass of something red and alcoholic in her hand. The uniform and the wine made an odd mix.

'So, this is what Galway's regional public health nurse gets up to between house calls, is it?' Imogen said.

'Ha ha, very funny. It's Friday evening, and I'm officially off-duty,' Shannon said, raising her glass. 'Sláinte.'

Freya had stopped whatever she was doing with a pair of pliers and a piece of tempered silver. A half-empty goblet was next to her. 'Would you like a glass yourself there, Imogen? It's a fruit wine made with elderberries mixed with damson and sloe.'

'That sounds interesting and like something Nan and her group would have a go at making.'

Freya elaborated: 'Oisin's been staying in a farmhouse near Killorglin. His friend was housesitting it for his aunt and uncle, and he helped himself to a couple of bottles of their homemade wine. They've enough to open a winery, by all accounts.'

'It's not bad,' Shannon said, her lips tinged purple. 'I'm on my second.'

Imogen nodded. She would like to try it, thinking how apt the name Freya had chosen for her business was. Mermaids. She looked like a mermaid with that mane of hair. Although how she managed to create anything working amid all that chaos was a mystery. Her gaze swept over the mysterious-looking tools and lumps of metal cluttering the bench behind which Freya was seated on a stool.

'Help yourself. You'll find an extra glass in the cupboard out the back, and you could fetch another tub of Pringles while you're at it. I buy them in bulk when they're on special now Shannon's home, and your sister's after making short work of the last one.'

'That sounds about right,' Imogen muttered.

'I'm comfort-eating. I miss James.' Shannon slid the remains of the tube into the palm of her hand and tapped the bottom of the container to ensure it was empty.

Imogen and Freya exchanged a knowing glance over Shannon's penchant for emotional eating before Imogen went to find a glass and another container of crisps.

When she returned, Freya downed tools and grinned, holding her hand out for the Pringles. 'Give me those. She's not the only one with an absent boyfriend.'

'Nev's not here, either. So...' Imogen peeled back the lid and foil, helping herself first and through a mouthful muttered, 'Besides, sour cream and onion is my favourite.'

Imogen was usually fastidious about avoiding junk food, but a girl was allowed some weaknesses and she tipped out another handful.

'Shannon said your fella's coming down for St Paddy's, though. Oisin will be here too.' Freya's expression at the mention of her artist boyfriend was wistful as she waited for the crisps, but Shannon grabbed them first.

'Well, James isn't, so I need these more than you two.'

Imogen and Freya laughed, although Shannon's glum expression as she began scarfing the crisps said there was nothing amusing about her boyfriend being in Boston.

'Sorry, Shan.' Imogen nudged her sister with her hip, the ruby red drink swishing in the glass as she tried to jostle her out of her fug.

'Don't be annoying.'

'I can see a smile,' Imogen persisted.

'So can I,' Freya added, leaning her elbows down on the workbench and resting her chin in the palms of her hands.

Shannon's lips twitched. 'Stop it. I want to wallow.'

Imogen gave her one more nudge for good measure.

'I am looking forward to meeting Nev next weekend, at any rate.' Shannon beamed.

'Me too,' Freya added, straightening as she gave up on the crisps and returned to her pliers and silver.

'Although I'd not want to be in your shoes when Mam and Dad meet him.'

'Thanks a million,' Imogen said, seeing her sister shudder. She didn't want to talk about that. 'What are you working on, Freya?' she asked instead.

'This.' Freya pushed a notebook toward her. It was open to a sketch she'd done.

Imogen picked the book up and studied the pencilled drawing. She was talented, even if all those Celtic swirls did remind her of the playdough snails she'd liked making when she was little. 'This is great. It's very... er, Celtic.'

The corners of Freya's mouth raised but she didn't look up from what she was doing. 'It's for a client in Canada. A lot of my orders come in online these days.'

Shannon wasn't letting the subject drop so easily, though.

'There's something else about this Nev fella, Imo. I can feel it in my water.'

'Jaysus, Shan! You sounded just like Mam then.'

'Is he married?'

The horror on Shannon's face would have been comical if Imogen wasn't annoyed with her. 'No. He's not. He was, but that's none of your business.' She held her hand up. 'And before you go there: No, it wasn't me who broke his marriage up. He's been divorced five years, thank you very much.'

'It's just the age thing that's an issue, then?'

'Sure, it's not for him or me. It's only a few years.'

Shannon's eyebrows raised at Imogen's use of 'only a few years'.

'All right, quite a few years older.' Imogen sighed. 'Listen, it's no big secret. Nev's got children. Grown-up, of course. Three needy daughters and a Rottweiler ex-wife. They all hate me and do their best to make things difficult for us. I've been reluctant to invite Nev home to meet you all for obvious reasons, and he's been on at me about that, which proves he's serious and I'm not arm candy.' She eyed Shannon.

'I never thought that.'

'Yes you did.'

'Now, now, you two,' Freya said. 'There'll be no more wine for either of you if you don't stop bickering.'

'Now you sound like our mam, Freya.' Imogen couldn't help but grin. Sorry,' she tossed over to Shannon, her gaze swivelling back to Freya as she added, 'But it's her.'

Shannon poked her purplish tongue out, making Imogen laugh.

'Anyway, Nev's promised to stop being at the beck and call of his ex and their daughters. So, we're solid now.'

Shannon nodded, satisfied.

The subject was closed, and Imogen sipped from her glass,

enjoying the unusual tang the fruity wine had while listening to Freya and Shannon chatting.

Freya was imitating a broad Australian twang as she told them about a group who'd piled out of a minivan and into the gallery pretending to be interested in the art adorning the wall. Freya, however, suspected they were scoping the place for a loo. 'If they'd asked, I would have told them the Shamrock was only down the road and to call in for a pint and a visit.'

Shannon topped her friend's tale by sharing how she'd spent half an hour that morning trying to locate a set of false teeth belonging to one of the elderly women on her rounds. The woman was in a panic because her gentleman friend always called in on a Friday after the pensioner's lunch special at his local pub. She tucked her lips in over the top of her teeth. 'Janey Mack! I know they're here somewhere, Shannon,' she imitated, before adding, 'I asked her when she'd misplaced them, and she said sometime after dinner. They'd been in then because she'd had a nice chop for her dinner.'

Imogen giggled despite the odd mood her conversation with Shannon had put her in. That, and the thought of seeing Lachlan tomorrow. She drained her glass, seeing that sediment had settled at the bottom. 'Thanks for that. I called in to look around the gallery because I need four paintings for the guestrooms I'm working on up at Benmore.'

'Do you have anything specific in mind, or will you know it when you see it?'

'A little of both. It would be nice if the artworks all ran along a particular theme.'

Freya set the pliers and silver to one side. 'There is a series of paintings that might work.' She hopped off her stool and gestured for Imogen to follow her. They crossed the hardwood floors and stood shoulder to shoulder to look at the cluster of landscapes. 'They're original acrylics of Connemara.'

Imogen studied the five paintings. The first depicted a group of Connemara ponies poised by a stream, alert to whoever was sitting behind the easel. Next, a solitary cottage where Imogen could sense the isolated lifestyle of the farmer it belonged to. And then she ran her eyes over a scene in which the familiar mounds of the Twelve Bens loomed large. She felt she was standing on the shore looking out at the misty morning lake, appraising the following picture, but her eyes lingered on the fifth painting. The reeds bowing gently to the wind and the rippling water with a stormy backdrop 'spoke to her', as they said in the art world.

'What do you think?'

'Freya.' Imogen wrenched her eyes away from the arresting images and gushed, 'They're perfect.' Then she leaned in closer to inspect the price tags on the discreet pieces of card beneath each frame. They weren't exorbitant by any means. She couldn't believe her luck and was so pleased she'd stopped by Mermaids on her way home. The first four paintings would find a home at Benmore, but the fifth picture would return to Dublin with her. She loved it. Whenever she felt the itch to be far from the hustle and bustle of city life, she could lose herself in the painting and feel like she'd been whisked away to the wilds surrounding her home.

'You haven't looked at the signature, have you?' Freya looked amused. 'Shannon told me you were working with him up at Benmore.'

Imogen, curious, leaned in closer and read the name scrawled in the bottom right-hand corner of each of the paintings. 'Ryan O'Malley,' she whispered incredulously. Then, looking back to Freya: 'But he's a builder, not an artist.'

'Can he not be both?' Freya asked.

Imogen had no answer because Ryan O'Malley, the once-accused bra-pinger, clearly had hidden depths.

ONE WEEK UNTIL ST PATRICK'S DAY

May you have...
enough happiness to keep you sweet,
enough trials to keep you strong,
enough sorrow to keep you human,
enough hope to keep you happy,
enough failure to keep you humble,
enough success to keep you eager,
enough wealth to meet your needs,
enough enthusiasm to look forward,
enough friends to give you comfort,
enough faith to banish depression,
enough determination to make each day
better than yesterday.

— IRISH BLESSING FOR ST
PATRICK'S DAY

19

Imogen had slept late and felt battle-weary after a Friday night full of song and dance at the Shamrock Inn. A strong brew would sort her out because today was going to be a big day. Her horoscope had said as much, she thought, making her way downstairs.

Today, her past would meet her present.

'Where's Shannon?' she asked over the racket of the old-fashioned hand beater her nan was giving what for as she mooched into the kitchen.

Kitty Kelly was adamant new didn't necessarily mean better, and there were some things modern technology couldn't replace. It was much debated with Nora as she didn't think an electric beater was in the same class as the latest smartphone.

Imogen preferred to stay neutral on the subject, and she pulled out a chair and sat down at the breakfast table, helping herself to tea from the pot.

'Finally, the dead awoke and appeared to many.' Kitty leaned the beater against the side of the bowl to give her arm a break and wiped floury hands on her pinny. 'Your sister, in her role as a taste-tester for this trial run of my top-secret entry in the Great Emerald Bay Bake-Off next Saturday, has nipped across the road for a bottle of essence. And don't ask me what flavour essence because that will give the game away, and I'm not telling.'

Liam breezing into the kitchen caught the tail end of the conversation and, after planting a kiss on top of Imogen's head, said, 'I tell you, Rose, my mother's lips are sealed tighter than the Hoover Dam when it comes to what she's after making there. I've been banished from my own home for the morning, so I have.'

Imogen felt warm hearing her dad's pet name for her as he came around the table to swoop on the last piece of toast. He was dressed from head to toe in khaki as if he were about to undertake an army exercise instead of wandering the country-side in search of flora and fauna.

Liam Kelly's hobby was an unusual one for a publican: botany. When time allowed, he loved nothing more than to seek out the wildflowers of Connemara. Hence, after the fragile white guelder rose, Imogen's pet name was Rose. Liam had bestowed all five of his daughters with the name of a regional wildflower. But Imogen fancied hers was the best, making her a clear favourite in her father's eyes.

'I'd like to spot an Orchis Mascula,' he mumbled, brushing crumbs from his jacket.

'Speak English, son.'

'The early purple orchid, Mam.'

'Good luck,' Imogen said over the rim of her teacup.

'Thanking you.' Liam looked up at the ceiling. 'I shall slip off before your mam finds me a job. But not before I do this!' He lunged for the baking bowl and stuck his finger in the batter, earning himself a swat from his mother as she herded him out the door. 'Get off with you.'

'Tell your mam I'll be back for lunch,' he called to Imogen before Kitty shut the door on him.

'He's incorrigible, that lad of mine,' Kitty tutted fondly as she returned to her beating.

Imogen finished her tea. Should she have something to eat? Her eyes flitted to the toaster in contemplation. Probably, but she wasn't hungry. The thought of seeing Lachlan after so long had her keyed up, and her eyeballs ached. An indicator she'd had one too many last night and would be helping herself to the paracetamol she knew to be in the bathroom cabinet upstairs when she went up for her shower.

As she'd told Nev she would, Imogen had volunteered her services behind the bar last night, giving her mam an evening off. How had his gala dinner gone? she wondered, reaching for her phone to text him but realising it was still upstairs. Later, she told herself. And where was Ryan last night? She'd been desperate to tell him she'd bought five of his paintings, four on behalf of the Leslies. She wanted to know why he'd not mentioned he painted. Talk about hiding your light under a bushel!

He'd said he'd see her at the pub, and she'd kept looking to the door each time it opened, but there'd been no sign of him. It had been deflating, and later, when she was tucked up in bed, she'd done her best not to think about Ryan, Lachlan or Nev.

Now she willed her headache away. Evan Kennedy was to blame for her sins, she decided, remembering how he'd insisted she and Father Seamus have one for themselves each time he appeared at the bar. And Father Seamus on Bushmills finest too. The priest had told Evan generosity was a virtue.

It was very out of character for Evan, but he'd had a windfall on the horse racing, and Imogen decided it would have been rude to say no. Usually, the Shamrock Inn regular relied heavily on the generosity of tourists to supplement his ale intake. He was a seasoned pro when it came to garnering their sympathy by sharing how he was a distant relative of the late great John F. Kennedy, who also suffered the curse of the Kennedys.

Ryan sprang to mind again. He'd missed a good night. The craic was mighty with Dad on his tin whistle, Dermot Molloy on the pipes, Ollie Quigley playing his fiddle and Shannon singing. A memory of Rita Quigley hitching her skirts up and dancing a jig extinguished her annoyance over Eileen Carroll gossiping in the bookshop owner's ear and, forgetting about her headache, she smiled into her empty cup. Pushing her chair back, Imogen got up and slinked upstairs, glad Nan was too engrossed in sprinkling flour into her mix to notice she'd not eaten.

She passed her mam in the hallway with an armful of sheets.

'It's a great drying day, Imogen,' Nora informed her, carting them down the stairs.

What was that outside her bedroom door? Imogen approached the mound on the floor warily lest it was still alive and, crouching down, exhaled seeing Napoleon had gifted her with a pair of Shannon's knickers this morning. Yesterday it had been socks. There was no sign of him as she muttered a 'Jaysus wept' and kicked them up the hall to her sister's room. She prayed Shannon had the sense not to wear those things around James, at least not this early in the piece. They put her in mind of the parachute at the music group the other day.

When Imogen returned to her room, she found Napoleon playing lord of the manor on her bed. Upon seeing her, he cocked a leg and began washing his nether regions.

'Don't be doing that on my bed, thank you very much. So off you go now, and I know you mean well, but the presents are to stop. I don't want any more knickers or socks. Do you hear me?'

Napoleon paused his grooming to fix her with a haughty gaze before lowering his leg, leaping off the bed and sauntering down the hall to keep guard at the top of the stairs.

Imogen shook her head and shut the door. It was time to begin the taxing task of deciding what to wear to wow an ex-boyfriend when you didn't want to look like you'd made any effort.

Five minutes later, clothes were strewn across her bed and, with the blazer, shirt and jeans she'd settled on draped over her arm, Imogen made for the bathroom. She slid the lock across the door and thought if anyone wanted to use it in the next forty minutes they were out of luck.

'Imogen's here.' Shannon kicked back at the kitchen table, tasting duties done judging by the smear of batter around her mouth, and angled the phone so Imogen could see James. He waved to her.

'Hello, James. You're looking sweaty.' Imogen waved back.

'I was up early for a Saturday morning run.' He grinned out of the phone at her.

'What time is it where you are?'

'Six a.m.'

'You're mad, so you are.'

'It's the highlight of Harry's week. He brings the lead into the bedroom on the dot of five,' he replied, referring to his beagle. His smile was wide as he told her how his mam, who hadn't been doing well the last few weeks, had rallied lately. He was putting it down to Maeve.

Imogen mirrored his expression even though his words made her sad. Tough times lay ahead for Maeve, James and the Cabot family, as Shannon had told her on the quiet that a sudden rallying before passing could happen with cancer patients; it was something she'd seen before in her work as a nurse. James was going to need her sister's strength, Imogen thought.

The conversation moved on, with James asking how the Benmore House project was coming along, and then Imogen was elbowed out of the way by Kitty. She'd closed the oven on her secret baking and was keen to tell James about the St Paddy's Day Bake-Off.

James had her beaming by saying she was sure to win and how he couldn't wait to get back to Emerald Bay to sample some of her wonderful cooking again.

Imogen and Shannon exchanged a look knowing the key to winning Kitty Kelly over was to praise her cooking. James had well and truly cemented his place in their nan's heart. Imogen thought she would have to remember to tell Nev to compliment Nan on her cooking. He was going to need all the brownie points he could get.

'Ah, no. Here she comes,' Shannon muttered.

Imogen looked to where their mam had just dropped the laundry basket and was honing in on the phone Shannon was still holding.

'I'm sure she has some sort of potential son-in-law-on-the-phone sixth sense,' Shannon said, and Imogen sniggered.

This time it was Nora doing the elbowing as Kitty harrumphed back to the worktop. She began telling James all the news from Emerald Bay.

Shannon snatched the phone away as Nora started giving him the minutes from her Menopausal and Hot Monday group meeting. 'He's my fella, Mam. Stop hogging him. James, I'm taking you upstairs to the privacy of my room.'

'Remember whose roof it is you're under,' Nora called as Shannon thundered up the stairs.

Imogen rolled her eyes as her sister reached the landing and she heard her say, 'And who do we have here? It's Napoleon. Say hello to James. You miss him, don't you?'

The sooner Shannon married James Cabot and got on with the business of having children, the better!

Nora turned her attention to her second-born child. 'You're looking glamorous for a young woman who's about to hang the washing out and give her mammy a hand with the hoovering. I see that ankle's all better now, if those shoes you've on are anything to go by.'

'Mam, I can't right now. I'm sorry, but I've got an emer-gency up at Benmore House.' Before her mam could press as to what the emergency was, Imogen had headed out the back door.

She was off to confront her past.

20

'Brr,' Imogen shivered inside her blazer as she marched toward her car. The garment was more about style than practicality. This time of year, the mornings still had a bite and, come four o'clock, the heat went out of the sun. The fire roared inside the Shamrock each evening and would do so until at least mid-April. She got behind the wheel of her car, only dimly aware of the bees humming this morning, and, without pausing to second-guess her decision to visit Benmore, gunned the engine.

A group of teens were slouched outside the Bus Stop, vaping, as she turned out onto Main Street. Imogen felt their pain at being fourteen and utterly bored, remembering it well. She was sure she'd never worn six inches of tangerine foundation, though, she thought as the one with the belly piercing tucked her hair behind her ears. In her mind, she was already jotting down that orange foundation was never a good idea in the *Don't* section of the make-up tips in her Lottie Book.

Life in Emerald Bay was carrying on, as usual, she observed waving out at Mrs Sheedy and Mrs Brady. Had Mrs Brady made the fatal error of asking how Mrs Sheedy was keeping? The woman was a right Moaning Minnie, never happy with her lot, and she'd be bending her ear for an age if that was the case. It must run in the family because she was Mrs Tattersall's first cousin.

Imogen passed Mermaids, busy with Saturday-morning visitors thanks to a coach parked on the other side of the road, and then she left the village behind. Her eyes were trained on the road ahead, but her resolve began to wobble as she drew close to the castle ruins.

What was she doing? She slapped the steering wheel as her phone simultaneously announced she'd received a text message. It was a reminder that she still hadn't been in touch with Nev to find out how his evening had gone, but before she could think about it, she'd turned off the road. Her car bounced into the beach access parking near the ruins of Kilticaneel Castle, where only one other vehicle was parked.

Imogen pulled up down the far end to the other car, and her hand reached for her phone, fully intending to ring Nev, but before she grasped hold of it, her gaze trekked toward the castle. She'd ring him later, she told herself for the second time that morning, not wishing to examine why she felt sneaky and something else. Disloyal.

'You're being silly, Imogen,' she said out loud. 'All you're doing is collecting your laptop. You don't even know for certain you'll see Lachlan.'

This sentiment was true because he might be out doing whatever it was you did on all that country acreage, but the idea after all this build-up of not seeing him was crushingly disappointing. She knew no matter what she told herself it was much more than just a laptop she was collecting this morning.

Perhaps she should put the radio on and just sit here for a few minutes. At the very least, it might stop her from talking to herself. She wasn't in the mood for music, though. Not even Justin. And then there was no more time for introspection because she opened the door and got out of her car.

The sudden blast of salt-laden fresh air chased away the remnants of her headache as she carefully picked her way to the castle. To explore castle ruins hadn't been on her agenda when she dressed earlier, and the last thing she needed was to turn her ankle again when it was still weak.

Today, no children were keeping watch for marauding pirates from the imposing fortification. Over the crash of waves below, she could hear a dog barking and a child's laughter. She pictured a stick being thrown and a dog bounding into the icy water as she stepped inside the crumbling fortification.

The ruin was as much a part of the landscape here as the bogland itself. All was silent now as the thick walls encased her apart from the wind's whistling. It sneaked in through the holes where cobbled stones had toppled over time. Always too, there was the shushing of the sea.

Imogen stared up at the tower, seeing a bird's nest tucked perilously into a groove in the stones. Picking her way across the sandy soil and broken flagstones, she emerged into the open courtyard area. The ground here was rough with weeds and spiky coastal grass.

Overhead, the sky couldn't decide between blue or grey, and the sun was equally indecisive. Why hadn't she put a sweater on under her blazer? she mused, wrapping her arms around herself, but practicality was never a feature in fashion.

When the castle was deserted like so there was a powerful sense of the past, Imogen always thought. She could feel energy contained within the partitions, and making her way over to the far wall, she leaned back against its solidness. These ramparts had withstood the passage of time and coming here always put her problems into perspective. Throughout the centuries, so many stories had played out in this courtyard, and she'd know that what seemed impossible right now was a mere blip in time. It would be irrelevant in the days, weeks, months or even years to come because time did not stand still. Not for anyone.

A seagull screeched, gliding low for a second in search of scraps before following another's call, and Imogen closed her eyes. Lachlan had pressed her back into this wall that summer. The thrill of those remembered kisses swept her back in time...

It had been Lachlan's suggestion they come to the castle that night. His parents had returned, and Benmore House was no longer theirs to roam freely. They were having a garden party that evening, so even the grounds were off limits. Her curfew was eleven o'clock, and she'd told her mam and dad she was going to Fi's to watch a film. A story her pal was complicit in. They hadn't questioned her, being run off their feet as they were with the pub, but never so busy they didn't keep an eye on the clock for curfews.

The night had been dark and moonless initially, thanks to cloud-cover, and Imogen held tightly onto Lachlan's arm when she got out of the car he'd borrowed from his parents. Their eyes were wide, trying to adjust to the inkiness, and the ruin they were making their way toward was no more than a jagged outline. When the curtain of clouds suddenly parted and the moon appeared, it bathed their surroundings inside the castle in an eery glow.

Imogen had stared through the arrow slits out to sea, thinking the silver path tracing its way across the waves looked magical. But, when she turned back, Lachlan had disappeared.

'Lachlan!' Her voice bounced off the stone walls. 'That's not funny.' There was no reply, and she ventured deeper into the ruin with a nervous giggle.

He jumped out at her as she stepped into the courtyard, and even though she'd guessed that was where he was hiding, she still emitted a soft cry before thumping him playfully.

He'd taken her by the hand and then led her to the wall.

They'd stood with their backs against the stones as hers was now. And their necks craned upward to the stars.

'Do you believe we're connected to the stars?' Imogen asked.

There'd been a fortune teller in the village once. It was when the Travellers had set up camp in a field. Sergeant Badger had tried to get them to move on, but they'd refused to leave until they were ready. Imogen and Fi had been desperate for a reading but, simultaneously, terrified to venture into the camp.

'I don't know.'

Imogen risked a glance at Lachlan, whose expression was earnest.

'What if they could tell us what lay ahead?' she persisted.

'I know what lies ahead.'

'What do you mean?'

'I'm a Leslie. I know what the future holds.'

She nudged him playfully, 'You're not a fortune teller.'

'I don't have to be. My future is mapped out for me.'

'How?'

'I'll finish school, go to university, and probably transfer to America for a year as Matthew did. Then I'll come back for you, and we'll go away together and have this amazingly exciting life.'

'Really?'

'Really.' He turned so his body angled toward her. 'But you're going to have to wait for me.'

'I can wait.' Imogen knew she would wait forever if she had to.

'Promise.' He traced a finger down her cheek.

'I promise.'

He positioned himself so his body pressed into hers. They'd kissed under a canopy of stars sealing the deal. As the kisses increased in urgency, Imogen knew she would never feel this way about anyone else again. She gave her heart and everything to Lachlan that night because they would be together forever. He'd promised.

Now she blinked, aware of the presence of others. A young couple were stepping into the courtyard. They were clad in the outdoorsy wear of backpackers and hesitated, seeing her there. She must look an odd sight, Imogen thought. They probably thought she fancied herself as that Claire one from the Outlander stories, trying to find a crack in the stones to whisk her through a time portal. She supposed it was what she had been doing in a way, pushing off from the wall. It was time to go and, uttering a greeting, Imogen hurried as quickly as her shoes would allow away from her memories.

A camper van was parked up now, but she barely registered it. She'd kept her promise, waiting for the longest time, but Lachlan had never come back. He'd never even replied to a single letter, and she'd sent them off to him religiously in the beginning. Although, looking back now, she didn't know what she'd found to write about week after week.

Was Fi right? She'd given her short shrift when she'd gotten maudlin one night, knocking back the cocktails at the hen night of some friend with whom they'd since lost contact. 'You need to get over yourself, Imo. He was an arse who sweet-talked you into having sex with him, but you have to sift through the arses to meet Mr Right. And I don't mean fall for their lines and shag them either.'

'It was making love, not shagging, Fi,' had been her holier-than-thou reply, and now she cringed at the memory. It was a lofty way of describing a few minutes huffing and puffing with her back scraping against the castle's stone walls.

At the time, she'd been annoyed with her friend for not understanding that she couldn't possibly ever feel the same way about another man, but now she wondered. Had she cast herself and Lachlan in the roles of a romantic melodrama? She climbed behind the wheel of her car and shook her head. There was more to it than that, though. There was the way Mrs Leslie had sneered at her with such contempt.

Imogen knew it was the voice of common sense telling her she didn't have to prove herself to anyone, let alone Lachlan Leslie. But going to Benmore with the intention of seeing him today wasn't about common sense; it was about banishing that girl who still lurked inside her, telling her she wasn't good enough. She needed closure. The thought of what Fi would say if she were to mention the 'C' word almost made her smile as she pictured her friend placing her hands over her ears and telling her it was a bad word, right up there with 'journey', and should be banned from the English vocabulary.

She knew, too if she were to be a decent role model for her god-daughter Lottie, then this was something she needed to do.

Imogen reversed past the camper and pulled back out on to the road. She was heading for Benmore.

The house was pulling her in like quicksand.

21

The silver Merc was gone, Imogen noticed, pulling up outside the house, which somehow managed to seem even more imposing than usual this morning. An SUV had replaced the car. Hired, she assumed, parking next to it and trying not to think about Lachlan, his fiancée and their wedding planner driving toward Emerald Bay, full of excitement for the weekend ahead. Instead, she angled the rear-view mirror and checked her make-up, giving her hair a fluff before reaching for the door handle. A swarm of butterflies batted their wings in her belly, but Imogen steeled her resolve. She knew she had no choice but to get out of the car now because if anyone glanced out of one of the windows and saw her just sitting there, they'd wonder what she was up to.

Imogen had no wish to look like an eejit, and she took a steadying breath, opening the door, conscious of alighting with grace in case anyone was watching. Then, holding her head high and with her chin jutting forth, she trekked across the length of the drive and up the stairs to press the doorbell.

She heard the bell pealing inside and imagined the sound bouncing off the walls. Would Francesca answer the door, or did she have Saturdays off? It was hard to imagine Sigrid and Matthew whipping up much in the kitchen if left to their own devices, and how they'd cope with guests to boot, she didn't know. Perhaps Francesca had left a casserole or lasagne for them to heat and eat. Jaysus, her mind was wandering, but at the same time, it was razor-sharp thanks to a cup of tea you could stand a spoon up in earlier, paracetamol and the salt air. Sigrid would no doubt be suffering today after the nudge she and her friends had given it yesterday, and she was glad she wasn't in her shoes.

Footsteps sounded, audible despite the thick wooden door between them, and her heart began jumping about madly. *Stand tall and hold your head high, Imogen,* she told herself, pushing her shoulders back. The lock clicked, and then the door swung open. As she registered who was standing there, her lips parted, and her mouth formed an 'O'.

It wasn't Francesca or even Sigrid but Lachlan himself, and she wasn't prepared for that. She took a step back, and his hand shot out to grasp her forearm.

'Careful,' he said, sounding more Londoner than Irish.

Flustered, Imogen looked down at her heels, seeing she was only a whisper away from toppling backwards off the steps. 'Thank you,' she managed to croak.

Lachlan, satisfied she wasn't going to do herself an injury, let go of her arm. Her gaze clung to him greedily. If possible, he was even more handsome than she'd remembered. His classic good looks had become leaner as the puppy fat of youth melted away to be replaced with chiselled masculinity. He was wearing a white shirt and jeans, and she could smell the spicy notes of his aftershave. His relaxed stance was at odds with his older brother, who somehow managed to look stiff and formal even when he was dressed casually.

'Er, can I help you?' He was looking at her appreciatively,

amusement dancing in his eyes in that way of a self-assured, attractive man.

Imogen stared at him, wondering how he didn't know who she was. It had thrown her. Of course, she'd changed, but not so much she was unrecognisable as the teenage girl she'd been. She would have known him anywhere. 'Lachlan?' Her voice trailed away lost, and her legs felt weak.

He studied her face curiously then, and finally, something clicked. 'My God, Imogen? It's been years.' He slapped his forehead. 'Of course, it's you. When Sigrid mentioned your name earlier, she said you were a local, but I didn't put two and two together. You're the interior designer she's employed.'

Imogen nodded, not trusting herself to speak.

'Come in.' He stepped aside and, somehow, she put one foot in front of the other and stood opposite him in the foyer. There was no sign of anyone else. It was just the two of them.

'It's so good to see you again. How are things? You look great, by the way.'

As she bloody well should, given the amount of time and effort that had gone into her casual but groomed look. 'Thanks, and I'm good. Excellent, in fact.' What was wrong with her voice? She sounded like she had swallowed sandpaper.

'Sigrid mentioned you'd travelled from Dublin and were staying with family. I can't believe I didn't guess it was you. We had some laughs that summer, didn't we?' His face glazed over nostalgically.

Laughs? Was that all they'd had? Imogen forced herself to speak, trying to adopt the same carefree manner and suspecting her smile looked like she was baring her teeth. 'Yes, we did.'

'Do you remember how we had the run of this place? I was like lord of the manor, and you were my lady.' He grinned. 'Good times. I'd love to chat over them with you.'

Did he mean he wanted to relive his glory days? Imogen

wondered, sensing his reference to being lord of the manor wasn't just a throwaway remark. There was something about the inflection in his voice. She also didn't trust herself to trip down memory lane with him. He'd presented her with the perfect opportunity to blurt the question she wanted an answer to. Why hadn't he come back to Emerald Bay as he had promised? And if his life had moved on as she suspected it had, why hadn't he contacted her to break things off? To leave her hanging had been cruel.

However, the moment came and went as he asked, 'How's Dublin treating you? I'd imagine it was some change after Emerald Bay.' He found his observation funny.

Lachlan sounded like an arse, she thought, wishing he wasn't so attractive as she fibbed her reply: 'Not really.' Despite her bravado at the time, she had struggled with the impersonal nature of city life. No one had dropped off baked goods or called by to invite her to any of the local happenings. 'I'm based in Dublin, but my work as a designer takes me all over the country. So I could work from anywhere I wanted to.'

'Yes, Sigrid said you're in high demand. Good for you. The country girl made good.'

Was that condensation she was picking up on? Or was she super-sensitive, thanks to his mother's throwaway remark that she was a silly little girl? Lachlan would forget all about her once he returned to school, she had sneered. She suspected it was a little of both because his mother had been right, and Mrs Leslie's pinched-over powdered features blurred her vision for a moment.

'Lachie,' a whiny voice with a cheap accent called from somewhere deeper in the house. 'Jean-Paul wants to show us the drawing he's just sketched of where the tables should go. He said he's channelling his inner muse.'

Lachlan smirked, rolling his eyes at Imogen as though they were sixteen-year-old co-conspirators again.

She couldn't help herself, spontaneously smiling despite all the conflicting emotions.

He made no move, asking, 'Are you married?'

'No.' Imogen gave a brittle laugh. 'I've been too busy focusing on my career for marriage.'

'But there must be someone serious. You're far too beautiful not to be spoken for.' Somehow, he managed to sound charming, not cheesy, and a magnetic current was pulling her toward him.

'And you're far too kind,' she rebutted, beginning to relax in his presence as she caught glimpses of the lad she'd fallen for that summer. 'I have a partner. Nevin. He's in large-scale property development.'

'Well, if you decide to take a whirl down the aisle, here's some advice. Do not hire Jean-Paul.' Lachlan looked over his shoulder, but there was no one there. He still mouthed the word 'nightmare' instead of saying it out loud.

Imogen couldn't suppress her grin. 'I won't.' Then, remembering her manners, added, 'Congratulations, by the way.'

He ignored that, telling her once again how good she looked.

She was falling into the deep pools of his eyes, and to break the trance, she asked, 'You work in finance?'

'I play the stock market.' Again, amusement flickered as he spoke with the casualness of someone born to wealth.

'Jean-Paul doesn't like to be kept waiting, Boo-Boo.'

Imogen's eyes tracked the source of the whine to a willowy rake with a mane of tawny hair, cheekbones that could cut glass and lips so full they'd surely been plumped. She was standing near the stairs with her hand on a bony hip, appraising the situation.

Boo-Boo? Imogen had noticed Lachlan flush at his bride-to-be's use of the pet name. Although she wasn't in a position to judge, not when Nev called her Bunny.

He muttered under his breath, 'You'd think he was paying us, not the other way around.'

Imogen picked up on the woman's proprietary tone. She held her own as Lachlan's fiancée gave her a slow, condescending once-over before toying with the ends of her hair. A ploy to be sure Imogen got a good long look at the enormous rock glinting on her ring finger.

Lachlan smoothly introduced his ex-girlfriend to his fiancée. 'Vicky, this is Imogen. She's the designer working on the guestrooms. We knew each other when we were kids. I'd forgotten what a small world Emerald Bay is.'

'Victoria Baré,' the stunning apparition said, gliding toward them. 'Lachie's fiancée.'

As if she didn't know that! Imogen thought she'd probably added the accented 'e' to her surname and that it was pronounced bare, as in bear. She stared at the outstretched hand and, for a split second wondered if Victoria meant for her to curtsy and kiss it. Thankfully she came to her senses in time to grasp it. The woman's handshake was like a limp lettuce leaf.

'Sigrid didn't mention you were working today,' Victoria said, her jewel-like eyes glittering with suspicion. 'Or that you and Lachlan knew each other.'

Imogen thought he would have his work cut out for him with this green-eyed monster, explaining she'd forgotten to take her laptop home last night and had swung by to collect it.

'Well, since you're here. I don't like the colours you've chosen for the room you've started work on. And I trust you're familiar with the rules of feng shui. Jean-Paul says to have the right feng shui is imperative. He had to rearrange the furniture in the room Sigrid put him in last night because he said he wouldn't be able to sleep in there otherwise.'

'Vicki darling, the guestrooms are not our domain. Benmore isn't our house, remember.'

Imogen detected Lachlan's bitterness at being the younger son in his remark.

'But I want everything to be perfect. And things are already going wrong,' Victoria moaned.

'You're overwrought, darling. Nothing is going wrong.'

'Everything's going wrong,' the model sniffed.

'Like what?'

'Like me telling Sigrid when we arranged this weekend that myself and Jean-Paul embrace the keto lifestyle, and she still went and served quiche for supper last night and a bean salad. Everybody knows legumes are out on keto. And there's the bad bedroom feng shui.'

Imogen was amazed Sigrid managed to serve anything for supper. She wondered if the quiche was a leftover from yesterday's luncheon because, from what she'd seen, there wasn't much in the way of eating going on.

'Vi-Vi, none of that matters, darling.' Lachlan turned to face his fiancée, taking both her hands in his. 'You will have the perfect day.'

'Promise, Boo-Boo?'

'I promise.'

Imogen was feeling surplus to requirements as they eyeballed one another lustily. What would old Mrs Leslie have made of her son's choice of bride, she wondered, and felt a modicum of spiteful pleasure at the thought she'd be turning in her grave.

The sound of clapping echoed about the foyer just then, and the loved-up duo sprang apart as a diminutive but plump man with a beret angled jauntily on his head and, dear God, a cravat. He was wearing a cravat. As he strode toward them, continuing to clap, he reminded Imogen of one of those Paris fashion designers applauding themselves at the end of a fashion show.

'Chop-chop, love birds! We have a lot to do. And you are...?' His eyebrow arched beneath the beret in Imogen's direction.

'She's the interior designer working on the guestrooms, Jean-Paul,' Victoria supplied before Imogen had the chance to open her mouth.

'The feng shui in those rooms is terrible.' He sniffed.

'I've told her that,' Victoria grovelled.

Imogen almost apologised.

'Come, come.' He clicked his fingers, and Victoria began trotting dutifully after him, a leggy gazelle to his stumpy corgi.

'Lachie.' She swished her hair back, eyes flashing in annoyance.

'Good to see you again, Imogen. Duty calls.'

Imogen knew good manners dictated she should wish them a wonderful wedding day, but she wasn't feeling polite. Her eyes widened, however, as Lachlan looked back over his shoulder and mouthed, 'I'll be in touch.'

Had she imagined it, she wondered, knowing her eyes hadn't been playing tricks on her as she stood frozen in the foyer for the longest time. All the while trying to comprehend what had just occurred. The half-lidded look Lachlan had given her made it clear that it was more than a chat about old times he was after. Did he think he could have one last fling before tying the knot? Was that it?

She had come here this morning intending to finish what had always felt like unfinished business and, as ridiculous as it now seemed, show Lachlan what he'd missed out on. 'You're an eejit of the highest order, Imogen Kelly,' she whispered, her face hot. The man for whom she'd carried a torch for so long was a gobshite, and she'd been nothing to him. A summer dalliance. Worst of all, his boyish charm still affected her. What would she do if he did get in touch with her? She wasn't hard to find. A quick google search would give him a contact number.

Fi's comment about her starring in a romantic drama of her

own making was on the mark. 'What were you thinking? You're a grown woman, for feck's sake. And if he does phone or text you, then you're to ignore it and block him,' she said, knowing it was what Fi would say to her, and she'd be right.

Instead of walking out of Benmore House with her laptop tucked under her arm, feeling like she'd cast off the shadow of that summer, she would be leaving having proved the late Mrs Leslie right.

She was a silly little girl.

22

Imogen didn't want to go home to the pub where either her mam, nan or Shannon would be sure to detect something was up. When it came to it, her dad's sensitive side had been finely honed after raising five girls, and not much got past him either. No matter if she burst through the door with the brightest of smiles, they'd figure out something was up. They always did, and she wasn't able for the Spanish Inquisition.

Nor did she want to have a heart-to-heart with Fi about what a fool she'd been. Fi wouldn't rub her nose in it or say I told you so, but the fact was she had told her so. Then there was Nev. Thinking of him gave her a guilty twang, and checking her phone as she idled at the bottom of Benmore House's driveway, she saw she'd missed a call from him. Right now, though, she didn't want to talk to anyone, not even Nev. The only thing she wanted to do was drive, so instead of indicating left and returning to the Shamrock as she'd planned, she flicked the lever down to the right and drove away from Emerald Bay. Some soulful Bieber was needed, too, so pushing play on her Justin compilation, she hit the open road.

There was something soothing about driving with no destination in mind, and Justin on the radio, of course. Imogen imagined she was on a road trip heading down Route 66 as her fingers tapped out the beat, and for some reason, in this particular daydream, she looked like Susan Sarandon and had a headscarf on. Mam had loved *Thelma and Louise*, and they'd all sat through it many times. It was a good film, and Brad Pitt was at his golden best in it, all the Kelly women had agreed on that. She blinked because the apparition on the road ahead wasn't in faded denim and a white Stetson, and thank goodness, he had his shirt on.

A tweedy farmer with a cloth cap had opened a gate, and a flock of recently shorn sheep piled forth, filling the road, and she slowed to a near stop. A dog that could have been Shep's twin began bossing them along, and the farmer held up a hand, acknowledging Imogen. She silently cursed, crawling along a safe distance behind the skittish animals for what felt like forever. At last, however, they turned down a winding lane, and after a dramatic few moments involving much whistling and barking as two sheep attempted to make a break for it like Bonnie and Clyde, the road was once more clear for her to accelerate down.

Imogen wasn't paying attention to where she was going and was only dimly aware of the County Mayo scenery with craggy hills always in the background as she passed by lakes and turf bogs with twirling giant windmills standing sentry. So it was a surprise as the wild vista turned to worked farmland and a sign loomed for Charlestown, the crossroads of the West. As she revved toward the town, she played with the idea of driving to Knock Airport. It was only five minutes or so away. She could park up, buy a ticket, and wing her way... where?

This was whimsy, though. Imogen knew she would finish the job at Benmore and return to Dublin, putting all of what had happened this morning behind her. She wouldn't risk her hard-won reputation in Irish interior design by running off and leaving a job not even half finished. That would mean Lachlan would win twice, even if he didn't know it. She felt the sharp sting of not having been so much as a blip on his radar once he'd left Emerald Bay at the end of their summer together.

A farmer bobbing along on his tractor was ploughing a field on one side of the road, and her curiosity was piqued by a cluster of aluminium caravans set up on the adjacent land. She eased off the accelerator to see horses grazing in the long grass and dogs puttering about as though they'd somewhere important to be but weren't quite sure where. On makeshift lines, washing fluttered, and two women dressed in sweatshirts and jeans were chatting near the fence line while a group of young children kicked a ball about. There were no men in sight, presumably off working for the farmer, but at the far end of the field, she could see a young man who appeared to be training a dappled horse.

Travellers, she thought, wondering what it would be like to live a nomadic lifestyle. Right now, she'd embrace the ability to pack up one's life and move on to new horizons.

A little way from the campsite, another caravan was parked off the road. It was fortunate there wasn't another soul on the empty road because Imogen's car was barely moving as she checked out the sign leaning up against the caravan.

Gypsy Maria's healing cards and psychic and clairvoyant readings were in bold black print, and the sign was interspersed with images of cupped hands, stars, moons and crystal balls, even though the latter didn't appear on the list of services.

The caravan wasn't the romantic horse-drawn wagon of old, looking instead like a rusting one-berth from the seventies.

Imogen knew she'd drive on if she had any sense, but she'd already proved she was lacking in that department. Besides, the plastic chair outside the door was empty, which meant there was probably no one about anyway. The door was open, though, and against her better judgement, she pulled over a stone's throw in front of it. What did she have to lose?

So it was that Imogen came to be standing outside the home on wheels. She caught a musky whiff from inside that reminded her of the joss sticks Hannah enjoyed burning.

'Hello?' She tapped on the door.

A phlegmy cough sounded, and for a fleeting second, Imogen thought about hotfooting it back to her car, but an older woman had appeared in the doorway, blocking the light from inside. Imogen assumed this was Maria, taking note of the shocking pink hair and spiky cut. It smacked of a Nessie Doyle special. The flowing top over her blue trousers was as flamboyant as her hair.

'Sorry, I didn't mean to disturb you.' Imogen was still poised for flight. 'I was passing, and I saw the sign.'

Maria's coal eyes were ringed in thick matching liner, and her lipstick a slash of vermillion. 'It's a tenner a reading, and I don't take credit cards,' she informed Imogen in a voice suggestive of a pack-a-day habit. A further clue in the odour of a freshly smoked cigarette clinging to her.

'Er, I'm not sure I have cash.'

'Cash only.' Maria hoisted her trousers up.

Imogen knew she'd a tenner folded behind the cards slotted inside her phone case. It was her emergency stash for those moments when only cash would do, like now. She put her hand in her bag to find her phone, thinking all she had to do was present the coins she knew lurked down the bottom and shrug. Then she could be on her way. But what if Maria, being psychic and all, already knew about the note she had tucked away? Wasn't it bad luck to cross a Traveller? She wasn't prepared to risk it, so she pulled her phone out and dislodged the note behind her Visa card.

Maria's hand reached out faster than a cobra striking to snatch it from her.

'You'd better come in.' She turned away and disappeared inside the caravan.

There was no going back, Imogen thought, stepping inside to see Maria stuff the note inside an old tea caddy – the type of tin you paid a fortune for these days because it was retro. She placed it on a shelf and closed the cupboard before telling Imogen to have a seat.

While Maria busied herself filling a kettle and, after the third attempt, managing to get a flame flickering on the two-ring cooktop to place it over, Imogen slid in behind the table. She sat down on the foam bench cushion covered in orange flowery fabric and took advantage of the chance to check out her surroundings unobserved.

The caravan was like stepping into a seventies time warp with the curtains matching the cushion coverings. It was cluttered, too, but it would be hard to be minimalist in a small space, no matter what your George Clarke man said.

The source of the musky fragrance was a smouldering joss stick burning on the table at which she sat. It did little to mask the stale smell of butts coming from the full-to-overflowing ashtray next to it, but aside from that, a packet of Pall Mall and a small bottle of essential oil, there was nothing else on the table. So where were the tarot cards or other tools of the trade Imogen had expected to see laid out?

'I'll have the kettle whistling in no time. Do you take milk in your tea?'

'A splash of milk, please.' There was no point asking for a sweetly spiced chai, even if she had just handed over a tenner.

'It's fresh from the farm today.' Maria fetched a small glass bottle from the tiny fridge to the side of the cooktop.

'Lovely,' Imogen murmured. She was gasping, now she thought about it, and observed Maria warming the pot before scooping loose-leaf tea leaves into it. She fetched a cup and saucer next, which looked far too delicate in her meaty hands with the stacks of silver rings adorning her fingers, and true to her word, the kettle was soon singing.

'We'll give it a minute to brew,' Maria said, placing the teapot down on a stand in the middle of the table before she squeezed in opposite Imogen. Her knee knocked against Imogen's under the table, but she didn't appear to notice as she reached for the Pall Mall and thrust the packet at her. 'Smoke?'

'No, thanks,' Imogen replied, primly happy to see Maria put the packet down without fetching a cigarette to smoke herself.

The silence that followed felt awkward to Imogen, but Maria didn't seem bothered as she sat breathing noisily. Perhaps she was channelling her energy or something, Imogen thought, toying with the pendant on her necklace. It was a relief when she poured the red-brown brew.

'Sugar?'

'No. I'm sweet enough.' Jaysus, she was feeling antsy because that was the sort of eejitty thing her mam would say. She blew on the hot tea and took a tentative sip. Whatever blend of leaves Maria had used hit the spot, Imogen decided, enjoying the refreshing flavour.

'You'll want to leave a little at the bottom for the reading.' Maria's cup had a red imprint on the rim as it hung between lips and saucer.

'Pardon?'

'For the tea-leaf reading, like.'

'Tea-leaf reading?' Imogen frowned. 'Er, there appears to be some confusion.'

'No confusion.'

'But on the sign outside it says psychic and clairvoyant readings.'

'That's Maria's area. I'm the tea-leaf lady. I work Saturdays.'

'Sorry, I assumed you were Maria.'

'No. I'm Fran, and it's the tea leaves or nothing.'

'But what will the tea leaves tell you?'

'What's in your heart.'

Was she being deliberately obtuse? Imogen couldn't tell, but she couldn't very well ask for her money back now she'd all but finished her tea. For the price of it, a biscuit, at the very least, would have been nice. But, tea and biscuits aside, Fran was a little scary with her overbearing presence and gravelly voice.

'That's settled then,' Fran said.

Was it?

'Take your cup by the handle with your left hand and then in your mind seek guidance from the universe or ask what it is you want an answer to.'

Clearly it was settled, Imogen thought. She followed Fran's instructions, not that she believed in any of this leaf nonsense. Tea was for drinking, and yes, OK, a good cuppa was hard to beat, but a cup of Rosie Lee wasn't going to reveal the secrets of the universe. Nevertheless, she searched her brain for what she wanted to ask, studiously avoiding wasting more of her time on Lachlan Leslie. The usual suspects cropped up, like *Will I win the lottery?* and *Will I find lasting love?* Or, more to the point, was Nev the one? If there even was such a thing. Would his daughters come to accept that they were an item? Would her mam and dad be OK with the age difference between them? She'd like to know where they'd be as a couple in a year's time.

The tea leaves might think her greedy, demanding answers to all those burning questions, though, and finally, she settled on *Have I met my soul mate yet?* Happy she'd wrapped all her concerns into one concise, straight-to-the-point query, she opened her eyes and looked at Fran to signal she'd done as she'd been told.

'Good. Now swirl the dregs there around three times counter-clockwise.'

Imogen swished the liquid in the bottom of the cup anticlockwise, unable to fathom how those black ant-like leaves would tell Fran anything.

'Stop.'

Imogen froze, cup in hand.

'Place the saucer over the top of the cup. That's it. Now tip it up so the liquid drains into it quickly.'

Imogen managed to do this without spilling a drop, and then Fran took the cup, staring into the contents. The leaves were stuck to the sides of the bone china and puddled in the bottom. How they'd tell her anything other than she'd need to give it a good rinse before putting it in the dishwasher was beyond her. Fran begged to differ, though, as she gently turned the cup, studying it from various angles.

The clock on the wall ticked loudly in the silence, broken only by Fran's wheezy breath and the odd car rolling past the caravan. Their occupants were smarter than her, Imogen thought, wishing Fran would do her stuff so she could make a U-turn and head for home.

'I see a hammer,' Fran finally announced, looking up and pinning Imogen with her black eyes.

'Pardon?' Her unwavering gaze was unsettling.

'A hammer.'

That's what she thought she'd said. Jaysus. Fran had seen her coming.

'That's not all, though.'

There was hope then.

'And I see a village.'

Given that she hailed from a village, as did a fair portion of Ireland's residents, this was hardly illuminating. The tea leaves showed Fran a hammer and a village. So much for revealing what was in her heart.

Fran leaned back against the cushion, looking pleased. Her job was done.

Her top clashed violently with the orange flowers, Imogen

thought, wishing she could wipe the cat that got the cream smirk off her face as she asked, 'Is that it? Is that all they told you?'

'The tea leaves never lie,' Fran replied enigmatically.

Imogen had had enough, and she inched her way off the seat. She was annoyed at herself for wasting her time and money.

'Well, thank you,' she said, remembering her manners and that it was bad luck to cross a Traveller as she made for the door, suddenly desperately for fresh air.

'A hammer and a village,' was rasped after her.

23

Imogen pulled into the car park behind the Shamrock Inn after an uneventful journey home. This time around, there were no straggling ducklings or farmers herding sheep. She hadn't even put Justin on for company as she drove along in silence with the words 'hammer and village' echoing in her ears.

She thought the whole day thus far had been disconcerting, relieved to be home as she picked her phone up from the passenger seat. A number she didn't recognise showed up on the screen as a missed call, and if she'd been amid an ECG, she'd have had the machine's alarm bells ringing. Was it from Lachlan? He'd said he'd be in touch.

'Breathe, Imogen,' she told herself, checking her text messages and seeing the same number. The top line was visible without opening the text, and she read the words *I can get away this...* in disbelief. It was from him! She hadn't misread the way he'd looked at her. She knew a booty call when she got one. Lachlan was after a last hoorah before he got married. Well, he could feck off! It showed how little he thought of her. And something else, she realised. It brought home to her what a lucky escape she'd had, because Victoria

Bare, or Baré, whichever way you said her name, was welcome to him.

Imogen's finger hovered over the message, torn between opening it and deleting it. 'There's nothing to be gained by reading it, Imogen Kelly,' she murmured, steeling herself, and before she could wobble, she hit delete and blocked Lachlan's number. He'd get the message, she thought with pride at closing the book on that part of her life that had haunted her for so long.

Then, feeling lighter, she fetched her laptop and bag, locking the car before heading toward the back door. Something buzzed past her ear, and she instinctively swatted it away. It made a second pass like an aeroplane attempting a landing and, flapping her hand, she muttered, 'Don't even think about it. If you know what's good for you, go away!'

However, the honeybee was smitten, hovering close by like an unwanted stalker. Her perfume was Marc Jacobs, Daisy. It probably found her irresistible, she mused, knowing she might as well be a whopping great daisy to the bee. She was nearly at the door now. So far, so good. Watching it dart off, a black dot in the direction of the hive, was a relief. Before she had a chance to grasp the knob, it was back.

Only this time, it had brought company.

Imogen battled a spike of panic, thinking the fecking thing had spread the word: there was a lovely big daisy bobbing about in the beer garden. To be stung would be the final straw today, and her hand settled over the doorknob, twisting it frantically, but it refused to open. Vowing to have words with whoever had locked it, her hand shot to her handbag, faltering on the zipper. Why didn't she keep an orderly bag with her key in the side pocket for moments like these? But no, it was Sodom and Gomorrah in there and with the bees determined to invade her personal space, this was not the time to spend rummaging around its chaotic depths. So instead, she dashed for the side door, all but falling into the pub.

'Jaysus, Imogen! Are you after driving through a puddle at speed on Main Street again? Is it Sergeant Badger or the Hounds of the Baskervilles themselves you've got chasing you there?' Liam looked up from where he was making the pouring of Enda Dunne's pint of Guinness into an art form and past his panting daughter.

'It's just me, Dad, and don't be bringing up the puddle thing again.' The whole debacle was still mortifying even now. Who knew driving through a puddle and splashing a pedestrian in Ireland was illegal? She certainly hadn't as she zipped around the village streets, proud of having recently passed her driving test.

Mrs Tattersall had known, of course, because she'd wasted no time informing Sergeant Badger of Imogen's teenage misdemeanour after being on the receiving end of a drenching outside Heneghan's Pharmacy. To appease the woman who ran a hotline to his desk with her daily tip-offs about the local hooligans, Sergeant Badger had arrived in the village with his siren blaring. He parked outside the pub, leaving the blue Gardai light flashing lest anyone not be aware something was going down in Emerald Bay.

Now, this part of the memory got a little murky because, in Imogen's mind, she had Sergeant Badger kicking in the door of the pub, but she thought that embellishment was a result of PTSD. However it had happened, the officer had entered the Shamrock and stood in the bar with his Garda cap in hand and asked Liam to fetch her, which he did as a law-abiding citizen.

Imogen recalled standing in the pub with her knees knocking as Sergeant Badger got his notebook out and relayed the charge against her. She'd heard her mam snicker but couldn't be sure because her future behind bars stretched long before her eyes. The thought of wearing a stripy jumpsuit for the rest of her days filled her with fear. Stripes did nothing for her.

In the end, her dad had bought the sergeant off with a free pint and packet of pork scratchings, and Imogen had got away with nothing more than a telling-off and a telephoned apology to Mrs Tattersall.

Her father had brought the incident up regularly ever since, thinking it hilarious.

Mercifully, Liam registered his daughter's pale face as she caught her breath and refrained from going there today, asking instead, 'What's after happening then?'

'Fecking Hannah and her bee crusade is what's happened.'

'You've not been stung, have you? Your mam's out the back. Sure, she'll sort it for you if you have.' Liam released the Guinness tap and adjusted the angle of the pint glass.

'No, I haven't, and it's almost a miracle worthy of St Bernadette in Lourdes that I wasn't because I was swarmed, so I was.'

Enda sat up a little straighter at the bar then. 'Well, you know now, young Grace, bees sense when you're scared of them. They're like dogs in that respect, so they are. Were you flapping your arms about and carrying on like so?' Enda gave a demonstration that made him look like a scarecrow on a windy day.

A bee was nothing like a fecking dog, Imogen thought, in no mood for Enda Dunne's words of wisdom. 'I'm Imogen,' she stated shortly. 'And, no, I did not flap about like so.' She had. 'And I fail to see the similarity between bees and dogs.'

Enda had thick skin and carried on undaunted: 'And did you know, Ava, a bee is after having five eyes? Can you imagine that?'

Jaysus wept, she was having a conversation with Emerald Bay's answer to Sir David Attenborough! 'No. I can't, and it's Imogen.'

Her father came to the rescue, placing Enda's pint in front

of him. 'There we are, Enda, my man. That will put hairs on your chest, so it will.'

'Thanking you, Liam.' The older man looked at his glass lovingly before taking a sip, leaving behind a foamy moustache. 'Ahh,' he said, satisfied with his lot. 'I'd be hard-pressed to find a finer pint in all of Ireland.' Then he used the back of his hand to wipe the froth away.

Liam looked pleased even though Enda said something along these lines each time he received a fresh pint of the black stuff.

'How was your morning's rambling?' Imogen asked. She was safe now, and her equilibrium was slowly restored as the adrenaline left her body. 'Did you find your orchid?'

'No. I did not, but I enjoyed the peace wandering none-theless, and I picked a posy of early cornflowers for your nan.'

Imogen laughed. 'She still won't let you sample whatever it is she's after baking, Dad. Nan can't be bought.' Unlike Sergeant Badger, she thought.

'Never a finer woman roamed Eire than Kitty Kelly,' Enda rhapsodised, looking to the door separating the pub from the Kellys' living quarters wistfully, but there was no sign of his lady love.

Jaysus wept, Imogen thought, shaking her head as she strode toward the same door, eager to make her escape. Nan had bagged herself a prize there if she was so inclined, which she was adamant she was not.

'Before you go, I've some sad news, Imogen.'

Imogen froze, and her body tensed the way it did when you weren't sure what you were about to be told. Her dad had a poker face, and she couldn't read whether someone had died or whether they were out of the Black Jack sweets he was partial to over at the Bus Stop.

'What is it?'

'Don O'Malley's after being taken to hospital with a

suspected second stroke this morning. Ryan rang the ambulance, and then Shannon went around to sit with Don until the ambulance arrived. Aileen went in with him, and Shannon followed behind, but we've not heard how he's getting on.'

Imogen was stricken. *Poor Ryan*, she thought, her body fluctuating between hot and cold. For a moment, she put herself in his shoes, imagining how she'd feel if it were her dad in the same boat. It made her feel physically sick and frightened.

'Your nan and mam are busy cooking a storm up in the kitchen. Meals like.' He shrugged. 'Sure, what else can you do in tough times but make sure the family is fed?'

Imogen nodded, opened the kitchen door, and was hit by the smell of meat and onions.

Nora was stirring lamb mince in the pan along with onions, carrots, peas and sprigs of thyme while the lid of a saucepan on the cooktop rattled, a plume of steam escaping.

Kitty, meanwhile, was shaping the dough for her soda bread on an oven tray.

'Imogen,' Nora said. 'You're just in time.' She put the stirring spoon down and reached for her daughter, pulling her into the small workspace. 'Get those sleeves rolled up. You need to drain the potatoes and mash them with milk and butter. We've shepherd's pie to be making for the O'Malleys.'

Imogen didn't need to be asked twice.

24

'The coast is clear, Mam,' Imogen said, stepping into the beer garden to see the bees were busy in the lavender bushes on the far side of the garden. Two leather-clad men sat at one of the picnic tables with pints in front of them, their motorcycle helmets on the wooden seats next to them. They glanced over to see Imogen warily casing the area while Nora Kelly looked over her shoulder. Her mam gave the fellas a wave which they acknowledged before returning to their ale.

'Tell the family I'm going to light a candle for them,' Nora called from the doorway as Imogen trooped over to her car. She carried a weighty, still-warm dish of tinfoil-covered shepherd's pie and a loaf of Nan's soda bread wrapped in a tea towel to keep it hot. The bread was balancing on top of the tin foil, and the combined yeasty, savoury smell would have been tempting if her stomach wasn't in knots worrying about what poor Ryan and the rest of his family were going through.

'I will, Mam. Catch you later.' Imogen placed the dish on the passenger seat. It was strange to think that less than a week ago, none of this with the O'Malleys would have registered, other than for her to think it was sad. Ryan was no longer the annoying boy she'd gone to school with. Instead, he was the sometimes irritating and often amusing fella she worked with. She suspected if the shoe were on the other foot, he'd be around in a flash to check on her. To drop in a meal was the least she could do.

She set off, resolving to drive slowly around the streets leading to the yellow house. The pie would be no good in a heap on the floor of the car if she had to stop suddenly, and she didn't relish the thought of scraping up mince and mashed spud.

Young Kyle Hogan, Emerald Bay's notorious criminal guilty of the great faux perfume bottle heist at Christmas from Heneghan's Pharmacy, was paying the price for his crime and mowing the lawns in the park as she crawled past. Little children were playing on the recently upgraded equipment, with either their mam, dad or older siblings keeping an eye on them.

Imogen thought the old swings and slide were far more exciting than these new tamer versions, even if, according to Health and Safety, they'd posed a risk.

She glimpsed the teens huddled at the park's far end near the prickly holly bush. Why did they always look like they were up to no good? Probably because they were, she mused, recalling illicit cigarettes and snogging by the holly bush when she was their age.

As she pulled up outside the O'Malley house, Doctor Fairlie's wife, Helena, had her hand on the door handle of the staid brown car she'd driven for as long as Imogen could remember. The pie and loaf hadn't moved an inch, and getting out, she dangled the keys loosely from her fingers, shouting over a hello to Mrs Fairlie. Her silver hair was shorter than the last time she'd seen her, Imogen noticed. The jaw-grazing hairstyle was a little severe, but her smile was as kindly as ever as she greeted Imogen in return.

'It's work up at Benmore House that's brought you home, isn't it, Imogen?'

'Yes, it is. Ryan's working up there, too, as it happens. How's yourself and Doctor Fairlie keeping?' Imogen asked.

'We've nothing to be complaining about. Poor Aileen will be beside herself, though. It's just Ryan and his sisters home. You probably know your Shannon went into the hospital with Aileen and Don.'

Imogen nodded. 'We've not heard from her.'

'Well, as they say, no news is good news.' Mrs Fairlie's deep hazel eyes flitted to the house. 'There's enough food on their kitchen worktop to feed them for a month. I hope they've plenty of room in their freezer.' She gave a wry smile. 'It's what people do, though, isn't it, when there's nothing else they can do to help? Cook, I mean.'

'It is,' Imogen agreed. 'I've got a shepherd's pie and soda bread to drop off.'

'Well, I'll let you get on your way then. I need to get home and check on the chicken I've left roasting in the oven. My husband may know how to cure everything apart from the common cold, but he can't cook to save himself. It was good to see you, Imogen. You take care now.'

'You too, Mrs Fairlie, and say hello to Doctor Fairlie from me,' Imogen said, smiling at the image she'd painted of the hapless doctor. She'd always liked him because he had a jar of jellybeans brought out whenever an injection was needed. He'd also always let her take two or three if it was a particularly nasty needle.

She fetched the food from the car and advanced on the front door, thinking about how the Emerald Bay community always banded together in times of need. Who would drop her a meal around if she was sick in Dublin? The answer was depressing. Nev didn't cook, for one thing, favouring Uber Eats or dining out. She had friends, but they weren't Fi sort of friends; they were friends you air-kissed cheeks with at glamorous events. The sudden image of herself greasy-haired and poorly in her PJs with no food in the fridge made her sad.

As she juggled the dish and loaf in her arms so she could press the doorbell, Imogen pondered how she could be surrounded by people in the city but still feel lonely sometimes. Then, telling herself to stop being silly because she was living her dream in Dublin, she shook the thoughts away as the door opened, and Ryan's oldest sister, Jenny, greeted her with a weary smile.

'Hi, Jenny. Sorry to disturb you, and I know you've been inundated with food, but...' She held up her offering. 'We're all thinking of you at the Shamrock, and Mam said to tell you she's lighting a candle for your dad and your family.' She could see glimpses of Ryan in his sister. They had the same jet eyes and strong jawline, for one thing, but Jenny's hair, which Imogen knew to be as dark as her brother's, had been highlighted with reddish glints and curled into gentle waves. She was a pretty woman.

'That's very kind of her. Is that Kitty's famous soda bread you have there?' She gestured to the tea towel parcel.

'It is.'

'Well, you'd better come in then.' Jenny stepped aside, ushering Imogen in, then plucked the precariously balanced loaf off the top of the dish. 'I'll take that for you.'

Imogen's first impression of the interior of the O'Malleys' home was that it was as welcoming as the buttery yellow exterior. Oh, it wasn't modern by any means, nor did it have the charm of an olde worlde cottage. The wall coverings and carpet were dated, but there was a homeliness to it in the cluster of photographs decorating the wall here in the hall.

The family's milestones and achievements – university graduations and grandchildren – were proudly displayed in frames. She eyed the antique telephone table with its fresh flowers giving off a sweet scent. That table was class, she thought, but the family portrait above it caught her attention, and she lingered there to look at it for a moment. The style of jeans Ryan's sisters wore, low-rise flares, hinted at the earlier 2000s. Imogen was no historian, but she knew her stuff where denim was concerned.

It was Ryan she studied, though. The photographer had posed him for what looked like a studio portrait with his hand resting on his dad's shoulder. The shock of black hair, skinny frame and spots were how she remembered him from their schooldays. Not that she was judging. Her mam could produce a stack of pictures of awkward teenage-phase photographs that Imogen would rather never see the light of day again. His eyes and smile hadn't changed, though. They still made you think he was secretly laughing at something.

Jenny was padding toward the kitchen, and Imogen stopped gawping at the picture and followed her, hearing the low murmurs of conversation coming from the front room where the door wasn't quite closed. It creaked open, and a tiny dachshund waddled forth with a stripey sweater over its long torso.

'That's Lulu, Mam and Dad's baby. Although she might as well be Ryan's – she dotes on him since he came home,' Jenny informed her, turning at the dog's yap.

'She's so sweet,' Imogen gushed. As Lulu looked up at her curiously, her tail wagging, she wanted to stoop down and pet her, but that would have to wait until she'd offloaded the shepherd's pie.

The kitchen Imogen stepped into with Lulu on her heels was light and spoke of home baking and herby meals. Indeed, the worktop was laden with scones, cakes and various dishes covered in foil like hers. No matter what stresses and strains lay ahead for the O'Malley clan, they'd not be going hungry, that was certain, she thought, waiting while Jenny shuffled dishes about to make room for hers.

'There we go.'

Imogen placed it down and bent to pat Lulu. The little dog lapped it up, and when Imogen straightened, she went and sat by the back door and stared up. A leash was hanging off the hook.

'One of us will take her out for a W-A-L-K later.' Jenny spelled it out, but the dog's softly floppy ears pricked anyway. 'Ignore her. She's a master manipulator.'

Imogen grinned, and movement through the window caught her eye, along with a shriek. She looked out to the south-facing garden to see Wonder Woman, Ella from *Frozen*, Spider-Man, Batman, an Arabian princess, and a Storm Trooper charging about on the lush grass. The weather was holding despite Mam announcing they were in for rain as she swirled her fork across the top of the shepherd's pie earlier. Imogen had watched, fascinated, as decorative peaks formed in the mashed potato.

Jenny tracked her gaze. 'Wonder Woman and the Storm Trooper are my two. Batman's Kelly's, Ella and Princess Jasmine are Jody's and Spider-Man and Luke Skywalker there are Lexi's. Their nana and granddad keep a box of dress-ups for them to play with whenever we call around. They love it, and that get-up out there keeps them entertained for hours once they stop fighting over who gets to be who.'

Imogen found this amusing as she took note that it was only Ryan who hadn't settled down and had children.

Jenny sighed. 'The poor wee dotes don't understand what's going on.' She blinked furiously, and her bottom lip trembled. 'We were told there was a higher risk of a second stroke occurring in the first three months after the initial one. But Dad was doing everything he was supposed to be doing.'

Imogen instinctively reached out and patted the hand resting on the worktop. 'Well, that's got to go a long way now, Jenny.'

Jenny mustered a grateful smile. 'Everybody's being so

kind.'

'I thought I heard your voice.'

Imogen turned to see Ryan filling the space in the doorway. Seeing him without the tool belt draped around his hips was odd. Today he was dressed in a sweater and jeans, and his hair was mussed like he'd been running his fingers through it constantly. He needed a shave too, but given the circumstances, stubble would hardly be a priority.

'Hi. I've just dropped some food off.'

'People have been amazing, eh, Jen?' Ryan said.

'I was just saying that.'

Imogen wasn't sure how to word what she wanted to say but knew it didn't matter because they'd understand what she was trying to convey. 'Ryan, Jenny, I, er, we, that is, we're so sorry to hear about your dad.'

Ryan ran his fingers through his hair. 'Thanks. We're not writing him off just yet, though. He's a battler, you know.'

'He is.' Jenny smiled. 'If anybody can pull through this, it's him.'

'I'm sure you're right.'

A scream sounded from the garden, and Jenny swivelled back in that direction. 'Christ. Bloody Wonder Woman's after lassoing Princess Jasmine again. I told her she was to use her magic powers for good. What's Jasmine ever done to her?' Jenny stalked to the back door and shooed Lulu – who was still trying to hypnotise the leash – out the way. Her growly voice was audible even though she'd closed the door behind her as she sorted the upset out.

Imogen glanced uncertainly in Ryan's direction, unsure what to say to him. He shoved his hands in his pockets and leaned on the door frame as he spoke up.

'That lot in there is driving me mad' – he angled his head down the hall – 'it's all doom and gloom and endless cups of tea.

And Jody's husband, Pete, is an eejit. A small-dose-only type of fella, you know?'

'Jody married Peter O'Shea, didn't she?' Imogen asked, picturing an eejit from school who was a huge Beckham fan.

'Yep. Remember how he always got his hair styled however David Beckham happened to be wearing his?'

'Oh my God, the boy-band frosted blonde hair.' Imogen snorted despite the sombre situation and was pleased to see Ryan crack a grin too.

'The braids were worse.'

They found the memories of Pete O'Shea arriving at school with cornrows of braids hilarious.

'And he used to date whatshername who sported a Posh do.'

'Yeah, that was our Jody. She still does.'

Imogen's eyes widened, and she cringed. 'Sorry. Foot in mouth there.'

'Not at all. It's not my fault I'm related to Emerald Bay's answer to Posh and Becks.'

Imogen's shoulders were still shaking as the door opened, and Jenny, who had a firm grip on a tearful Wonder Woman's shoulder, frogmarched her daughter through the kitchen. Ryan stepped out of the way to let them pass.

Lulu moved toward Ryan and sat at his feet, gazing up at him mournfully with glistening brown eyes.

'Listen,' Ryan said to Imogen. 'Lulu's desperate for a run or waddle. Do you fancy coming down to the bay with us? I need to get out myself.'

After the day she'd had, Imogen thought a spell down by the water would be cathartic, and she sensed Ryan wanted the company. 'That sounds good. I'll drive.'

25

Imogen's phone began ringing as she followed Ryan down the hall. The noise was jarring and, pulling the culprit from the pocket of her tracksuit bottoms, she swiftly put the ringer on silent. The call was from Nev. He must be beginning to think something was wrong because they never went this long without touching base. Feeling bad, she sent off a quick *call you later* as Ryan stopped outside the front room, poking his head around the door.

She heard him tell his family he was taking Lulu to the bay and that his phone was on if they heard anything in the interim. There was no such thing as a quick getaway in an Emerald Bay home, and Jody called out, 'Imogen, don't be rushing off. Come and have a cup of tea with us.'

Imogen pushed past Ryan to stand in the doorway and greet the solemn group of adults seated on over-stuffed sofas and armchairs angled around an enormous flat screen. Wonder Woman sat on the floor eyeing the plate of shortbread, but after her golden lasso incident didn't dare take a piece. Imogen would have slipped her a square if she could.

'Hello there,' she said, feeling self-conscious. 'I called by to drop a meal off. I'm sorry you're all having such a hard time.' She didn't dare let her eyes linger on Pete, sporting a Beckham-like gentleman's pompadour. No small feat, given his thinning thatch.

'Bunch up, Kelly, so Imogen can have a seat,' Jody bossed.

'Thanks, but I really can't stay.'

'You're needed back at the pub, I suspect,' Lexi said, her brown eyes sad.

It was a white lie, that was all, Imogen thought, nodding as if this was the case. If she said she was going down to the bay with Ryan, there'd be no getting out the front door in a hurry.

'Well, we won't keep you then,' Jenny said. 'And thanks a million for the food. I'll be sure to tell Mam how wonderful everyone's been rallying around like so.'

'We're all thinking of you,' Imogen said, holding a hand up in a half wave before saying goodbye. It was easy to see why Ryan needed some air, she thought, stepping outside after him and Lulu.

Imogen was already jangling the keys to remind Ryan who was driving, and a moment later, as he folded himself into the passenger seat, he muttered, 'I don't think sports cars are designed for fellas like me.'

He had a point, Imogen thought as she slipped behind the wheel, because his knees were up around his ears, and his head was grazing the roof. A grin danced, thinking how incongruous he looked squished into her coupe. Now, if she had a sunroof, she could open it so he could stick his head through. The thought of cruising through the streets of Emerald Bay with Ryan's head poking out the sunroof made her mouth twitch, especially picturing Mrs Tattersall's expression. 'You got in, didn't you?' she said unsympathetically, and then, twisting her neck, looked back to check on Lulu.

The well-behaved little doggy was sitting on the back seat, tail thwacking against it and her tongue lolling as she panted, looking eager for the off. The dachshund was more at home in the car than Ryan, and she gave Imogen a reassuring yap when she asked her if she was all right in the back. Satisfied, Imogen twisted back to face Ryan. 'If it were warmer, I'd put the top down. You'd be grand then.'

'I'll have to take your word for that. I've never been big on having the wind in my hair.'

Imogen started to giggle and then felt terrible, given the solemnity of the circumstances.

'What's so funny?'

'Nothing.'

'G'won, share. I need all the laughs I can get,' Ryan said, pulling the seat belt across himself and clicking it into place.

'Well, you probably won't find this funny, but when you mentioned not being keen on having the wind in your hair, I got this vivid picture of you in my mind with long curly hair like those old rockers you're so fond of. So there we were, cruising down Main Street with the roof of my car down and your bad perm blowing behind you. And you should have seen the look on Mrs Tattersall's face.'

Ryan's eyes shone. 'You missed my man-bun phase.'

'No! You didn't?'

'Yeah. I did.'

For some reason, they both found this very, very funny.

Laughter was probably a stress release for Ryan, Imogen thought. It was supposed to be the best medicine, after all. Still laughing, she started the car and pulled out onto the empty street, her speed tootlingly sedate for Lulu's sake. Less than a minute later, as she veered onto Main Street, she'd concluded that Ryan was a fiddler; the sort of fella who'd have you using bad language if he ever got hold of the television remote because he'd flick through channels just as you got to the good bit in the programme you were watching.

She slapped his hand away as it reached for the hazard

lights switch. He'd already had the windscreen wipers on and the air con blasting out.

'Sorry,' he muttered, placing his hands deliberately on his denim-clad thighs. 'I'll behave, I promise. It's a terrible habit, I know.' A split second later, his hand snaked out, contradicting what he'd just said as he pushed a button. Justin Bieber blared, and Ryan swiftly twiddled with the volume knob before looking at Imogen quizzically.

'What?' she asked sheepishly.

'Bieber?'

'Bon Jovi?' she countered, fast as lightning.

'Touché.'

'Anyway, it's my car, my music. I've had to listen to enough of your rock power ballads.'

'Fair play to you, but Bieber?'

'Oh, shut up.' She laughed.

'Ah, Jaysus. Pretend you can't see them,' Ryan muttered, trying and not succeeding in slinking down in the seat.

Imogen slowed, seeing Eileen Carroll waving determinedly. She was hard to miss in her vibrant pink twinset. This afternoon it was Isla Mullins with whom Eileen was chatting; she was equally hard to miss in her hoodie sweatshirt proclaiming it was Guinness Time. The owner of Isla's Irish Shop believed the best way to sell the clothing items she stocked was to wear them, and her wave was equally determined.

'I have to stop, Ryan, or they'll tell my nan I was rude, and I'll be for it. Sure, they'll only want to let you know they're thinking of you.' Imogen pulled over to the side of the road without waiting for any argument from him.

Isla reluctantly scurried inside her shop after a potential customer while Eileen bustled across the road, self-importantly checking to see if it was clear. Imogen was reminded of a strawberry-flavoured lollipop as she wound her window down and greeted the owner of the Knitter's Nook. 'Hello, Mrs Carroll.'

'Hello there, Imogen. I see you've Ryan O'Malley in the car there with you.' Eileen's bust heaved from the exertion of her robust waving, and she leaned in the window, puffing.

Imogen flattened her head into the headrest, trying to avoid the woman's sausage roll breath.

'You two have been pally of late.' Eileen's eyes soaked up the scene. 'Don't think it hasn't escaped my notice. I've seen you gallivanting along Main Street in that big truck you drive, Ryan.'

'It's a Hilux, Mrs Carroll, and it's a good work wagon.'

'Sure, we're after working together up at Benmore House, Mrs Carroll,' Imogen supplied, keen to nip in the bud any ideas Eileen might be getting where she and Ryan were concerned.

Eileen sucked her teeth for a moment before remembering why she'd charged across the street in the first place. 'Any news from the hospital as to how your dad's doing, Ryan?'

'Not yet, Mrs Carroll.'

'A lovely man is Don O'Malley. We're all praying for him. You be sure to tell your poor mam.'

'I will, Mrs Carroll. Thanks.'

Eileen made no move to be on her way. 'Is it the hospital you're off to now, then?'

Ryan nudged Imogen with his knee in an unspoken *Tell her nothing*, but that was easier said than done where Eileen, a consummate professional in the art of gossip, was concerned.

A diversion was crucial for making a quick getaway, Imogen decided. 'Sorry, Mrs Carroll, but I think you've got a customer there.' She looked past the woman to the window of the Knitter's Nook.

Eileen removed her head from the car and turned away, shading her eyes toward her woollen shop. 'I can't see anyone.'

'I definitely saw someone, and I know how you pride yourself on your customer service. You wouldn't want to keep them waiting now, would you?'

'No. I wouldn't. Remember me to your mammy now, Ryan.'

Imogen didn't hang about as she pushed her foot down on the accelerator.

'Well played. I like your style,' Ryan said, hands on the dashboard.

'Thank you.' As they passed by Mermaids, Imogen broached the subject of Ryan's painting. 'There should be a nice commission coming your way.'

Ryan frowned. 'Commission on what?'

'I called by Mermaids last night and bought your collection. All five paintings. Why didn't you mention you're an artist?'

'Because it's no big deal, and it never came up. Besides, I only dabble. It's a hobby of mine, is all. I'm hardly an *artist*.' He made the inverted commas sign. 'Selling the odd picture pays for the canvases and paints. I don't get it though, you said you bought the whole collection?'

'Exactly that. And you don't just dabble, you're very talented. The paintings were just what I was looking for to hang on the guestroom walls at Benmore. I think Sigrid will enjoy telling guests the artist's not only from the village but worked on the renovations at the house too.'

'Either that or she'll think you wasted her money. But hang on. I don't understand. There are only four bedrooms and five paintings in the collection. You said you bought them all.'

'I did.' Imogen kept her eyes firmly on the road ahead, knowing her cheeks had turned pink. 'The fifth painting's for me.'

26

It wasn't long until the sporty red car pulled into the parking area near Kilticaneel Castle for the second time that day. Ryan had let the conversation about his artworks drop, and they'd lapsed into silence. Imogen's eyes flickered briefly toward the stark ruins before she got out of the car. Her day had panned out so differently from how she'd thought it would. A creeping melancholy stole over her at her stupidity because she hadn't chased the ghosts away. But then, glancing across to where Ryan, having untangled himself from her car, was stretching, she decided he needed her to be a cheerful distraction for him. What he was going through worrying about his dad was so much worse than realising, even though you'd faced your insecurities, they'd always lurk.

The sight of Lulu yipping and yapping as Ryan set her down on the ground a moment later chased the last of her despondency off. She'd love a dog even though she'd given Shannon grief about Napoleon being a precursor to children. It was an unwritten rule that hypocrisy was allowed between sisters; dogs, however, weren't allowed in her apartment building. The management company had a blanket no pets policy.

'Will she need to be on a leash?' Imogen asked, thinking most dogs she saw on the coastal path and down by the water were usually roaming with their owners keeping a watchful eye nearby. Lulu was so small, though and wouldn't be able to hold her own if she encountered a big unfriendly doggy. It was hard not to feel protective of an animal so tiny and sweet, but she knew, too, it would be unfair of her to carry the excited wee madam down to the beach.

'No, sure, she'll be grand running about here.'

Ryan didn't seem perturbed in the least, Imogen thought, keeping a watchful eye on the dog as she trotted off ahead of them. She was grateful that, for once, she'd chosen well by wearing her Sweaty Bettys and the expensive running shoes that usually only had an airing when she hit the treadmill at the gym. She'd be able to jog after Lulu if the need arose.

The grasses on either side of the path were overgrown with the advent of spring and would soon be cut back for the summer months. Yet, amidst their spiky splendour were daubs of purple flowers bending in the breeze. Her dad was sure to know their name, Imogen thought, inhaling the tantalising whiff of aniseed off the wild fennel.

Lulu trotted ahead with her tail wagging as she paused to sniff here and everywhere.

They rounded the bend and, under a deepening sky, Emerald Bay's horseshoe arc of wet golden sand was revealed. The tide was retreating and would have left pools in the rocks clustered at either end of the beach. Imogen had loved exploring those when she was younger. They were full of unusual wonders.

Ryan stopped and held a hand up to his eyes to gaze at the scene but was still squinting as he said, 'I never get tired of that view. It's different from one day to the next.'

Imogen nodded, knowing what he meant. The sea this evening was soothing, and some days it could be tranquil, as it was now, or rough, the seething body of water's fury reminding the residents of Emerald Bay of nature's power. The only certainty was that the beach was in constant flux.

They carried on to the sand, sinking into it as they watched Lulu dash as fast as her short little legs would let her down to the distant water's edge. The sun lowered in the sky, turning it pinkish orange. Aside from the owner of a Labrador dancing about in the shallows, the beach was deserted. Imogen watched, ensuring the golden Lab was friendly as the dog splashed over to greet Lulu.

'Lulu will play for ages. Especially now it looks like she's made a friend. You're not in a hurry, are you?'

'Not at all. Shall we find a dry rock to sit on?' Imogen suggested.

'Sure.'

By the time they reached the pile of rocks that looked like the Atlantic had been angry one day and tossed them off the ocean floor so as they landed in a higgledy-piggledy heap, Imogen could feel gritty sand in her shoes. She'd also found treasure in a pale pink scallop shell she was clutching as if it were gold.

They scrambled over the rocks seeking a suitable dry flattish mound to perch on while watching Lulu play.

Imogen bypassed a rockpool with a lone crab scuttling about and limpets clinging to the sides; then, spying a suitable candidate, she sat down. She slipped her sneakers off and shook the sand from them.

Ryan dropped down next to her, and even though no parts of their bodies were touching, Imogen was conscious of his proximity.

Ryan, however, seemed oblivious as he inhaled deeply. 'I missed that when I lived in London.'

'The smell of the ocean?'

'Yeah. The Thames wasn't the same.'

'I'd imagine not. I know of an essential oil diffuser blend that smells like the ocean. I recommend it to clients who are after a beachy vibe. Although, when I need a blast of salt air, I drive out to Greystones.' Not that she did very often because her time was consumed in Dublin's cafes, restaurants, and wine bars when she wasn't working. The waves and shifting pebbles at the beach, thirty minutes or so drive from her apartment, always chilled her. She promised herself to get off the treadmill her life had become and take the time to recharge at the beach more often. It was good for the soul.

'There's nowhere quite like Emerald Bay, though, is there? I mean, this is home.' He gestured around them. 'It's where we grew up. All of this was our kingdom when we were kids.'

Imogen nodded. He was right. 'We were lucky to have the run of this place and the freedom we had.' A strong pang passed through her for the carefree days of childhood. You thought it would never end when you were small, she mused.

'We were. Good times.' His expression was contemplative. 'I never thought about it before. My old man getting sick, like. Mam and Dad, they're this solid, invincible team, you know?'

Imogen nodded, tucking her hair behind her ears as the breeze ruffled it. She knew what he meant because her mam and dad were the same. There was comfort in knowing they were a unit that always had her back, no matter how bad things got messed up. She didn't know what she'd do if the tables were turned.

Ryan's gaze fixed on the retreating tide. 'The stroke was a warning he needed to slow down, eat better, all that stuff we know but don't pay attention to until something happens.' Ryan slapped his thigh, making Imogen jump slightly. 'He did all of it. This shouldn't be happening.'

Imogen reached out then and laid a hand on his forearm.

His gaze was watery. 'We knew there was a chance of

another stroke, but Dad was doing well. I don't know what we'll
do if he doesn't pull through.'

'Don't think like that, Ryan. There's power in positive
thoughts.'

He didn't seem to hear her as he picked at a loose thread on
his jeans. 'I was working in St Albans, in Greater London, when
Mam called to tell me what had happened. I remember being
annoyed when I saw her name pop up because I wanted to get
home in time to watch the rugby. I couldn't even tell you who
was playing now.' He shook his head at the irony. 'I almost
didn't answer her call because you can't get Mam off the phone
once she gets going. I mean, she'd ring me all the time. I love her
dearly, but the woman could make a story out of hanging the
washing out.'

Imogen tinkled. 'That's the Irish mammy for you. Mine's
the same, and my nan before her.'

This time he looked at her, and they smiled at each other in
complicit understanding.

'Something made me answer her call that afternoon,
though.' He ran his fingers through his hair.

It was a habit when he was anxious, Imogen picked up.

'It was like some sort of sixth sense that something was up,
and as soon as I heard her voice, I knew whatever it was, was
bad.'

A joyous ruff-ruffing wafted up the beach, but Ryan and
Imogen were too lost in their conversation to acknowledge Lulu.
The dachshund had joined in on a game of fetch with the
Labrador and its owner.

'Dad asked me to promise once, if anything happened to
him, I was to look after Mam and my sisters.'

Was that selfish of Mr O'Malley? Imogen wondered. It was
a load to place on a young man's shoulders, but then family was
family and who was she to judge? 'You've kept your promise. I
think your dad must be very proud of you. You gave up your

business, relationship, everything to return to Emerald Bay. It's a big call.'

She asked herself whether she'd do the same if she were in Ryan's shoes. She liked to think she would if her parents needed her, but it was hard to imagine how it would feel having the independent life she'd carved out snatched away by fate not by choice.

Ryan shrugged. 'I didn't have to think about it. When Mam phoned to tell me what had happened, I knew I had to step up. And not once has it felt like a sacrifice.'

'Because it was the right thing to do.'

'Because it was the right thing to do. And because I knew I'd be back one day. It was just sooner than I'd planned.'

'But what about having to break things off with your partner?' The answer to this question was suddenly of burning interest to Imogen. What was she like, she wondered. Was she a fashion plate like awful Victoria? Or more down-to-earth? She'd go with the latter, she decided. Ryan didn't strike her as the type for whom all the superficial stuff mattered; for some reason, she thought of her Instagram account. Shiny, glossy, superficial.

Ryan didn't answer right away, and she thought perhaps she'd probed too deeply. After all, it was none of her business. She was about to apologise when he spoke up.

'As I said, Emerald Bay's home, Imogen. But Ireland wasn't for her.'

'And she wasn't for you? You could have tried a long-distance relationship.' Christ, she was being a Nosy Nelly.

'Neither of us could see the point in that, and I realised she wasn't the person I wanted to spend my life with when she made it clear she couldn't understand my choices. In the end, the feeling was mutual, and we agreed to disagree and part ways.' He shook his head as though ridding himself of unpleasant memories. 'What about you? Is there someone special in Dublin?'

Imogen nodded, reluctant to tell Ryan about Nev, but fair's fair, and he'd confided in her. 'Nev. He's a developer.'

'As in property development?'

'Yeah, but big projects. Nev travels a lot, finding investors. He's coming to Emerald Bay next weekend for St Patrick's Day.'

'You don't sound very excited about his coming here.'

Imogen raised her shoulders, letting them fall again. 'I'm looking forward to seeing him, but I don't think Mam and Dad will approve. He's older than me.'

'A lot older?'

'Twenty-seven years.'

'Right.'

Was that disapproval she was picking up on? 'Sure, you'll see for yourself when you meet him that it's no big deal. He's a great guy. You'll like him.' Imogen was uncertain why his approval mattered. It was bad enough worrying about what her parents would think.

'Imogen, you're a grown woman. You don't have to explain your choices to me or anyone.'

'What about my mam and dad?' she asked in a small voice.

'Liam and Nora are reasonable people. You said he's a great guy. They'll come round.'

Imogen wasn't so sure.

'Is that what's been getting you down?'

She looked at him sharply.

'Sorry. I don't mean to pry, but you've seemed preoccupied. And, earlier at the house, I just picked up on a vibe, is all.'

He was perceptive, considering everything he had going on, Imogen thought, studying her shoes. She wanted to offload, but it wouldn't be fair to.

'It's not a big deal. And it's not worth bending your ear.'

'Bend away.'

'No. It's beyond stupid and trivial.'

'If it's getting you down, it's not trivial or stupid. Come on, I could do with the distraction, to be honest. Waiting to hear what's happening is driving me mad,' He pulled his phone out of the pocket of his sweatshirt and checked it before putting it away. 'Still nothing. C'mon then, talk to me.'

'OK,' Imogen relented. 'But you're not allowed to say I'm a total eejit. Deal?'

'Deal.'

She bit her bottom lip, tasting salt as she pondered where to begin. Then, taking a deep breath, Imogen started at the beginning.

27

'Do you remember that summer when we were sixteen, and Lachlan Leslie started hanging out at the bay with us?' Imogen sneaked a peek at Ryan.

'I remember he hung out with you that summer,' he replied, not looking at her.

His expression was odd, and something in his voice warned Imogen not to go there, so she ploughed on. 'I fell head over heels for him. Lachlan and I were always together, either at the beach, in the castle ruins or up at Benmore. God, it sounds like a bad Netflix teenage melodrama, I know.'

'I've four sisters like you, Imogen. I grew up with teenage-girl melodrama. I get it.'

She gave a wry grin. 'Are you sure you want me to go on, because you've probably had your quota of first love angst?'

'Try me. I'm a good sounding board. My sisters will tell you that. They used to come to me for the male take on whatever drama was happening in their love lives. Still do, for that matter. I've got to watch what I say now they're married, especially where Pete's concerned.'

Imogen's shoulders relaxed a little, and she smiled. 'No, I

don't suppose you can tell Jody that Pete looks nothing like David Beckham.'

'She'd be shattered if she took her blinkers off. For one thing, David's not got a beer belly or bald spot,' Ryan said, and they both laughed. 'Listen, nothing you say will shock me. I promise.'

Imogen believed him, and it would feel good to finally offload the baggage she'd carted about for so long. 'OK, but don't say I didn't warn you.'

He gave her a gentle nudge. 'Duly warned.'

'Lachlan told me he felt the same way I did, and we made plans to be together once he'd finished school for good. He'd come back to Emerald Bay for me, he said. And eejit that I was, I believed every word of it because I wanted to.' Her nails dug into her palms as she squeezed her hands shut and leaned forward, staring at where the sky disappeared into a greyish-blue line with the sea. She couldn't add that this was why she'd given in and slept with him. A quick fumbled encounter against the walls of Kilticaneel Castle. It was her first time, and she'd been unable to accept for a long time that Lachlan had told her what she wanted to hear so she'd have sex with him. The idea made her feel stupid, used and dirty, and she blinked, skipping on. 'Of course, he never came back. I waited for word from him all year, but it was radio silence, no calls, no emails, no texts, nothing. It wasn't a term we used then, at least I don't remember it, but he ghosted me well and truly once he left the bay.'

A sigh escaped, recalling the rollercoaster ride each time she'd texted or tried ringing, holding her breath, waiting to see if, this time, he'd respond. She remembered the cold sensation in the pit of her stomach when her period was late, how she'd spent a terrified fortnight trying to figure out what to do if she was pregnant. The thought of telling Mam and Dad made her physically sick. At least that hadn't come to fruition, and she'd put being late down to the upset of not hearing from him.

Fiona had told her to let Lachlan go, and she knew her behaviour of constantly reaching out to him was desperate, but she couldn't stop. 'Emotions are so intense at that age,' she said now.

'I remember.'

'See. I told you, total eejit.'

'I don't think you were an eejit.'

'Really?'

'Really.'

'I was, though.'

'Finish your story, Imogen. I'm not judging you.'

She'd never shared her encounter with Mrs Leslie with anyone. Not even Fiona. She'd been too mortified. But it was high time she got over herself because she'd let the old witch win by saying nothing.

'That year seemed to go on forever. Time seemed to move slower when we were young.'

'It did. The years speed up as you get older.'

Imogen nodded. 'By the time summer rolled around again, I'd had enough, and I didn't think what I did next through properly, which is something my mam will say is a character trait.' She sensed Ryan's half-smile. 'I borrowed Shannon's old bicycle and pedalled up to Benmore wearing the dress I'd wheedled Mam and Dad into forking out for by saying it was for the disco over in Kilticaneel. It was ridiculously impractical to wear, but I loved that dress.' She recalled the shimmery faux silk and how it had felt like cool water cascading over her when she'd slipped it on.

'Jaysus, I was a wreck by the time I got there.' She shook her head at the memory, remembering how her hair had been plastered in strands to her forehead. 'It was so hot, and I had to push the bike up the drive because I skidded and came off when I turned off the road and hit the gravel. I grazed my knees and hands and tore my dress too. Mam went mad when I got home. Of course, I fibbed and told her I'd stumbled on the rocks here at the bay. That went down like a lead balloon. Sure, what was I doing wearing my new dress at the beach anyway? I should have had the sense to come up with a better story.'

Imogen held her hands out in front of her, palms up. In her mind's eye, she could see the dirt and stone embedded in them. Her throat thickened at the memory of fighting tears as she road home, her knees stiff and her hands sore. Her mam had cleaned her cuts. But all the while had given her an ear-bashing that didn't finish until she'd applied the antiseptic.

She placed her palms down on her knees.

'I should have gone home when I toppled off the bike. But I didn't. Librans can be very determined when they want to be. Dramatic too.'

'I'd never have had you down for being either of those.'

Imogen looked at Ryan, who was feigning innocence, and elbowed him. 'Ha ha. I'm pouring my heart out here.'

'I know. Sorry. I won't interrupt again.'

'OK, so I should have gone home, but instead, I knocked on the door expecting the housekeeper to open it, but it was Mrs Leslie herself. Honestly, Ryan, it was like a scene from *Great Expectations*. Your woman looked like she belonged in a different era and seemed far too old to be Lachlan's mam. I knew he was a late baby, but she was older than my nan. I was terrified, to be honest, but I'd come this far, and my knees were bleeding. I thought she'd fetch me a plaster at the very least and maybe offer a glass of water, given how hot it was, but all she did was look at me like I was something nasty she'd trod in.' Imogen shook her head. 'Awful, awful woman. She made me feel so cheap in my dress, which I'd thought made me look all sort of Keira Knightleyish, you know, from that film *Atonement*? I knew then that even if my dress wasn't torn, I'd never wear it again.'

Ryan nodded. 'I'm sorry she made you feel like that. And you do look a little like Keira.'

'Without the cheekbones. Thank goodness for highlighter.' Imogen tried to make a joke, but it fell flat. She'd forgotten Ryan wasn't supposed to be interrupting. A look passed between them, and Imogen murmured, 'Thanks.'

'You're welcome. What happened next?'

'I stood there like this orphaned waif struck dumb.' Mimicking Mrs Leslie's proper voice, Imogen went on, 'And she said, "Has the cat got your tongue?" I tried to speak, but nothing came out, and in the end, it didn't matter because she said it all.' Her voice faltered because this was the painful part that made her face heat up even now.

'What was it she said?'

Imogen clenched her jaw so hard it hurt, then took a deep breath. 'She said, "I take it you're the girl from the village Lachlan was sneaking about with last summer." I must have looked surprised that she knew. I mean, we thought we were invisible when we were at Benmore. There were so many places to hide away, and his parents never seemed very interested in his comings and goings. My reaction made her sneer even more. "I see. You thought I wouldn't know what was happening right under my nose?" I stammered out a sorry or the like, but she was on a roll. "Lachlan's been and gone, I'm afraid," she said. "Did he not contact you while he was here?" She relished every word; I could tell, and I must have looked like I'd been slapped, realising he'd been here in Emerald Bay.'

Imogen wanted to hug the hurt young woman she'd been and tell her it didn't matter. But it had mattered then. 'You know, sitting here now telling you this as an adult, I can see what a bitter woman she was and to have behaved like so she must have led an unhappy life. But she was the adult, not me, and when she told me I was a "silly girl" for thinking Lachlan would see the likes of me as anything other than a distraction over the summer. It crushed me.' She clenched her fists again. 'And it makes me so angry that I let it.'

Ryan reached over and wiped the tear she hadn't even known was trickling down the side of her face away. She didn't flinch from his touch even though she knew she probably should, and the next part of her story came out in a confessional blurt. 'I deliberately left my laptop behind at Benmore yesterday so I'd have an excuse to go back to the house today when Lachlan and his fiancée were there.'

'Why? What did you have to prove?'

'I thought I had everything to prove. Mrs Leslie's long gone, but I wanted to show Lachlan how I've done much more than just mouldering away here in Emerald Bay.'

'And did you?'

Imogen realised Ryan was keeping his promise. There was no judgement in his question. She shook her head. 'He didn't remember me at first, and then when he did, he laughed about our summer fling. It was nothing but a bit of fun to him and I think he was keen to see if I was up for a ride down memory lane with him before he gets married. His mother was right. And I was back there again feeling like that sixteen-year-old girl being sneered at.' Imogen took a shuddering breath. 'Don't say it. I know I shouldn't have gone there in the first place, but I couldn't help myself. I suppose I thought I'd get...' Imogen's voice trailed off. She knew the word she wanted to use but couldn't bring herself to say it.

'Closure,' Ryan supplied.

'That's it exactly, but I hate that word.'

'It is an awful phrase.'

'Yes, but to be honest I do feel like I've drawn a line under the whole sorry thing. At least there's that,' Imogen blurted. 'Ryan, do you think I'm mad?'

Ryan laughed.

'It's not funny.'

'No, it's not, but you've always been a little mad, Imogen. That's what I like about you.'

Imogen turned to look at him then and swallowed hard, trying to read the look in his eyes.

'You are worth so much more than the Leslies. Don't ever let anybody make you doubt your worth again. OK?'

'OK.'

'Pinkie promise.'

'What?' A smile formed, seeing him close his hand, leaving his pinkie finger sticking out. He waggled it at her. 'And you said *I've* always been mad.'

'A *little* mad.'

Imogen entwined her little finger through his. 'My nan used to say this was a fairy handshake. It was our thing, and I pinkie — fairy promise.'

Ryan's eyes, locked with hers, were soft black velvet. With a burst of clarity she knew that if he were to kiss her right now, as she sensed he wanted to, she wouldn't push him away even though it was wrong.

Droplets of frigid water sprayed them, and they sprang apart as Lulu shook herself off and ruffed as if to say, 'Cut it out, you two. I'm back now.'

Imogen blinked, coming out of a trance, as did Ryan, and they focused their attention on the dog. For her part, Imogen couldn't believe what had just happened even though nothing had happened per se. It would have, though, if Lulu hadn't picked that moment to return and shake herself off.

The ping of an incoming text saw both of them start, and Ryan thrust his hand into his pocket, fumbling with his phone before looking at the message.

'It's from Jenny,' he said, not meeting her questioning gaze. 'I need to go home.'

'Yeah, of course.'

They made their way back to the car park, not speaking,

and the ride to the O'Malley house was equally silent. Imogen didn't know what to say. Everything sounded trite, and there was an awkwardness between them that hadn't been there before. Ryan stared out the window, obviously preoccupied with what he'd find out when he got home. As she pulled up outside the house, she thought about offering to go inside with him, but would that be presumptuous? Before she could dwell on it further, Ryan muttered a gruff thanks and climbed out of the car, opening the back door to let Lulu out.

'Bye, Lulu. Ryan, will you let me know how your dad is?' she asked, unsure if he heard because he was already closing the back door.

Imogen waited until the house swallowed them up. Then she drove home, not daring to examine what had just happened between them down at the bay and praying that Mr O'Malley would pull through.

28

Imogen was sitting on her bed, twiddling her toes, literally. It was quiet in her room, apart from snuffled snoring. The chatter and laughter from the pub, which would be filling up now, given it was Saturday night, didn't reach this far.

Curled up at the bottom of her bed, Napoleon had made the most of her earlier absence by sneaking into the room. She'd come upstairs after picking at her dinner to find him curled up on her black jeans. They were strewn across the bed where she'd tossed them during her morning outfit-finding frenzy, and her eyes had travelled the length of the bed to where the scraggly remains of Napoleon's adored toy mouse had been plopped in the centre of her pillow.

Shannon would say it was a love token, but as she still wasn't back from the hospital, it was up to Imogen to deal with the ganky thing. She heaved a sigh, telling herself that she'd have to remember to close the bedroom door after herself. Then she'd picked the soggy toy up by what was left of its tail gingerly, carrying it down the hall to her sister's room before flinging it in the door.

A funny thing had happened on her return, however.

Imogen fully intended to scoop Napoleon up and chuck him out. But, instead, she'd gazed down at the contented tortoise-shell ball of fluff, thinking he was rather sweet even if he had a squashed face. Not to mention that he was getting fur all over her favourite jeans. The antihistamines were working their magic too.

'All right. You can stay. But you're not to let on to anyone that me and you have come to an understanding. And under no circumstances are you to let off. Do you hear me?' His nose had twitched in his sleep, and she'd taken that as a subliminal yes. Then, climbing onto her bed, she'd picked up her phone, willing herself to call Nev. It was guilt holding her back, but she knew she had nothing to feel guilty about.

'It was nothing, Napoleon. Just a silly moment. I had a crap morning, and Ryan was stressed out, that's all.' So then, having got that off her chest, she'd put on her brightest and breeziest voice and hit the green call button, having decided a phone call was safer than FaceTiming.

As it happened, the conversation had been cut short anyway because he was dining with clients.

Instead, she'd tried Fiona, suddenly desperate to share everything that had transpired that day with her best friend.

'Imo, it's not a good time,' Fiona said a few rings later. 'All hell's let loose because I didn't mash the potato like Euan's mam.'

Imogen was affronted on her friend's behalf that her husband should be carrying on like so. 'Fi, Euan's no right to be kicking off because the mash isn't to his liking!'

'Not Euan, you eejit. Lottie.'

'Oh, sorry.'

A piercing squeal sounded, and Imogen held the phone away from her ear, wincing.

'Shite, I've got to go. She's just picked the bowl up and dumped it on the floor.'

The line went dead, and Imogen tossed her phone down, thinking she'd have to have a word with her god-daughter about the starving babies around the world who'd give anything for a bowl of spuds, creamy or not.

And now here she was, twiddling her toes, wondering how Mr O'Malley was, and how Ryan and the rest of his family were, with the evening stretching long.

'There's nothing else for it, Napoleon. I'll give Mam and Dad a hand behind the bar.'

Once more, it was a one-sided conversation. Swinging her legs off the bed, she tidied herself up and ventured downstairs to volunteer her services.

'Are you not feeling well? Do you need your temperature taken there, Imogen? Nora, quick, c'mere, Imogen's after having a funny turn. She's offered to help behind the bar,' Liam said, grinning at his wife.

'Stop being a smart arse, Dad, or I'll pour myself a wine and join Freya and that lot over there.'

'Oh no, you won't,' Nora called over. 'Not when there're pints that need pulling.'

To echo Nora's sentiment, Cathal Gallagher raised his empty glass at Imogen.

Half an hour later, Imogen saw Shannon talking earnestly to their dad and overfilled Michael Egan's pint. She wanted to drop the pint glass and charge over to find out how Mr O'Malley was, but she couldn't very well abandon the pint.

'Sorry about that, Michael,' she said, dragging her eyes back to the task and tipping a little of the beer out. It was an act she knew would be considered sacrilege by the fisherman. Then she picked up a cloth and wiped the glass before passing it to him.

Michael pressed the correct money into her outstretched palm and gave a begrudging grunt she chose to take as a thank you before strolling back to the table his dad and brothers were clustered about.

'Surly fishy fecker,' she grumbled under her breath. You'd have thought it was Conor and Michael who'd stepped out with Ava and not Shane, the way they'd behaved toward the Kelly girls since her younger sister had broken up with him. All three of them needed to grow up. 'Ouch!' she exclaimed, receiving an unexpected slap of the tea towel on the back of her legs. 'What was that for, Mam.'

'Don't think I didn't hear you using the language, my girl. There's no need for that even if he is a surly fecker,' Nora said, the irony of her comment not escaping her.

'Surly *fishy* fecker, Mam. Get it right. Look.' She pointed to where her sister was still talking to their dad near the back entrance. 'Shannon's back.'

Colm Nolan – the octopus, as she and her sisters, along with a good portion of the ladies of Emerald Bay, called him – was waiting for a pint, and Dermot Molloy was clearing his throat, wanting to be served too. It was going to be a mad night, Imogen thought, smiling at Dermot, leaving her mam to tend to Colm. He was her cousin, although that was not something you'd want to be shouting about, Imogen thought, imagining the faint sound of banjos as a certain scene from an old movie played out in her mind.

'How're you, Mr Molloy?' She smiled, ignoring Colm, who'd lost another front tooth since she'd last seen him. Emerald Bay's butcher was surrounded by miniature versions of himself and his wife, all vying for his attention.

'Dad, can I have the salt 'n' vinegar crisps?'

'I like the sour cream ones, Daddy.'

'Plain for me, Dad.'

'Grand, Imogen,' Dermot beamed. 'This lot will have a lemonade each, please. I'll have a pint of Harp and a glass of your house white for Mrs Molloy over there.'

Mrs Molloy waved, and Imogen nodded and smiled back before filling the row of glasses she'd lined up on the bar top with fizz. Dermot was busy sorting out the crisp order for his brood of mini Molloys.

Imogen was taking Mr Molloy's money when she saw Liam setting a chair by the side of the fire. It was just ticking over tonight with sputtering flames because it was a mild evening. She rang Dermot's order up and nearly dropped his change as her father made her and probably all the pub's patrons jump by blowing hard on his tin whistle.

Shannon was standing alongside him, and the whistle saw the general din settle down to a low curious hum.

'Listen up now,' Liam said, helping Shannon onto the chair. 'Shannon's got something to tell youse.'

Shannon cleared her throat. 'Good evening. Well, as most of you will already know, Don O'Malley was taken to hospital this morning after having a suspected second stroke.'

The hum grew louder, and Shannon coughed, waiting until she had everyone's attention once more. 'He's since had tests done which confirmed he'd had what's called a haemorrhagic stroke. This causes a ruptured artery and leads to bleeding on the brain.'

The gathered locals compared war stories of family members close or far who'd suffered similar events.

Shannon held her hand up to signal she hadn't finished. 'The rupture was small and quickly brought under control. Mr O'Malley is on an IV drip and needs rest, but he will require ongoing occupational therapy. He'll be admitted to the South Infirmary Hospital in Cork to begin rehabilitation in the next day or two... Thanks,' Shannon finished, leaning on their dad to step off the chair.

Liam spoke up next. 'The family will need our support, so let's put our hands in our pockets. Every penny counts.'

Enda had already whipped his cloth cap off, placing his donation in it before passing it on.

Imogen watched the cap making its way around the pub, feeling proud at how the community pulled together when one of its own was in need. Then she went back to pulling pints and fetching crisps and pork scratchings.

'I could do with a wine, Imo,' Shannon called to her sister as she made her way to the bar. 'I'm knackered, so I am.'

'Fair play.' Imogen fetched the chilled, open bottle. They weren't supposed to help themselves to the family's livelihood, but Shannon had earned a drink on the house. 'Will he make a full recovery, Shan?' she asked, the wine glugging into the glass.

'He's a long road ahead of him, and he'll likely need to spend time at the National Rehabilitation Hospital in Dublin too,' Shannon said, listening as Imogen filled her in on her visit to the O'Malleys'.

'There's hope, though,' Imogen stated rather than asking. She was thinking of Ryan and his family. They'd been so fraught waiting for news about what was going on that afternoon.

'There is.' Shannon gave her a weary smile. 'Thanks for this. I'll have a drink with Freya and then go through and talk to James.' A smile danced as she said his name, even though her eyes were sad.

'You miss him, don't you.'

'Yeah, I do.'

Shannon made to turn away, but Imogen stopped her by asking, 'Shan, do you think he might be the one?'

'Where did that come from?'

Imogen shrugged.

'All I know is every time I think of James, I smile.' Her mouth did exactly that.

'I can see that. I don't remember you smiling much when you were with Julien. It was like you were trying to do that cool, moody French girl thing.' Imogen made her camera-ready sultry face.

'Feck off with you. I didn't go around looking like the long-lost sixth Kardashian sister.'

'The long-lost sixth, *French* Kardashian,' Imogen corrected.

'Why are you asking anyway?'

'I don't know.' She didn't.

Shannon left her to it. And Imogen, ignoring Colm's brother Tom, whose finger was exploring his nose as he waited to be served, silently said Nev's name, trying Nevin for good measure too. She wanted to see if her mouth would take on a life of its own, but nothing happened. It wasn't surprising, given Tom was now inspecting his finger. Her mam was serving Rita Quigley, and she pulled a face knowing she'd no choice but to ask the King of the Nose Pickers what he was after. Her mouth was set in a grim line, thinking if he handed her his money with his right hand, she'd down tools and walk off the job.

He didn't.

'We've over one hundred quid in here,' Liam said, looking pleased as he emptied the contents of Enda's cap into the tin produced for various good causes from time to time. He placed it on the bar before writing in black marker what the donated funds were for on the piece of card he'd found goodness knows where.

It was then Imogen had an idea. A very good idea, if she did say so herself.

29

'Imogen Kelly, and to what do we owe this honour?' Father Seamus asked as his congregation trickled out the door, congratulating him on a lovely Mass. 'I thought the sacramental wine had been spiked and I was seeing things when I saw you sitting next to your mammy and nan in all your finery this morning. That, or I'd somehow lost time, and it was Easter already.'

Imogen's face creased, well used to the priest's tongue-in-cheek sarcasm where her and her sisters' sporadic church attendance was concerned. She'd made a concerted effort with her outfit: a suitably chaste, long-sleeved, floaty maxi dress with a high neck and delicate flower pattern. It was billowing about in the breeze as she stood alongside her mam on the church steps. A little like the parachute at Lottie and Ben's music group the other day. She clutched a handful of fabric to stop it from blowing up.

'She came of her own free will, Father,' Nora butted in.

'She did, Father.' Kitty backed her daughter-in-law up. 'T'was a miracle, so it was.'

'There's a chance for one of them, at least,' Nora said.

'Excuse me. I'm right here.' Imogen was also well used to

her mam and nan's cynicism when it came to matters of
theology where she and her sisters were concerned. So it had
been no surprise her mam, dad and nan had spluttered into
their cereal when she'd wafted into the kitchen and announced
she was going to church that morning. She might as well have
informed them she was off to live in a kibbutz in Israel, judging
by their incredulous expressions.

'Ah, you know yourself, Nora, Kitty; God loves all his children, even those with poor church attendance. He's good like
that.' He winked at the two women while Imogen pursed her
lips, wishing they'd disappear so she could tell him about the
idea she was after having.

Appeased, Nora went to chat with Clare Sheedy, waving
her over while Kitty made for Eileen Carroll.

'And what is it that brought you to us this fine Sunday
morning, Imogen, because you don't look starved or thirsty, so I
take it it wasn't the bread and wine.'

'I'm after having an idea, Father.'

'An epiphany.' The priest looked encouraged.

'Er, no, just an idea.'

His shoulders sagged.

Imogen carried on, undeterred. 'What it is, is this: I understand it's the church committee organising the St Patrick's Day
festivities?'

'That's right. The proceeds will go towards new curtains for
the hall. They've been hanging since the 1960s, and it shows.'

'Father, the thing is, we've got a family in need here in
Emerald Bay, and I wondered if the curtains could wait another
year. The funds raised could go to the O'Malley family instead.
Shannon's after telling me Mr O'Malley is in for a lengthy
rehab period, and he'll likely be staying in Cork and Dublin
hospitals for some time. Mrs O'Malley will want to be nearby
and accommodation... well, you know yourself, Father, it
doesn't come cheap.'

'I don't know. I've got a bargain-priced holiday cottage I'm fond of visiting each summer in Dingle,' Father Seamus retorted.

'Yes, but Dingle's not Cork City or Dublin now, is it?'

'I suppose not.' Father Seamus tilted his head to one side and rubbed his chin thoughtfully. A light began to dance in his blue eyes as he pondered what she'd said. 'You know now, Imogen; I'm thinking we could call you having an idea to help others an epiphany after all.' He looked pleased. 'Listen, there's a meeting in the hall about the St Patrick's festivities this afternoon at two o'clock. I think you should be there to put your suggestion to the committee. You'll have my full support.'

'Two o'clock?'

Father Seamus nodded. 'I'll see you there.'

'Thanks, Father.' Imogen beamed, skipping down the stairs to join her mam. This morning not even Clare Sheedy's moaning about how her son wasn't coming home from New York for Easter and her daughter would be spending it in Dublin with her family could rub the shine off her mood.

'We're very proud of you, Imogen,' Liam said, stroking Napoleon, who'd clambered onto his lap. 'We never thought we'd see the day, did we, Nora?'

'No,' Nora agreed, wiping down the worktop. 'And look at you, dressed appropriately for once. The pearls are a nice touch, although your sister will go mad if she finds out you took them without asking.'

'It's a shame your nan's not here to see you. Pearls, no less,' Liam said.

The smell of the roast in the oven filled the space with the promise of dinner to come.

'Are they too much?' Imogen twiddled with the single strand. She was usually confident in her clothing choices but felt less so after a strong gust lifted the back of her dress while waiting for her mam to finish listening to Clare Sheedy's list of complaints outside church earlier. Her reaction had been swift, and she'd got things back under control, but she couldn't tell whether she'd mooned Father Seamus. Fingers crossed he'd missed her display because she needed him on her side.

As for her mam's comment about Shannon going mad, well, it was about time the shoe was on the other foot, she thought, having lost count of how many times her sisters had raided her wardrobe. Admittedly, the blush pink sweater and white capris were not her usual style, but the church committee needed to take her seriously this afternoon.

'Not at all. You look very smart.'

'Mam, don't say smart. Say I look like the sort of woman who'd fit in at a church committee meeting.'

'Oh, you do, doesn't she, Liam?'

'She does. Our daughter is off to a church committee meeting. Who'd have believed it?'

'Oh, pipe down, Dad,' Imogen huffed, heading out the door.

'Good luck, Imogen,' her mam called after her.

She'd walk around to the church hall, Imogen decided, noting the wind had died off and that the bees were more interested in the attractive tanned, toothy, blonde couple supping their pints as they batted at them and tried to admire the rural outlook. There was a camper van parked by her car. It was no bigger than the decorator's van that had been parked up outside Benmore during the week. She guessed it belonged to Barbie and Ken over there, and shook her head at the mystery of how two people could sleep in a van without access to a shower and still manage to look like an advert for some sort of multivitamin.

'Imogen. You're looking smart today,' Carmel Brady called out. The Silver Spoon café was closed on Sundays and she looked to be enjoying her day off relaxing in the sun.

Christ on a bike, that word again. 'Thanks a million, Mrs

Brady,' Imogen replied through gritted teeth. The woman was enjoying her usual Sunday afternoon port and lemon with Mr Brady, who was savouring his Guinness. 'I'm, er, I'm just off to a church committee meeting.'

She left Mr Brady slapping his wife on the back as she spluttered away on her port and lemon and strode off. The ballet flats, also pinched from Shannon, were surprisingly comfortable, she mused, thinking that striding made a change from tottering.

The door to the church hall was open, and Imogen marched purposely through it. She was on time and looked the part. A quick survey revealed all the chairs, set out in a semicircle with Isla Mullins at the helm, were taken by the usual suspects. It reminded Imogen of an AA meeting. Not that she'd ever been to one, but she'd seen enough of them in films and on TV to come to this conclusion. All eyes turned toward her, registering surprise at the newcomer.

'Imogen.' The souvenir shop owner bristled, importantly puffing up inside her Rub Me, I'm Lucky shamrock sweatshirt. 'If it's the jacks you're after wanting, I'm afraid you'll have to hang on until you get home. We're about to begin our meeting.'

Isla was an Aries, Imogen surmised. Give her a pair of Princess Leia buns on either side of her ear and she'd look like a ram too. 'I know, Isla. The church committee meeting. That's what I'm here for. Father Seamus suggested I come along.'

A reverent whisper at the good Father's name went around the group as Imogen glided across the polished wooden floors in her ballet flats to the far side of the hall where the rest of the chairs were stacked. She bypassed the trestle table laid with a white cloth and sagging under the weight of the plates of biscuits, scones and precision-cut triangle sandwiches for afters. The ancient water boiler started to whine from the kitchen in preparation for the tea. She began wrestling with a chair to free it. 'For feck's sake, it's jammed on.'

Mrs Tattersall's disapproving voice rang out. 'Imogen Kelly, it's a church meeting you've come to. You'd do well to remember that.'

Imogen looked over her shoulder, 'Sorry,' she mouthed, giving the chair a final tug and nearly toppling over as it came off.

'You can sit between me and Mrs Lafferty, Imogen dear.' Helena Fairlie smiled kindly, beckoning her over as she nudged up next to Mrs Greene to make room.

'Thanks.' Imogen dimpled gratefully, watching as the women shifted and bunched up before slotting her chair in the mix and sitting down.

Isla looked pointedly at her watch and announced it was one minute past two o'clock and time to get the meeting underway. 'Let us pray.'

Imogen dipped her head and whispered in Mrs Fairlie's ear: 'When does Father Seamus put in an appearance?'

'Two thirty. In time for the afternoon tea. You can set your watch by him.'

Imogen tried not to smile at Mrs Fairlie's comment as she waited for Isla to say Amen so they could get the show on the road.

Things were still ongoing, though, because there was the mini devotional to get through and then, finally, Isla brought them around to the business side of things.

Imogen raised her hand to signal she'd like to speak, but Isla ignored her, scanning her notes before announcing, 'We need a volunteer to dress up as a lady leprechaun and ride alongside Lorcan McGrath on his tractor, tossing out sweets to the children. But, of course, I'm supplying the costume, so I'm exempt.'

Imogen forgot that her hand was still raised.

'Thank you, Imogen. I'm sure you'll make a fine Ms Leprechaun.'

Feck, Imogen thought. *How did that happen?* 'But—'

Isla, however, had moved on to discuss the Great Emerald Bay Bake-Off.

Imogen turned to Mrs Lafferty and said, 'But why Ms Leprechaun?'

'Because we pride ourselves on being progressive in Emerald Bay,' Mrs Lafferty replied. 'And Isla's sold out of the male leprechaun outfits. She had a run on them last week when a Nordic tour bus stopped.'

Despite her distress at inadvertently volunteering to be Ms Leprechaun and sitting beside Lorcan McGrath throughout the parade, Imogen sniggered. It was the thought of all the leprechauns on the loose around the Norwegian fjords.

'What brought you along to the meeting today, Imogen?' Mrs Greene asked, receiving a glare from Isla for crossing the line and speaking before being invited.

Isla repeated Mrs Greene's question. 'Imogen, what brought you to the meeting?'

The floor-to-ceiling curtains on the raised stage area of the church hall were mustard-coloured and moth-eaten, Imogen saw glancing toward them. They needed replacing, but she was putting her faith in the group she was about to address, thinking the O'Malley family were a worthier cause. 'What it is,' she said, going on to relay her words to Father Seamus earlier and telling the group she had his backing for her idea.

'We'll put it to a vote,' Isla bossed. 'All those in favour of forgoing the curtains for another year to donate our St Patrick's Day proceeds to the O'Malley family during their time of need, raise your hand.'

It was unanimous. Imogen sat back in her chair, beaming.

30

The beer garden was deserted now the afternoon sun had dropped low in the sky. Imogen had her pashmina wrapped around her shoulders and a cup of coffee she'd carried outside on the table where she was sitting. The bees, she suspected, had gone to bed. Fiona had called her back, beginning the call by telling her Lottie had come down with a tummy bug which explained her behaviour over the mashed spud the day before. Now her friend's laughter echoed tinnily out of her phone as she told her woeful tale about inadvertently volunteering to be Ms Leprechaun at next Saturday's parade.

'It's not that funny, Fi. Shannon didn't even laugh that hard.' That wasn't true. She'd been bent double at the thought of her sister dressed as Ms Leprechaun, bouncing along next to Lorcan McGrath on his tractor as she tossed sweets to the village children. Imogen had been quick to remind her who it was had been dressed as an elf at Christmas with pointy ears on her woolly hat, carolling her heart out with the rest of the Emerald Bay Elves in the square.

'Sorry, Imo,' Fiona gasped.

Imogen took a sip of her coffee, and by the time she'd put it down again, Fiona had herself back under control.

'Oh, I wish I could be there. Make sure one of your sisters takes a video, won't you?'

'They're bound to want to record my journey along Main Street for posterity.'

'Seriously though, Imo, it was a great idea altogether getting the committee to agree on the funds going to the O'Malleys. What did Ryan say when you told him?'

'I texted him, but I'm still waiting to hear back.'

'Why didn't you call around to the house or ring? A text seems a little impersonal.'

Imogen didn't like the turn the conversation was taking. 'I didn't want to disturb him. He's a lot going on right now.'

'Imogen, what's going on?'

'Nothing's going on!' Jaysus, it was grand having a friend who knew you inside and out, until it wasn't.

'It's me, Imogen Kelly. Fess up. Are you after snogging him or something?'

'Why would you come up with something so random?'

'Because you've got that squeaky tone. And you always squeak when you've been snogging, especially if it's someone you shouldn't have snogged because you're seeing someone else.'

'I don't get around snogging people I shouldn't when I'm in a relationship, Fi, and I don't squeak!'

'Methinks she protests too much.'

'You're barking up the wrong tree.'

'But something happened.'

'It was nothing.' Imogen sighed, staring out at the evening shadow creeping over the fields across the way. 'It was a moment, is all.' She explained what had happened at the bay yesterday afternoon and how sure she'd been that Ryan would have kissed her if Lulu hadn't reappeared and broken up their weird vibe.

'Imogen, do not read more into it than what it was.'

'I wasn't.'

'Yes, you were; otherwise, you'd have called him or popped in to pass on your fundraiser news.'

Fi had a point, Imogen thought.

'You'll be ill-fated lovers next. You and I both know how it goes.'

Was Fi right? Imogen wondered. Was she reading too much into what had been something and nothing? There was no way she'd be confiding in her about her visit to Benmore House to see Lachlan yesterday because she'd been right about that. She had blown their short-lived fling into an epic romance. She'd not make the same mistake twice.

'OK, Fi. I am shelving it as a non-event.'

'Good. That's sorted, then. Lottie's desperate to have a word with you. She's lying on the sofa with a blanket over her. I'm passing the phone over.'

Imogen waited until she heard her god-daughter's heavy breathing before saying, 'Hello, Lottie. I'm sad you've got a poorly tummy.'

'I don't like mashed tato anymore.'

'Fair play to you, Lottie.' The little girl lamented on all the foods she no longer liked and Imogen listened with a smile, then, seeing the time, said she hoped Lottie's tummy was all better soon before asking her to put her mammy back on.

'Nev's FaceTiming me in a minute, so I've got to go.'

'Will you tell him you're after volunteering to be Ms Leprechaun, or surprise him on the day?'

'I think I'll surprise him.' She thought there would be a lot of surprises next weekend.

'You could always drop into the conversation that Nev's a little older than you before he arrives, Imo,' Fiona said again, having picked up on Imogen's train of thought. 'Soften the blow like.'

'I know I should. It's just, you know what Dad can be like.'

'A perfectly loveable teddy bear who puts his girls' happiness above all else.'

'Yeah, a teddy bear who can turn into an overprotective grizzly.'

'It'll be fine. Your dad will see that Nev makes you happy. I wish my family weren't coming to stay. I'd have liked to meet him.'

'Next time,' Imogen said. 'Or, better yet, come to Dublin for a weekend.'

'That would be great.' Fiona's sigh was wistful. 'One of these days.'

They said their goodbyes. Nev could always be relied on to be punctual, she thought as the familiar incoming bleeping sounded a few seconds later. Imogen fluffed her hair out and held the phone at what she knew to be a flattering angle before answering.

'Hey, you,' she held the screen closer as Nev's chiselled features appeared in front of her. He looked good for his fifty-nine years, not craggy like her father; but then her father had never had a facial in his life. Unlike Nev, who she knew took better care of his skin than she did.

'What have you been doing in the wild west today?' he asked, unbuttoning the neck of the polo shirt he wore to golf.

'Oh, nothing much. I just got off the phone with Fi, actually.' She didn't know why she was reluctant to mention having gone to church that morning or her chat with Father Seamus and the subsequent committee meeting. Instead, she asked him to fill her in on his day, knowing he'd met his girls for Sunday lunch and gone golfing near Wicklow in the afternoon. Both of which were about as appealing to Imogen as eating black pudding.

And she hated black pudding.

31

Imogen rapped on the door of Benmore House and stood back to wait for it to be answered. She wondered if the Leslies were early risers. Her money was on yes, apart from when Sigrid had her ladies around for lunch. Personally speaking, it wasn't in her nature to bounce out of bed with the birds, but here she was, bright-eyed and bushy-tailed before 8 a.m. on a Monday morning, despite Shannon hogging the bathroom. Even still, Ryan's Hilux was already parked up, which surprised her because she wasn't sure whether he'd be in. Although he'd mentioned that the joinery would be finished today, with the vanity, shower and bath scheduled to be fitted on Tuesday morning, it would have been perfectly understandable if he'd opted to spend the day at the hospital with his mam and dad instead.

His words to her on Saturday ran through her head once more: *Don't ever let anybody make you doubt your worth again.* And this was why she was standing a little taller in her Gianvito Rossi's when the housekeeper, Francesca, opened the door a split second later.

Imogen felt as though she were towering over the Italian woman.

'I know your nonna,' Francesca growled in a low, throaty voice, looking up at her. Her aproned girth blocked the entrance, and she fixed her nut-brown eyes on Imogen's.

The fierce glare was unnerving, and Imogen shrank back to her normal height, thinking a simple good morning would have sufficed. Instead, she felt like she was in the presence of Don Corleone's sister. 'Shall I tell her you said hello, Francesca?' she replied, expecting her to move aside and let her in the house.

'I hear things.' Francesca's sturdy legs stood firm, her arms folded across a bust jutting forth like a ledge.

'Er, well, Emerald Bay's a small place.' Imogen was unsure where this was headed, wishing she'd had a second cup of coffee at breakfast. She also wished the housekeeper would get out of the way so she could give Sigrid the rundown on the busy week ahead before the first of the expected tradespeople arrived.

'Things like your nonna is entering the Great Emerald Bay Bake-Off.'

'Yes, she is.' What did it have to do with her? Imogen wondered.

'It's a secret, her entry, no?'

'Yes, it is. Nan's been very tight-lipped about it.'

'Because I am wondering about things.'

'I see,' Imogen said slowly, but she didn't see. Not at all. Still, at this point, she'd say anything to gain access to the house.

'I, too, am entering the competition. And I am wondering what your nonna's nipotina may have seen or smelled working here.' Francesca tapped her nose to make her point.

Imogen didn't know Italian but guessed Francesca was referring to her being Kitty's granddaughter and implying a conflict of interest where the Great Emerald Bay Bake-Off was concerned. 'I'm sorry, Francesca. Do you think I've been spying on you for my nan? Because I can assure you, I haven't been.'

Sigrid appeared at that moment with a dainty milk jug in her hand. 'There you are, Francesca. Mr Leslie has been ringing the bell. He'd like more milk, please.' She held out the empty jug to the housekeeper.

Francesca was torn but, having picked up on the annoyance in her employer's voice, stepped aside to take the milk jug from her.

Imogen seized her chance and shot inside, closing the door behind her before the Italian woman had a change of heart.

'Good morning, Sigrid. Did you enjoy the rest of the weekend?' She didn't wait for a reply. 'Would you have a moment?' she asked as Francesca clutched the jug and made no move toward the kitchen.

'The milk, Francesca.' Sigrid made a clucking sound with her tongue, which, if Imogen had been in Francesca's shoes, would have had her frisbeeing a focaccia at her.

The housekeeper reluctantly moved off, shooting Imogen one last menacing glare before disappearing.

'That woman's head is elsewhere at the moment,' Sigrid said half to herself before inviting Imogen to follow her to the drawing room.

Adjusting the strap of her laptop case, Imogen did so. This time there was no cake on the table between them, nor would she hold her breath in expectation, not after Francesca's carry-on.

Was it only a week ago she'd sat in this very same spot? Imogen thought. So much seemed to have happened since then. 'Have Mr Lachlan and his fiancée returned to London?' she asked, opening her case to retrieve her notes.

'Yes.'

Imogen sensed a *thank God* hanging off the end as she flipped open her notebook and bit back a smile, aware the other woman was far too well bred to say it out loud. She might have only caught a fleeting glimpse of Sigrid's soon-to-be sister-in-law, but she'd had all the hallmarks of a bridezilla.

A hammering began upstairs, and the frown hovering on

Sigrid's forehead deepened. 'I shall be glad when this work is finished. It's very invasive.'

'Well, that's what I wanted to talk to you about this morning,' Imogen said, crossing her legs. 'I'm afraid this week is going to be rather hectic trying to get all the work completed by Friday, and then we'll all be out of your hair.' She was due to go back to Dublin after the weekend.

The Swedish woman looked decidedly unimpressed as Imogen began running through the order of work to be carried out, which would see a steady stream of tradespeople trooping up and down the stairs. Not to mention the deliveries Imogen was expecting.

'I think I shall suggest to Matthew that we spend the week at our apartment in Dublin.' Sigrid sighed when Imogen closed her book. 'We could leave this afternoon and be back by lunchtime on Friday.'

'For the big reveal.' Imogen smiled encouragingly. Dublin was a good idea. It would be so much easier not to have the disgruntled owners hovering, she thought. There was a lot to be said for the grand unveiling at the end of a project. She improved Sigrid's mood by showing her the pictures on her phone of the paintings she'd sourced from Mermaids, which Freya would drop off later in the week. She'd have liked to have said, 'You'll never guess who painted them?' but sensed Sigrid was in no mood for playing give us a clue, so informed her the man currently banging and crashing about upstairs had hidden talents.

Sigrid was duly impressed, and when Francesca ducked her head around the door to inform Imogen the decorators had arrived, she excused herself.

She was keen to organise her escape with Mr Leslie, Imogen supposed. Then she slunk past the housekeeper and up the stairs after the crew. They were starting to hang the modern wallpaper with its vintage print in the middle bedroom today while the plasterer patched the walls in the guestroom closest to the bathroom. The carpet was being laid over the next few days too, starting with the first room at the top of the landing. This meant it would be ready for Imogen to begin dressing tomorrow, her favourite part of the process. It was when she got to wave her magic wand and tie everything together.

To start with, though, she needed to say her good mornings. The decorators were draping drop sheets about the place and exchanging stories about their weekends. Imogen waved out as she passed the middle guest room and carried on down the hall to the bathroom, pausing to greet the plasterer. Upon seeing her, he tucked the cigarette he'd just finished rolling behind his ear and called out a good morning. He gave her the rundown on what needed doing in the room and then, leaving him to crack on, Imogen turned her attention to the bathroom. How to play it? she wondered. Cool and professional would seem cold, but she didn't want to act like she and Ryan were best buddies now, either. She'd strive for middle ground, she decided, knocking on the door.

'Morning, Ryan. How're you?'

Ryan swung around, pointing a nail gun at her, his standard power ballad playing on the portable player.

She put her hands in the air. 'Whoa, I surrender. And who is that?' She pointed to the stereo.

'Scorpions, "Winds of Change". You've no clue when it comes to the classics.' He shook his head, then, realising he was still wielding the nail gun, let it fall to his side. 'Sorry, I was squaring a few things off.'

Imogen let his musical jibe slide. 'I thought you might be at the hospital today.'

'No, I was there yesterday with Mam and my sisters. So I'd only be underfoot today.'

'Fair play. How's your dad doing?' Imogen could see the

fatigue in the tiny lines spidering around Ryan's eyes and felt a tug toward him that was not cool and professional.

'It's a setback for him, but he's determined. He's in great hands too. The hospital staff are brilliant like.'

'That's good. And is your mam coping all right?'

'She's had her quiet cry. Now she's ready to roll up her sleeves and get on with things.'

Imogen nodded. She'd imagine her mam would be much the same if faced with a serious trial. 'Did you get my message about the fundraising for St Patrick's being donated to your family this year? To help with ongoing accommodation costs in Cork and Dublin, that sort of thing.'

'Everybody's been so kind.' Ryan shook his head, processing what she'd said.

'People want to help.'

'Whose idea was it?'

Imogen didn't want to sing her praises. She hadn't gone to the meeting wanting a pat on the back, and her mouth worked trying to come up with an answer.

'You did?' Ryan's eyes widened.

She shrugged. 'The money raised was only going toward upgrading the curtains in the hall.'

Ryan's eyes were suspiciously bright, and she wanted to reach out to him but kept her hands pinned to her sides.

'Mam's overwhelmed by all the support,' he said, turning away, his voice suddenly gruff. 'It was good of you to think of us, Imogen. I'm going to finish this up, and then I'm off to start a new job in Kilticaneel. I'll be back to finish fitting out the bathroom. You'll ring me when the vanity, shower and bath are delivered, right?

'Right. Well, I'll let you get on then...' Imogen's voice trailed off, but she couldn't think of any excuse to linger longer. Then the smoke alarm began screaming and she charged into the room next door, guessing the fecking plasterer had lit that cigarette he'd rolled!

He was standing by the open window, wafting his hand back and forth to clear the smoke, and she disabled the alarm.

'Fecking thing's sensitive,' he said, glancing at the ceiling.

'Smoking is outside only, and if you'd pick up the butt you dropped into the courtyard when you next go downstairs, I'd appreciate it,' she said, making her annoyance known before exiting the room. Sigrid and Matthew were standing at the bottom of the staircase and she called down to assure them everything was fine. Then, satisfied peace was restored, Imogen went into the guestroom and eyed the linen packages delivered late Friday. She was looking forward to opening them. There was something about the smell of fresh sheets.

Ten minutes later, unable to resist seeing if the quilt was as gorgeous as she remembered, cardboard and plastic were strewn about the room the carpet layers were due to get to work in. She sat in the midst of the mess and rubbed her temples. Her stars had said she would face challenges today. They were spot on, she thought, eyeing the still-folded sheets and quilt: the wrong bedding had been sent.

It was a precursor to the rest of the week.

TWO DAYS UNTIL ST PATRICK'S DAY

May the road rise up to meet you.
May the wind be always at your back.
May the sun shine warm upon your face,
The rains fall soft upon your fields,
And, until we meet again,
May God hold you in the palm of His hand.

— IRISH BLESSING FOR ST
PATRICK'S DAY

32

How was it Thursday already? Imogen thought as she drove towards the village, mulling over her week thus far. She'd barely come up for air since Monday, or that's how it felt. No project was ever without its dramas, but something had challenged her every day at Benmore, and poor Shannon had been the one on whom she'd offloaded each evening. Nev didn't need more drama than he had already with his daughters. She was his sounding board, not the other way around.

With the project due to be finished by Thursday afternoon, it was a relief the Leslies weren't about to witness her Wednesday-afternoon meltdown, having taken themselves off to Dublin for a few days. The curtains being hung was one of her favourite moments in the design process, but on Wednesday it had seen her blood pressure skyrocket.

So far as Imogen was concerned, curtains were to a room what blusher was to the cheeks. An aesthetic of more importance than they were often given credit for. As for the pelmet, well, it was the crowning glory. In a cataclysmic moment, she realised the curtain maker had used the wrong side of the pelmet fabric for the room she thought of as Guestroom No. 1.

Not only that, the measurements for the drapes had been muddled up somewhere along the way. Her horror deepened on seeing the voluminous material sitting a full centimetre above the carpet they should have puddled onto. The only blessing to be gleaned was that the other rooms had been measured correctly.

Ryan, who was back to put the final touches to the bathroom a day later than planned thanks to the fixtures and fittings delivery not turning up until that morning, had happened past. He'd seen her ashen face and hands clasped in prayer, and suggested they step outside for an early lunch.

Imogen had numbly traipsed after him, having made a frantic call to the curtain makers, who'd assured her they'd work through the night if need be to have the correct drapes and pelmet ready to be hung by Friday morning. They sat on the front entrance steps with their respective lunch boxes on their laps.

The day was more summerlike than spring, and the sun was soothing as Ryan updated Imogen on his dad, who'd been moved to Cork with physiotherapy now underway.

'I heard a rumour that there's to be a Ms Leprechaun at the parade this year,' he said, examining the contents of his lunchbox.

'Don't,' Imogen warned, opening her own, which looked nowhere near as exciting as his. She wasn't hungry anyway. Stress always killed her appetite and at times like this she almost wished she smoked. 'I'm trying not to think about it.'

'Well, if it makes you feel better, you're not the only one stepping out of their comfort zone on Saturday.'

'Oh?' That caught her attention.

'I've spoken to Isla, and she's cleared it with the rest of the committee. I'm auctioning myself off for a date.'

'What?'

'It's called a date auction.'

'Like when people bid for a night out with you?'

'Yeah. A mate of mine volunteered his services as part of a fundraiser for his sister's kids' school in London. It went well. He was surprised at how much money he raised. And it doesn't seem right not to contribute something myself to Saturday's effort. It was the best I could come up with at short notice.'

'But you might wind up wining and dining Desperate Dee or something. Have you thought about that? And what about boundaries? You are going to have to set clear boundaries.'

'Who's Desperate Dee?'

'I made her up, but you get the idea.'

'It's just a bit of fun and a way I can do my bit.' He settled on a muffin and began unwrapping it.

The thought of Ryan entertaining some woman on a night out made her feel funny in a way she couldn't explain, but another thought popping into her head had her blurting, 'Oh my God. You could wind up taking Isla out.'

Ryan, who'd been about to take a bite of the cakey muffin, paused to add, 'Kiss-me-quick- I'm-Irish Isla? Christ on a bike! Thanks a million, Imogen, I'm about to eat my lunch here.'

Imogen started laughing, and so did Ryan. It had felt good to let go of the simmering tensions of the week with all the hold-ups and this morning's curtain debacle. There was no lingering awkwardness between her and Ryan, which was a relief.

The village loomed into sight, and she slowed the car to a crawl because Ned Kenny was puttering down the middle of Main Street on his motorised scooter. Outside Dermot Molloy's Quality Meats, Shep was enjoying a bone Dermot or one of his customers had tossed him to chew on. Paddy McNamara was swaying down the street in the direction of the pub, and winding the window down, she caught his off-key version of 'The Rose of Tralee' while Mrs Tattersall shook her head in disapproval, trundling past him with her trolley bag.

Imogen realised she was smiling at the comforting familiarity of the scene.

It dawned on her that she would find it hard to leave on Monday. As much as it pained her, maybe Ryan was right when he'd said she only thought she was a city girl. Because for whatever reason, this visit home had Emerald Bay getting under her skin.

The realisation was unsettling.

33

Imogen tried to relax in the wicker chair while waiting in the orangery, but it was impossible. Today, the citrussy aromas and misty panorama as a light drizzle set in weren't soothing, and she knew not even a triple gin and tonic would take the edge off. This jitteriness that had her swinging her crossed leg was nothing new. She experienced edginess every time a job concluded, and she was waiting for a client's final appraisal of their revamped spaces. It didn't matter that she was confident in her design ideas or that the client had been enthused. There was always the possibility they'd be unhappy with the end result.

This was the first chance she'd had to catch her breath since arriving at Benmore on the dot of eight that morning to be let in by a surly Francesca. The Italian woman had a streak of flour on her cheek even at that time of the morning and a yeasty smell clung to her, indicating she was making a fresh loaf of bread for the Leslies' return from their break in Dublin.

Despite fractious moments at the beginning of the week, to Imogen's relief, everything had fallen into place on the project at the last minute. The curtain makers had kept their word, and the van had skidded up outside the front door of Benmore shortly after 10 a.m. The new pelmet and curtains were now hung, and a courier had dropped off the replacement bedding. Imogen had busied herself making beds, smoothing quilts, arranging pillows, placing cushions, and artfully draping throw rugs. Then she'd moved on to arranging posies of dried flowers to be placed in vases on the various dressing tables before giving the carpet one last hoovering.

Ryan had done the Leslies proud with his workmanship in the bathroom, she'd thought as she stood in the doorway admiring the completed wet room. It was hard to believe that the flooring was bare timber boards and that the wall beams had been exposed a few short days ago. The result was an ode to the era of the Anglo-Irish house with its soft grey flooring, tiled shower and bath area, and gorgeous antique Victorian-style vanity. He'd also gone above and beyond the call of duty by saving her the job of wiping everything down, and the fixtures and fittings gleamed. She owed him a thank you when she next saw him. Just for a moment, she'd allowed herself to examine the peculiar feeling knowing she'd no longer see him every day left her with, but she chose to ignore what it might mean.

Sigrid and Matthew's car had purred up the driveway half an hour ago, and Imogen hastily straightened the recovered armchair in the guestroom closest to the bathroom before making her way downstairs to greet them.

The couple swept inside the house. Matthew, as per usual, was on a call and, with an absent-minded wave in her direction, headed for his study. Sigrid, annoyingly, declared she'd like to freshen up before viewing the finished design makeover and renovation. Imogen hadn't seen the need for this since she was as immaculately presented as ever, despite having sat in a car for hours. Still and all, Sigrid was the boss, so she'd done as suggested and taken herself off to the orangery to wait for her.

Now, as footsteps clipped down the hall in her direction,

Imogen stopped jiggling her leg lest Sigrid think she needed to visit the jacks and dragged her eyes away from the vista outside.

'That's better,' the Swedish woman announced as she glided into the glassed-in space looking no different than she had a half hour ago.

'Did you have a nice time in Dublin?' Imogen mustered a smile.

'No, since you ask. We had an unexpected visitor.'

'Oh,' was all Imogen said, not wanting to pry.

'You might as well know.' Sigrid's lips tightened. 'Lachlan turned up at the apartment to tell us the wedding's off.'

Imogen's expression must have revealed how gobsmacked she was by this news because Sigrid said, 'If you knew Lachlan. You wouldn't be surprised.'

If only you knew, Imogen thought. 'Can I ask why?' she stammered.

'He's a dumskalle, that's why.'

Imogen hadn't heard Sigrid drop a Swedish word before, and she didn't know what it meant, but she had a pretty good idea it wasn't flattering.

'Victoria found a text on his phone, suggesting she wasn't the only woman in his life, and she called the whole thing off. Accordingly, Lachlan has attached himself to his brother, which happens every time he messes up. I have a good mind to send him your bill. All that work and what for? He's out there now trying to talk her around, but if she has any common sense, she won't change her mind.'

Alarm bells clanged. 'Sorry? What do you mean by out there now?'

'In the driveway. He'll stay here until he either moves back in with Victoria or sorts out a place in London.' Sigrid's top lip curled, suggesting this was a less-than-satisfactory arrangement.

Imogen's instinct was to run to put distance between herself and Benmore. It wasn't a happy house, and she'd no wish to see

Lachlan. But Sigrid was already saying, 'Shall we?' and moving back down the hall, giving her no choice but to follow.

Her hand rested lightly on the banister rail as she trailed up the stairs in Sigrid's wake, with her mind elsewhere. She was on autopilot, going through the motions of showing Sigrid each of the bedrooms and, finally, the bathroom. All the while, Sigrid, cool as a cucumber, was unreadable. Finally, stepping out of the bathroom and closing the door behind her, she said, 'You've done a superb job, Imogen. I am very happy.'

If this were happy, Imogen would hate to see her sad.

Sigrid was still speaking, 'I would like you to relay this to Ryan as well. His artwork is also fantastisk,' she said, dropping her second Swedish word. 'A house like this' – she made a sweeping gesture – 'is always in need of work. We'll certainly be using him again in the future.'

'I'll let him know,' Imogen said, jaw clenched, wanting to make a getaway. Hopefully in the interim Lachlan would have come inside and made himself scarce. But, instead of fleeing down the stairs like Cinderella leaving the ball, she exchanged pleasantries with Sigrid, waffling on about what a joy and privilege it had been to work on Benmore. Blah, blah, then, finally, she could take her leave knowing word of mouth via Sigrid of a job well done would be invaluable for snaring future jobs.

Sigrid saw her to the door but didn't linger to wave her off. Imogen didn't mind because relief surged seeing there was no sign of Lachlan. The door clicked shut behind her and she hurried toward her car.

'Imogen!'

Imogen froze, toying with jumping in her car and speeding away, sending up a spray of gravel, but that would be stupid. Besides, she needed to face the man who'd broken her heart once and for all. It was time for closure, she thought, not quite able to muster a grin at the dreaded turn of phrase as, turning, she faced a dishevelled Lachlan. He badly needed a shave, she thought, squaring up to him.

'Yes?' Her voice was strong as she soaked him up. What did she feel, seeing him laid low and vulnerable like so? To her surprise, she realised nothing inside her had stirred. He didn't matter; it was enlightening, empowering in fact, because he was no longer relevant to her life or happiness. It was as if he were an ant squashed underfoot.

'I wondered if you might be free for a drink?' He tossed his head to flick his hair out of his eyes and then rubbed at the stubble prickling his chin before carrying on, 'Listen, Imogen, I understand you not responding to my message when I was here last week. It was presumptuous of me to think you'd drop everything to catch up on old times. We got off on the wrong foot.' He gave her a boyish grin. 'Do you think we could start over?'

God, he was unbelievable, Imogen thought, wondering how many women had had their hearts trampled on after falling for that smile of his over the years.

'Er, Victoria's no longer on the scene,' he added, as if his engagement being broken was no more than an afterthought. 'And I'd love to catch up properly.'

Imogen didn't have to think about her response. 'No. I'm sorry, Lachlan, I don't have time for a drink, so I suggest you find someone else to lick your wounds with.'

She tossed her hair over her shoulder and left him standing with his mouth agape to get in her car. Then, revving the engine, she cranked up Justin and drove away from Benmore without a backwards glance.

Lachlan Leslie was ancient history.

34

Imogen's phone bleeped as she reached the edge of the village later that Friday afternoon, and she suspected it would be her father texting yet again with an update on Hannah and the twins. Her instincts were right she saw once she'd pulled over, only this time he had an ETA for their arrival. They should be pulling up outside the Shamrock within the half hour. Ava and Grace had flown into Cork airport from London, and Hannah had picked them up to drive them home. She felt a bubble of excitement at the thought of seeing her sisters, whom she'd not caught up with properly since Christmas. No doubt they'd all be bickering in no time, but that was part and parcel of being a family. It didn't mean anything, she thought, indicating and pulling out onto the road.

Nev was due later tonight. She'd mentioned casually over dinner the other night that he was a few years older than her. Shannon's dinner had gone down the wrong way, hearing 'a few', but Imogen, once she'd slapped her sister on the back a tad harder than necessary, had kept her eyes on her parents, waiting for their reaction. Dad had mumbled something about 'What's a

few years' as he concentrated on spearing an extra potato off
Shannon's plate when Nora wasn't looking. Nora meanwhile
launched into a story about how there were nearly ten years
between Dennis and Mags Donovan, and sure she'd never
heard a cross word between them.

'I tried,' Imogen told Fi when she rang her mid-week.

Nev had charm on his side, she thought, and it was a bonus
her mam was partial to George Clooney. So maybe it would be
OK. She'd told Ryan there was power in positive thought, and
she'd put her money where her mouth was, she decided as she
drove down Main Street. The local businesses had been busy
because in her absence green and orange bunting had been
strung across the street, replacing the usual pastel triangles. A
banner with Happy St Patrick's Day had also been hung. The
shop windows all shouted about St Patrick's Day's specials and
ran with a cohesive green theme. In the houses surrounding the
village, the shamrock decorations would be draped across
mantels, and she'd spied an inflatable leprechaun in the window
of the Riordans' house. Perhaps she should ask if she could
borrow that and prop it up next to Lorcan?

There was a parking spot outside the Irish shop, and she
whipped into it, eager to get her costume fitting over and done
with so she could get home.

Isla's Irish Shop was a wonderland of souvenir tat, she
thought stepping inside and observing the twirly stand full of
fridge magnets. Isla was doing the hard sell on the couple
admiring a jigsaw puzzle with a map of Ireland on the box.
They'd have hours of fun piecing Ireland back together and
reliving their trip simultaneously, Isla was saying. Then, picking
up a bottle of Baileys and a box of Butler's chocolates, she
suggested they add a taste of Ireland to the mix as well. The
couple left five minutes later carrying an enormous shopping
bag.

Isla turned the sign in the door to *closed* behind them. 'Sorry about that, Imogen, but the customer always comes first.'

'Of course.'

'I hung your costume up out the back. Stocks are low,' she muttered, trooping out to her storeroom area to fetch it.

Imogen idly picked up a pottery mug with a sheep on it, wondering who would want to drink their morning tea or coffee out of it while she waited.

'Breakages must be paid for,' Isla trilled.

Imogen, not having heard Isla's return, fumbled the mug before hastily returning it to the shelf. She focused on the garment the shopkeeper was holding up.

'You can try it on in here,' Isla bossed, hanging the costume up in the curtained fitting room.

'Thanks.' Imogen entered the cubicle and pulled the curtain across. Her phone signalled a text, and a glance revealed her sisters were home. *Good*, she thought, undressing quickly and slipping into the white shirt. The green waistcoat with black trim was a snug fit. So far, so good. Then, attaching the bow tie, she unhooked the belt, wondering where the trousers or skirt were. 'Feck,' she whispered as it dawned on her that the belt was a skirt.

Jaysus wept. It barely covered her arse, she realised, having wiggled into it. 'Isla, it doesn't fit. It's far too short!'

'C'mere to me now, and let's have a look.' Isla didn't muck about, ripping the curtain open to find Imogen desperately tugging at the hem of the scrap of fabric.

'Sure, didn't they always wear short skirts to play the tennis? Just wear a pair of frilly green knickers underneath it and you'll be grand.'

What tennis had to do with a leprechaun outfit, and one designed to be titillating, was a mystery to Imogen. 'I can't wear this – I'll look like I'm touting for business on Main Street, Isla.'

But, even as she said it, Imogen knew she was wasting her breath because Isla Mullins hadn't been named Emerald Bay's businesswoman of the year three years on the trot by being a pushover.

Imogen exited the shop a short while later carrying a brown paper parcel in her arms, with a shiny green hat complete with gold buckle and elastic to secure it under her chin. Isla's instructions to assemble with the rest of the parade participants in the Shamrock's car park at 10 a.m. sharp in the morning were ringing in her ears.

The beer garden was deserted, and the car park quiet as she pulled in. A spark of excitement flared as she spotted Hannah's old rust bucket parked up. Families throughout Ireland would be getting ready for the big day tomorrow, she supposed, shaking her head at all the bee propaganda stickers decorating the back window of her sister's car. She nosed her coupe in a safe distance from her sister's and proceeded to unload her car. Then with her hands full and her chin resting on the hat, Imogen made her way to the back door. Rattling it was a juggling act, and she was annoyed to find it locked again. She'd have to have a word with Mam or Nan, whichever of them was the culprit. Probably Nan, she decided. No doubt there'd been a spate of burglaries on *Fair City*. Kitty Kelly took her favourite soap very seriously.

Rather than faff with her keys, Imogen stepped over to the pub entrance, which Mr Sheedy was exiting. He held the door for her, and thanking him, she stepped inside the pub. Her mam leapt out in front of her, making her jump.

'Jaysus, Mam. What's going on with you leaping out at me like that?'

'I've got a surprise for you.' Nora's face was shining.

Imogen glanced about. There was no sign of her sisters or

father in here. They were probably in the kitchen tucking into a treat Nan had whipped up. Dad would be making the most of Mam being through here, Imogen thought, amused, picturing him scoffing down his own mam's baking. She waved over at Chloe manning the bar, calling out a hello.

'I'm sorry to disappoint you, but I already know the girls are home. Dad's been keeping me updated on the half-hour since they left Cork. You know what he's like and, besides, you can't miss Hannah's car with all its stickers. What's for dinner, by the way? I'm starved.' The appetite that had deserted her at lunchtime had returned with a vengeance.

'Never mind that. Give me those there, and then close your eyes.' Nora took the leprechaun clobber off her and waited for her to do as she said.

'Why?'

'Would you do as I ask? You don't need to know the why's and wherewithal's.'

'Mam, I don't like surprises.'

'Sure, everybody likes surprises.'

'Not me.' Nevertheless, Imogen reluctantly did as she was told, allowing her mam to lead her to the kitchen. She was longing for the surprise to be food-related, given she could chew her own arm off about now.

The kitchen was quiet, apart from a running tap.

'Mind how you go, Imogen. You nearly trod on poor Napoleon's tail then.'

'Where've they all gone?' Nora asked. 'Don't even think about opening your eyes, Imogen.'

'Upstairs,' Liam replied, his mouth sounding suspiciously full.

'They were desperate to say hello to Napoleon,' Kitty added. 'But he must have been asleep on one of the chairs here because he's just appeared. Imogen, I'm filling the kettle to top the pot up.'

'Thanks, Nan. Is there baking on the table?' She didn't dare open her eyes.

'Scones with jam and cream,' Liam answered on his mother's behalf.

'Pass me one, would you, Dad.'

'All right. Hold out your hand now.'

Imogen did so, and once her dad had placed one of the scones Kitty Kelly prided herself on being light as air in her palm, she navigated it toward her mouth. Then she heard her mam bellow up the stairs that the cat was down here and Imogen was home. Thunderous footfalls and giggles followed.

'Are her eyes shut, Mam?'

Imogen recognised Grace's voice and grinned in that direction.

'They are,' Nora shouted back.

Kissy noises and mewling followed as they reached the kitchen, signalling that one of her sisters had picked up Napoleon.

'Right, so I'll do the count to three.' Nora began, 'One, two, three!'

'Surprise!' a cacophony of voices shouted.

Imogen blinked her eyes open and saw the grinning faces of her sisters and mam. Dad and Nan were looking pleased with themselves too. Napoleon was rubbing his furry face against Ava's, purring loudly, and Imogen briefly toyed with reminding her that he licked his bottom. She and Napoleon had come to an understanding, but some things were off the table, like the face rubbing. There was no point spoiling the moment, she decided.

Hannah still had her dreadlocks. The surprise wasn't her having cut the horrible things off then. There'd be no face rubbing there either because goodness knew what lived amongst them.

As for Ava, she was still rocking her sixties Marrakech vibe, while Grace was sporting the chin-length bob she'd had her hair cut into before Christmas, along with a preppy chic outfit. Nothing different there.

But hang on a minute. Standing at the entrance was a face she hadn't expected to see.

35

'James!' Imogen shrieked. Her mouth dropped open with one hundred and one questions as her sister's American beau stepped forward to squeeze her. He smelled of peppermint, Imogen thought as she face-planted against his chest.

'Great to see you again, Imogen,' he said, releasing her with a broad smile on his handsome face. Imogen's unconscious appraisal took in his casual travel-friendly clothing that didn't crumple. 'It's great to see all of you. It really is.'

'I told you you'd be surprised, and you've got cream all over your top lip there, Imogen – don't get it on James's shirt.' Nora hustled in with a tissue, and Imogen wiped her mouth.

'Did you know he was coming, Mam?'

'I did.' Nora looked pleased with herself. 'I made a bogus booking for Room 5 to throw your father off the scent because James wanted to surprise Shannon. So only myself and Kitty knew.'

Liam made rumblings about secretive women.

Nora ignored him. 'I told the girls yesterday because James flew into Cork on the same connection as Ava and Grace and they all travelled here together. It worked out grand.'

Imogen's second question had been answered, and she took stock of the Bostonian who'd won her sister Shannon's heart. Besides bloodshot eyes, understandable after his flight, not to mention the time spent in Hannah's old jalopy of a car and the lack of Gore-Tex or chinos, he looked no different from when she'd seen him at Christmas.

Hannah butted in. 'It's a whirlwind visit James is after having – he travels back Monday with the rest of us. We had a good chat on the drive here about airline CO_2 emissions, didn't we, James?'

James nodded.

'You want to have heard her, Imo. Poor James. And all the while she was carrying on, her car was belching out more fumes than the A380,' Grace stated.

Imogen was well able to picture the scene.

'I've written to Elon Musk about the possibility of Tesla sponsorship,' Hannah informed Grace, then, swinging back to Imogen, said, 'James has agreed to take a stack of Feed the World with Bees brochures back with him to put in the clinic where he works, haven't you, James?'

At the mention of bees, Imogen resolved to get in her sister's ear later about the danger run she was after doing every time she entered or exited the pub.

'I have.' James looked like he didn't dare say otherwise.

Ava gave him a sympathetic look as Napoleon nuzzled. She was looking a little thin on it, Imogen thought, now that she took a second look at the younger of the twins. Then she brought herself up sharp; worrying about what they were eating was Nan's department.

'Hannah, don't be mithering the poor lad,' Liam tutted, moving on from his slight at being excluded from the secret visit. He winked at James. 'Us lads have got to stick together. This one would have you taking a hive home with you if she thought you could get it through Customs.'

James laughed, but Hannah wasn't finished.

'Thanks again for the petrol money,' she said to him. And then, catching her mam glaring at her, added, 'What? I work for a non-profit. So until Elon comes through with the Tesla, there's no shame in asking for petrol money. And youse two can flick me a tenner each and all,' she said to Ava and Grace, palm outstretched.

Another question occurred to Imogen. 'Where is Shannon?'

'I asked her to call through Kilticaneel on her way home to pick up a leg of lamb. I didn't want her showing up before this lot arrived and spoiling the surprise,' Nora said.

'Would you believe Dermot Molloy's had a sign in the window to say they'd sold out of lamb since midday?' Kitty shook her head.

'I'm exploring the vegan lifestyle,' Hannah said.

'Well, you can explore it elsewhere.' Kitty's tone was clipped. 'It's the roast lamb we're after having. You can't have St Patrick's Day without a roast lamb with all the trimmings.'

'That's true enough, Mam,' Liam agreed, then rolling his sleeve up, checked his watch. 'I have an ETA for Shannon of five thirty-five. Someone needs to go and keep watch.'

Grace volunteered, and Imogen gave her a proper hello hug before she disappeared to the bar.

'Knock twice on the door as soon as she walks in, Grace,' Liam called after her.

'I will.'

Imogen greeted Hannah and Ava with a warm embrace, keeping a wide berth from Hannah's dreadlocks. Napoleon had jumped down from Ava's arm, tired of all the fuss, but had sat down at James's feet to allow him to pet him briefly before sauntering upstairs for some peace.

'Mam, Nan, what's for dinner?' Imogen asked, helping herself to another scone. It was alarming to note nothing was bubbling away on the cooker top, nor were the usual delicious aromas emanating from the Aga.

'I've rung an order through to the chipper,' Liam answered, referring to the Egans' fish shop where you could order the catch of the day fried in golden batter, served with a wedge of lemon and a scoop of chips. Rory Egan, a widower, was in partnership with his sister and her family. They ran the fish-and-chip side of the business.

Hannah pulled a face on Ava's behalf. 'We should boycott Egans'.'

'Don't be silly,' Ava said. 'Shane and I broke up ages ago and we've both moved on. Our relationship is ancient history. Besides, he only catches the fish, he doesn't fry it.'

'He hasn't. Moved on, I mean,' Hannah said, then she and Imogen chimed, 'And he's still a fishy, eejitty arse.'

Ava giggled.

'Stop your complaining. You're lucky it's not the bread and dripping for your supper like it was in my day,' Kitty tutted.

'Your nan's the reason we're having fish and chips,' Liam said, glee at the prospect of the greasy treat plain to see on his face. 'None of us has been allowed near the kitchen today, your mam included. Not while she perfects this secret entry of hers for tomorrow's bake-off. Only Shannon's in the know because she was the chief taster – which wasn't right, given I'm her son. 'Tis a serious business. I nearly got my head caught in the door earlier when she slammed it shut on me.'

'I told you not to be poking that big lug of yours in to see what I was up to. And you're right: when you're up against the likes of Eileen Carroll in the Great Emerald Bay Bake-Off, 'tis a serious business.'

'How does it work then, Nan?' Ava asked, curious. 'Will it be like the television programme with the tent and the cookers inside? Are any celebrity chefs coming to Emerald Bay to do the judging?'

'No. Sure, it was Rita Quigley who wanted to call the cake bake competition that. Her being a bookshop owner and all, she thought it was a clever play on words. It's going to run the same way it always does, with entrants dropping their cake along to the stall the church committee's set up and paying their entry fee.'

'I applied to the committee to be nominated as one of the business owners in the judging, but it was deemed nepotism, and Dermot Molloy pipped me at the post.'

'Just as well, or you'd have had to stand down, anyway,' Nora muttered. 'The cake-sampling isn't part of your dietary plan.'

'Dermot, Sergeant Badger and Father Seamus are the three judges, and they'll announce the winner at the pub in the evening. Imogen, tell your sisters the exciting news.'

'What exciting news, Nan?'

'The date auction your fella is after holding.'

'Nev?' Ava asked.

'No.'

'You've not found yourself a new fella already, have you?' Hannah asked. 'We didn't even get the chance to meet Nev. That was to be the highlight of my weekend. That and you being back in Emerald Bay, James,' she added, for once not wanting to offend.

'Thanks a million, Nan. Ryan O'Malley is not my fella.'

'Ryan O'Malley, the bra-pinger from school?' Ava and Hannah dueted.

'I remember you harping on about him back in the day,' Hannah added.

'He's not guilty. It was Declan Horan who was the culprit. Ryan's the builder at Benmore House. That's what Nan meant by "your fella", so you can all just settle down. Nev is very much on the scene, and he'll be here by nine o'clock tonight.' She wished she felt as confident about his arrival as she sounded.

She snuck a sideways glance at her father. As for the sleeping arrangements, she'd not broached that, but she was assuming Shannon and James would be sharing Room 5, so it was only fair she and Nev got some space to themselves too. She wasn't sure Dad would see it like that when he finally met him, and her toes curled inside her shoes, visualising the introduction. She'd cross that bridge when she came to it.

'Well, now that's sorted, where should James hide?' Ava asked.

'But I want to hear more about the date auction,' Hannah said.

'There'll be time for catching up on all the shenanigans later. James, g'won out to the hall there. You can jump out and shout surprise when Shannon walks in.' Nora jiggled up and down at the prospect. She was a little over-excited by all the surprises.

'Are you sure that's a good idea, Mam?' Hannah asked. 'You know what Shannon's like.'

'Hannah.' Nora's voice held a warning note as her eyes flitted to James, still engaged in tickling Napoleon behind the ear.

Imogen didn't know why Mam bothered. Hannah had no filter.

Hannah turned to Ava and Imogen. 'Remember how we thought it was gas to hide in the wardrobe and burst out when she was lying on her bed mooning over her JT poster? She used to wet her knickers in fright.'

The three sisters giggled over the shared memory while Nora looked thunderous.

James tactfully took himself off into the hall as a double knock sounded on the door, and the Kelly family held their breath in anticipation.

36

'Surprise!'

'Oh, oh, oh!' Shannon's hands steepled in front of her mouth, and she crossed her legs, blinking rapidly before looking to her family for confirmation she wasn't seeing things.

'I hope you don't mind me just showing up like this,' James said, grinning at her reaction and knowing full well that, once the shock wore off, she'd be over the moon he was here.

Grace, holding Shannon's shopping bag in one hand and steering her into the kitchen with the other, said, 'It's him, Shan. He's really here.'

Shannon burst into tears.

'She's like her mam,' Liam said to James. 'She cries when she's happy and sad. Sometimes she even cries when she's angry. I'm warning you now, son, it's very confusing.'

'These are happy tears.' Shannon sniffed. 'C'mere to me now, you!'

James didn't need to be asked twice, and Shannon threw her arms around his neck, standing up on tippy-toes to kiss him.

A collective 'Aah,' went round the kitchen.

'Get a room, you two,' Hannah said as the kiss went on and on.

Liam cleared his throat, and Kitty began banging a pot on the worktop that was waiting to be dried and put away.

'Aren't you going to clear your throat noisily then, Mam?' Imogen asked.

'No. I'm liberally minded, like the French.'

Imogen gave her mam an 'if you say so' look, thinking she could name many times Nora Kelly had been anything but liberally minded.

Imogen did the throat-clearing on her mam's behalf, watching with a pang as the reunited couple finally broke apart but their eyes remained locked on one another's. What James and Shannon had was something special, she thought, trying to recall if Nev looked at her with that same besottedness. Lustiness, yes, but she didn't like the question mark that hovered over besotted.

Liam announced he was off to pick up the fish and chips, and there was a mass scraping of chairs as they all piled in around the table, talking over the top of one another.

Hannah pressed Imogen about Ryan's date auction tomorrow, and seeing Grace's blank stare, Imogen started at the beginning and ended with: 'I don't know much about it other than it's being held here at the pub in the evening, and the highest bidder wins a dinner date with Ryan O'Malley.'

Grace's eyebrows shot up almost as high as her fringe, which sat well above her eyebrows these days in keeping with the 1920s-style bob she favoured.

'Don't say it.' Imogen held her hand up. 'It wasn't Ryan. It was Declan Horan.'

Nora, overhearing their conversation, said, 'Cathal Gallagher will run the auction. He always does the auctions.'

She said this as though auctions were a dime a dozen in Emerald Bay, Imogen thought.

'I want to know about Ryan's package.'

'Hannah!' Imogen spluttered.

'Mind out of the gutter, Imo. I meant, is it just a date he's after auctioning?'

'It's dinner, not a date,' Imogen replied, embarrassed at jumping to the wrong conclusion.

'And...?'

'Hannah Kelly, it's you who has your mind in the gutter. Your sister said *dinner*. Not dinner *and* dessert. Imogen, tell her about you taking part in the parade,' Nora bossed.

Hannah immediately dropped the date auction topic. She, along with Grace and Ava, was all ears as Imogen reluctantly explained how she'd come to be Ms Leprechaun in tomorrow's parade.

'Put the costume on for us now,' Ava urged when Imogen finished, having slunk down in her seat at the memory of the ridiculous outfit.

'Yeah, give us a giggle.' Hannah backed her up.

'Come on, Imo, make the three-hour drive in Hannah's tin can on wheels worth our while,' Grace said.

'No. Youse can wait until tomorrow.'

Imogen was spared the ribbing about riding alongside Lorcan McGrath by their dad bowling in with an enormous vinegary-smelling, grease-soaked parcel which was plonked in the middle of the table.

Kitty fetched a loaf of bread while Nora took the tomato sauce and butter from the fridge.

'Tuck in, everyone,' Liam said, unwrapping the bundle.

There was no need for plates with corners of the paper torn off on which to place the golden-crusted, flaky white fish and a handful of chips.

James observed slices of white bread being buttered before chips were placed on them. Then a dollop of sauce was squeezed on the chips before the bread was folded into a chip sandwich.

'Mm, chip butties are the best,' Hannah mumbled through her mouthful, egging him on to try one.

Shannon made James one up and passed it to him. He didn't even mind when she'd a big blob of sauce in the corner of her mouth, Imogen thought, as he took it from her as though her sister had just given him her hand in marriage.

Once the initial frenzy had settled down and everyone was assured that they wouldn't miss out, conversation resumed. James had them smiling as he told them Maeve was a firm favourite with his beagle, Harry, because she always slipped him tasty treats under the table. 'She's been a tonic for my mom, for all of us,' he added.

There were greasy-lipped smiles around the table, picturing the little Irish woman they were all fond of winning the droopy-eared dog over with clandestine treats.

'So come on, Imogen, tell us about your Nev,' Liam said, savouring the last of his fish. 'I won't make a good first impression if all I know about him when he arrives is that he does something or other in property.'

It was more Nev's first impression on him that she was worried about, Imogen thought, swallowing her mouthful. 'He's a developer, Dad, for big-scale projects in Ireland and overseas.'

'And, what else?'

'Er, well, he plays golf.'

'I'd have thought bowls would have been more his thing,' Hannah said.

Imogen shot her a fierce scowl, and Kitty looked at Hannah and then Imogen sharply.

'Golf? Well now.' Liam mulled this over, Hannah's remark having sailed right over the top of his head.

Imogen could see her father stashing golf away as common

ground to chat about, because he'd been known to play socially now and again.

This was her chance, Imogen thought. *Just say it!* 'Nev's a little older than me.'

'You said.' Liam was more interested in licking his fingers now after finishing his fish.

Imogen could feel her sisters all watching, waiting for her to fess up to the considerable age gap. She knew Hannah would be itching to make another smart crack. But, as it happened, it was Kitty Kelly who spoke up.

'Listen, Imogen, I might not be a woman of the world like you girls all fancy yourselves, but I do know this about men. They start out all full of vim and vigour and can't keep their hands off you.'

'Mam.' Liam left his fingers alone, frowning at her. 'Too much information.'

'How else do you think you got here, son? You weren't just a twinkle in your father's eye. And it's Imogen I'm talking to, not you, so cover your ears. Now then, where was I?'

'Er, vim and vigour, Nan,' Imogen supplied.

'Right. Well, after that comes the middle years when they start to get opinionated. They've something to say about everything – and don't get them started on the politics because it's only them who knows how to fix things and get the country running properly. The politicians aren't worth the salt they were born with. And, then, oh dear, they retire.' Kitty's expression was grim. 'That's when they discover the dust buster. Every time you turn around, they're lurking behind you with their equipment. You can't so much as nibble on a digestive biscuit without them bending down to suck up the crumbs. They'd drive you potty, so they would. Just ask any woman over seventy in the village. They'll tell you the same. It's a conspiracy, so.'

'The Dust Buster Conspiracy,' Grace said in a movie shorts voice, making them laugh.

'But what I'm saying to you now, Imogen, is' – Kitty's blue eyes held Imogen's – 'you've plenty of time for the opinions and the dust buster.'

Nothing got past Nan, Imogen thought, the fish and chips feeling like a brick sitting in the pit of her stomach.

It wasn't long until they were sitting back in their seats groaning about being full. With the clean-up being a matter of bunching up the paper and putting it in the bin, Kitty and Nora hurried off to the Vigil Mass, not wanting to be late, having secured promises that no one would miss the St Patrick's Day Mass tomorrow. Liam took over from Chloe behind the bar and the others decided to mosey through to the pub as well.

Imogen sat down to join her siblings by the fire, sipping on the Baileys nip, which sounded like a good idea, but the Irish cream liqueur wasn't mingling all that well with her greasy supper.

Freya, who'd joined them, was saying something, and she tried to concentrate on the conversation bouncing back and forth, but her mind was on Nev. He'd be here in a few short hours, and the excitement at seeing him bubbled up and overrode her anxiety. A phone was ringing, she realised, seeing the others patting down their pockets before she realised it was hers.

It was Nev.

'Excuse me,' she muttered, on tenterhooks he hadn't broken down in some tiny village where the only garage wouldn't be open again until Monday.

'Nev, give me a sec, I can hardly hear you,' she said, answering and moving out the door to the quiet of the beer garden. The night air was cool, and stars twinkled overhead as she sat at the picnic table.

'That's better. Is everything all right?'

'Imogen, listen, plans have changed—'

A chill settled over Imogen. She was dimly aware of a scuffling in the shrubs before a round shape scuttled across the grass. A hedgehog. She didn't say anything, but her grip on the phone tightened.

'Imogen?'

'I'm here. And what do you mean, plans have changed?'

'Deborah's here with me.'

'She's not coming with you to Emerald Bay?' Surely she wasn't in the car with him? Imogen couldn't keep the horror from her voice at the thought of a weekend spent in close quarters with Deb the Diva, his eldest daughter.

'No. I've not left. I'm still in Dublin.'

'What?' He should have got on the road hours ago, and why hadn't he said, 'not left *yet*'?

Silence stretched, and when Nev said, 'Listen, Imogen,' his tone was formal, an indication Deborah could hear what was being said. 'Debbie's in a state. She was in a car accident today.'

'Is she hurt?' Imogen gasped, clutching the phone tightly. She might not like the woman, but she'd not wish her any harm.

'Not seriously. A few bumps, bruises and a suspected concussion, but the real issue is that the Garda is involved because she was over the limit.'

'Did she hurt anyone else?' Imogen tried to get a clearer picture of what had happened.

'No, thank God. It was a lamppost she ran into. She'd been out for lunch and had a couple of glasses of wine with her meal. The car's in a worse state than she is.'

Typical Deb the Diva, ringing her father to bail her out, Imogen thought, her shoulders tensing at having to suppress vocalising this to Nev. Why was he so blind when it came to his daughters? I mean, drinking and driving? Deborah didn't think of anyone but herself and, given her propensity for drama, she was probably carrying on as though she'd broken bones and was facing life imprisonment. She hoped the Gardai would throw the book at her, and she'd have to face the consequences because Nev might hold a lot of sway with certain important people in Dublin, but his influence didn't extend to Ireland's police force. It would be a long overdue lesson learned for her.

'So you're at home?' she probed further. A woman's voice in the background, not Deborah's, made her clench her teeth together so hard they hurt. 'Who's that?' she managed to spit out.

Nev hesitated. 'Er, it's Genevieve. Debbie wanted her mother with her.'

'Well, let her sort it out, then, Nev.' Imogen's voice was verging on shrill. 'I'm sorry she's had an accident, but Deborah chose to get behind the wheel when she'd been drinking, and besides, from what you've told me, it was hours ago, and she wasn't badly hurt. So it isn't your problem to fix. She's a grown woman of twenty-six, for feck's sake. She doesn't need you and Genevieve carrying on as if she's a teenager.'

'Imogen, you're not being fair. The poor girl's in terrible shock.' His voice was clipped in that officious manner she'd heard him use when business deals weren't going his way. 'You're not a parent. If you were, you'd understand why I can't leave her.'

Imogen's eyes widened in disbelief, and she held her free hand to her cheek as though she'd just been slapped because that was what his words had felt like. 'I can't believe you just said that to me. I might not be a mammy, but at least I have some fecking common sense!'

'Christ, Imogen, I don't need this.'

'You don't need this?'

'Listen, I'll call you back. John, my solicitor, has just arrived to talk us through what happens next.'

'This was supposed to be our weekend, Nev,' Imogen said weakly, her shoulders sagging.

'I can't do this now, Imogen, but I'll do my best to get away tomorrow. I'll be with you in two ticks, John. Go on through. The girls are in the living room.'

'You can't do this to me. To us, Nev.'

'It's not about us.'

How could he not see that his decision to put Deborah first had everything to do with them? 'Don't call me back, and don't bother coming tomorrow either.' Her eyes filled with hot salty tears. She was done.

She could picture the tic at the corner of Nev's mouth. It flared when he was harried.

'I can't believe how selfish you're being. Try and understand.'

'But that's just it, Nev. I do understand. Please. I mean it. Don't call me back, and don't come to Emerald Bay. We're finished.'

She ended the call and switched her phone off.

37

Imogen didn't know how long she'd been sitting on the wooden bench trying to process her conversation with Nev. The darkness had settled over her like a blanket, though, and the hedgehog was still mooching about. She was getting chilled, thanks to the gentle night mist beginning to fall. The longer she'd sat there stewing, the more she'd realised that what she'd said about not wanting Nev to come to Emerald Bay hadn't been said in anger but with resignation and finality.

Nev had urged her to understand his predicament over the phone, and she had understood with an enlightening clarity that no matter what he promised her, she would always come last. It was a placement she no longer wanted. He wasn't solely to blame for the way things had worked out; that was down to them both, because he wasn't the one who'd changed. While his priorities were crystal clear, she was no longer sure what hers even were. Something had shifted inside her since she'd come home to Emerald Bay. The hard shell she'd built around herself had begun to crack.

That things were over between her and Nev hurt, of course it did, but it didn't hurt as much as she thought it probably should. She'd sat here poking and prodding at their relationship, concluding that a part of her had known this was how it would end. And not just because this morning's stars had alluded to plans going awry, but because Imogen knew she deserved more. Most of all, though, she wanted a man who put a silly smile on her face whenever she thought about him. And that man wasn't Nev. All of which didn't mean hot, angry tears hadn't burned as she thought about the good times they'd shared. They'd had plenty of those, but there had also been plenty of drama too. Her shoulders were heavy with sadness at how things had finished so abruptly. Because finished they had. Of that, she was sure.

Girlish giggling sounded on the road at the bottom of the garden, and young voices grew louder, along with the clink of bottles. The resident teen brigade was out and about and up to no good then, Imogen surmised. It was Friday night, after all.

The back door to the pub opened, galvanising her into action, and she wiped under her eyes, ensuring her mascara hadn't streaked or she'd have to face the Spanish Inquisition when she headed inside. How long had she been out here, she wondered.

'Is that you, Imogen?' a familiar voice called out, striking a match across flint as she made her way over the damp grass to where a flame briefly illuminated Evan Kennedy's face as he lit his smoke.

'It is, Evan. I needed a bit of quiet for a phone call. I'm heading inside now. Enjoy your smoke.'

'I will, ta, and hold your horses there while I get the door for you. Nobody can say Evan Kennedy's not a gentleman.'

'Thanks.' She managed a smile as she stepped back into the pub and the smell of ale and crisps washed over her. Her sisters and Freya were still fireside and hadn't noticed her come back in. Good, she thought, hoping to keep it that way, not wanting to explain what had happened with Nev, aware they'd have loads to say on the subject. There was no getting out of telling her dad though, or he'd jump to conclusions and think Nev had had a traffic accident when he didn't show up, convinced the journey from Dublin was perilous. So, with this in mind, she slunk toward the bar, not wanting to give any nosy punters a glimpse of her bloodshot eyes.

Her dad was down the far end of the bar, running a cloth over the wooden top as he chatted to Enda and Ned. Imogen waved out. He excused himself, looking about expectantly as he walked toward her.

'Is he here then, your man, Nevin?'

'No, Dad. Nev's not coming.' Imogen gripped the wooden bar, having decided the sooner she got to the point, the sooner she could go and hole up in her bedroom.

'What do you mean, not coming? Has there been a traffic jam?'

'No, Dad, nothing like that.'

'Sure, I was looking forward to telling him about the hole-in-one I scored on the Kilticaneel course.'

'That was mini-golf. And something came up, Nev can't make it.' Imogen's manner didn't invite debate. There'd be time for explaining he wouldn't ever be coming later.

Liam then eyed her with a bemused expression, which turned to a frown noticing her red-rimmed eyes. Imogen thought he might press her for more detail, but he knew her well enough to know when not to push things and let the matter drop.

'I'm heading upstairs, Dad, and if anyone asks, I've gone to get an early night before tomorrow's parade.' Imogen didn't wait for him to reply as she nodded hello at Rita Quigley coming out of the ladies before opening the door to the kitchen and breathing a sigh of relief at having escaped an interrogation. She closed the door, leaning back against the solid wooden slab, squeezing her eyes shut briefly before pushing off and heading for the stairs.

The landing was in darkness, and flicking the light on, she paused outside the twins' and Hannah's door, thinking she should move her things down the hall to her and Shannon's old room. There were so many things she wanted to write in Lottie's book, too, but she decided, like her clothes, that could wait.

Napoleon was asleep on Shannon's pillow, and he raised his head at the intrusion, yellow eyes glaring at her.

'Sorry,' Imogen mumbled, kicking her shoes off, drawing the curtains and flopping on her bed. 'It's been a shite night.'

Napoleon stretched, arching his back, and jumped down, leaving a gentle indent and pile of hair behind on the pillow. He meandered across the floor space between her bed and Shannon's, pausing to stretch once more before sitting down and eyeballing Imogen for an invitation to join her. She patted the duvet. 'Come on then.' He leapt up and turned around three times before snuggling in next to her with a snuffling sigh.

Imogen sneezed twice, but neither she nor Napoleon minded, and she stroked the purring bundle. She wondered if he knew she was upset, because his presence was comforting.

A soft tapping on the door saw her eyes fly open. Had she drifted off? A glance at her phone revealed half an hour had passed since she'd come upstairs. So yes, she must have. Breaking up was exhausting.

The tapping sounded again. There was no point telling whoever it was to go away because that would set alarm bells ringing, and reinforcements would be sent for. All four sisters would wind up drilling her as to what was wrong. It was much safer to say, 'Come in.' Besides, it was probably just Shannon wanting to grab something.

The door creaked open and, to her surprise, Nan was

standing there with a mug in her hand. 'I brought you a cup of tea with extra sugar.'

Imogen pulled herself up to sit, rubbing at her eyes. 'Thanks, Nan.' Dad must have sent her up to check on her, she thought, grateful for the tea because her throat was dry, feeling raw from tears shed and unshed.

Kitty put the tea down on the bedside table and made no move to leave, waiting while Imogen sipped at the sweet, milky brew.

'Now then, Imogen Kate Kelly,' Kitty said after a few seconds had passed. 'Why don't you tell me what's going on?' She didn't wait for an invitation as she sat heavily on the bed, causing Napoleon to mewl his indignation.

Imogen's bottom lip wobbled dangerously, and she put the mug down lest she spill what was left of the tea. Then, taking a shuddery breath, she poured her heart out to her nan about Nev.

When Imogen hiccupped out dramatically that she didn't know what she wanted anymore, Kitty leaned over and tucked her hair behind her ears, chucking her under the chin.

'Good care takes the head off bad luck.' Her blue eyes, surrounded by creases of a life filled with love, and laughter, smiled down at her granddaughter.

They were wise eyes, Imogen thought, even if she hadn't a clue what Nan was on about. She had an old Irish proverb for most occasions. They were nonsensical until you'd had the chance to turn them over in your mind, then you'd realise that they made sense in a mad way. But, whatever it meant, she felt better for confiding in her. 'Thanks, Nan. You won't tell Dad, will you? About the age difference, I mean. There's no point. Not now it's finished between Nev and me, and you know what he's like. He'll only go on.'

Kitty tapped the side of her nose. 'It's between you and me.

Fairy promise.' Then she clenched her freckled hand, holding her little finger out in invitation to Imogen.

Imogen's face reflected warmth as she remembered doing the same thing with Ryan a week ago. A calmness filled her as she linked her little finger through her nan's, and they shook on it as they used to when she was a girl.

She'd always been able to share things with Nan, knowing it would stay between them. It made her sad to remember when she'd stopped confiding in her. The secrets had started the summer she spent with Lachlan, but that was part and parcel of growing up. Still and all, sometimes it was nice to feel once again like that little girl whose Nan could make everything all right with a shake of their pinkies.

Untwining their fingers, Kitty's eyes lit up with an unmistakable twinkle as she asked, 'Will you come downstairs? Ryan O'Malley was asking after you earlier.'

Imogen's stomach flipped, and she wanted to ask, 'Really? What did you tell him?' But she didn't dare risk encouraging her nan down this track because the innuendo was clear. Subtle, Kitty Kelly was not; a trait passed down the line to Hannah. So instead, she said, 'Don't even go there. Sure, I've just finished telling you my heart is aching, and you're already lining up the next fella.'

'I've got a feeling that ache you're on about isn't anything that cup of tea there won't mend. And don't think I haven't noticed how your face lights up like Galway at Christmastime whenever Ryan's name is mentioned.'

'It doesn't,' Imogen was quick to toss back.

Kitty stood up, her knees clicking. 'It does. Sure, you're like a Cheshire cat grinning. You're doing it now, so.'

Imogen made a concerted effort to place her lips in a flat straight line as Nan made her way to the door. 'Well, if I can't tempt you downstairs, I'll leave you and your friend to it.'

'Thanks for the tea and listening like, Nan, but I'm going to get an early night.'

Kitty opened the door.

'Nan?'

'Hmm?'

'I love you.'

Kitty, never one for grand expressions of love, gave an unintelligible reply which Imogen took to be 'I love you too' before closing the door behind her.

'And you are imagining things where Ryan O'Malley is concerned!' she flung at the shut door.

There was no reply.

Imogen returned to petting Napoleon, thinking about what Nan had said. Did she smile whenever she heard Ryan's name?

Don't go there, Imogen, she told herself just as sternly as she'd told her nan.

ST PATRICK'S DAY

May the leprechauns dance over your bed and bring you sweet dreams.

— *IRISH BLESSING FOR ST PATRICK'S DAY*

38

Imogen took the stairs two at a time and burst into the kitchen. A Ms Leprechaun in a microscopic mini who desperately needed coffee.

'Sweet Mother of Divine!' Nora Kelly crossed herself, catching sight of her daughter.

''Tis a lovely belt you're wearing there,' Liam Kelly said, mopping the last of his egg yolk up with his toast.

Hannah, Grace and Ava were goggle-eyed, taking in the green apparition that had materialised before them. True to form, Hannah began laughing first, setting her sisters off.

'Are those my green tights?' Shannon asked, dragging her eyes away from James to inspect her sister's outfit. James seized the opportunity to scrape up the remains of the enormous fry-up Nora had placed in front of him with the emphasis on *son* as she told him to, 'Enjoy your full Irish there, son.'

They were Shannon's tights because Imogen wasn't about to waste good money on green tights when a pair was going begging in her sister's second drawer. But she wasn't admitting to anything.

'I can see what you had for breakfast.' Kitty frowned.

'I haven't had breakfast, Nan.' Imogen had forgotten to set her alarm and had slept in. She'd only woken because her mam had knocked on her door and said, 'Aren't you supposed to be in the car park out the back for ten o'clock?' That was at nine thirty. Imogen had never moved so fast in her life. Napoleon went flying as she flung the covers off the bed and stampeded toward the bathroom, which was occupied. Thinking on her feet, she'd shouted a bribe through the door, telling Grace if she got out of the bathroom right that minute she could have free spraying rights over her Versace Dylan Blue eau de parfum for the entire weekend. Her sister had emerged from the bathroom with soap suds still in her hair, wrapped in a towel. She'd left the water running for Imogen, who pushed her aside, slammed the door and jumped under the jets. The tights had taken some wriggling and jiggling to get into, but she'd pulled them up, thrown the rest of the ridiculous costume on, and now here she was. A leprechaun with minimal make-up and bad hair. She thought the hat was a blessing in that respect, adjusting the elastic under her chin because it was beginning to pinch.

'And whose fault is that?' Kitty tsked, pouring Imogen a cup of tea and pressing a piece of buttered toast into her hand. 'You've never been one to bounce out of bed with the birds. Now, get that down you. You've a busy morning ahead representing the Kelly family in the parade.'

'If she's representing the Shamrock Inn, then the general public will wonder what sort of establishment we're running here,' Liam mumbled.

Imogen, who thought coffee would have been better, gulped her tea. So much for treading lightly around her. She thought they must all know by now that Nev wasn't coming. Perhaps Nan had told them not to bring it up, knowing she'd no time for dwelling on things this morning, not with the parade of shame looming. She'd have hated having them all tiptoeing around her anyway, but they could leave off with the bad leprechaun jokes, she thought, trying to ignore her sisters, who kept sending each other off into fresh bouts of hysterics.

'Why did the leprechaun stand on the potato?' Hannah asked between snorts.

'To stop himself from falling in the stew,' Ava howled.

James looked bewildered and leaned into Shannon. 'I don't get it.'

She shrugged. 'Nothing to get. It's a stupid joke, like "Why are so many leprechauns gardeners?"'

'Why?' James asked.

'Because they're green-thumbed.'

James grinned. 'I get that one, but I still don't get the potato joke.'

'Would you all shut up?' Imogen said, banging down her empty mug and brushing the crumbs off her green vest before heading out the door. It was fifteen minutes until showtime by her watch.

'Don't forget midday Mass,' Nora called.

'Don't ladder my tights!' Shannon's voice wafted after her.

No, they definitely weren't treating her with kid gloves this morning, Imogen thought, stepping outside feeling disgruntled. Sure, a little concern for her well-being would have been nice. If it were Shannon, they'd all be subjected to Celine Dion or Whitney Houston for hours on end, but she wore her clothes, hair and make-up like a coat of armour. It protected her. How could she expect her family to be aware of the seismic changes she'd undergone since coming home?

So much had happened in the short time she'd be back in Emerald Bay. Seeing Lachlan, and being catapulted back to the emotions of her sixteen-year-old self. The realisation last night that it was over with Nev and, if she delved a little deeper, there was that moment down at the bay with Ryan too. She'd thought he was about to kiss her and, if he had, she knew she would have kissed him back. What did that mean?

All of it had carved great big chinks in that armour. She felt raw and exposed, not just because the plain black sensible knickers she'd pulled on over top of the green tights were on display either.

Imogen didn't feel like the same person who'd ridden into Emerald Bay on the back of a mobility scooter under a fortnight ago.

The sky was grey, but there were promising patches of blue beginning to appear, and it wasn't raining, which was the main thing.

She chased all thoughts of Nev away and joined the motley crew milling about the car park, no longer feeling completely ridiculous, given the state of the rest of the participants.

Imogen had found her people.

A frown creased her forehead seeing Dermot Molloy's young apprentice butcher being tended to by the St John's medic. It was too early in the day for dehydration or sunstroke and the like, both of which were highly unlikely to occur in Emerald Bay on St Patrick's Day anyway. And there was never any issue with the locals staying hydrated. As for sunshine, well, even if it appeared, it was hardly likely to be a scorcher. So, what had happened?

'Two bee stings,' Isla Mullins informed her, appearing seemingly out of thin air with a basket full of sweets. 'Both on the arm, but he's not allergic, so he'll be grand.'

Imogen took in Isla's headband with its twin shamrocks quivering like insect antennae on top of her head. She was wearing an oversized sweatshirt that came halfway down her thighs. She must bring it out for occasions like this, Imogen thought. It advertised Isla's Irish Shop on the front, and a giant green shamrock was on the back. She was wearing black leggings and shoes with green bows on them.

'Are you listening to me, Imogen?'

Had she been speaking? Imogen nodded, having decided Isla looked like an Irish version of Minnie Mouse.

'You're to portion these sweets out. Don't go throwing great big handfuls out to the crowds at the start of the parade only to find you've none left before you're even halfway up Main Street. We don't want you getting mobbed now. Things can turn on a dime at these sorts of events.'

Crowds? It wasn't the Dublin parade they were taking part in. As it was, a good portion of the residents of Emerald Bay were here in the car park, eager to advertise their wares with a splash of green tinsel for free.

'And be careful where you throw those sweets. They're hard-boiled, and you don't want to be taking someone's eye out with an orange barley sugar. I asked the Gallaghers to donate the wrapped fruit chews, but they weren't playing ball. So those there are obviously the ones that don't sell in the shop.'

Imogen took the basket of sweets and hooked it over her arm without comment, then deciding she needed a sugar hit, helped herself to a red one.

'And don't be eating them all yourself either.' Isla pinched a green one, then took a step back and surveyed Imogen. 'Now that I'm seeing you in the cold light of day, that skirt is on the short side.' She sighed. 'Well, we can't do much about that now, but if you drop anything, don't be bending over to pick it up.'

Imogen unwrapped her sweet with a groan while Isla's eyes drifted in the direction of the park. 'Right, so. I'm heading over to see if yer Mr Whippy man's arrived.'

The power of being chairperson for the church committee had gone to the woman's head, Imogen thought, pleased to see her go. A scan of the car park revealed no sign of Lorcan yet. Her stars had said to expect the unexpected today, and crossing her fingers, she wished for his tractor to have broken down. That way she could hop in the passenger seat of Dermot Molloy's van instead, which would be a much more dignified way to take part in the parade. The village's resident butcher had been put in charge of the sounds, judging by the loudspeaker attached to the van's roof. She looked to where Dermot was giving his children instructions.

The little Molloys, whose faces were painted white with a green and orange stripe down either side, were wearing green T-shirts with Dermot Molloy's Quality Meats screen-printed across the front. They each had a basket similar to Imogen's, and she sidled closer to see what they'd be handing out because it didn't look like free slices of the luncheon meat.

'Would you like one, Imogen?' Dermot asked, picking up on her curiosity and plucking a slip of paper from the smallest Molloy's basket.

Imogen glanced at it and thanked him for the 10 per cent discount on mince for one week only but passed it back. 'That's very generous of you, Dermot, but I've nowhere to put it.' She gestured to her costume.

Dermot coughed, his cheeks turned pink, and he dipped his head in a different direction. 'Did you cop a load of Niall Heneghan over there?'

A leather-clad man was sitting astride a gleaming Harley Davidson. Green streamers were attached to the handlebars. What was written on his helmet? Imogen wondered. Squinting, she tried to read it.

'Don't let hay fever get you down,' she read out loud, and then, as the motorcyclist lifted his visor, she saw it really was Emerald Bay's staid pharmacist. Well, well, well. She'd never have picked Niall Heneghan as having a wild side. He waved at someone, and a hush fell over the gathered group as Sandy from *Grease*, the saucy version at the end of the film, sashayed toward him. But no, wait a minute... Imogen blinked twice to be sure she wasn't seeing things.

Nuala McCarthy, Heneghan Pharmacy's assistant, had

discarded her sensible white uniform and flat-soled shoes to morph into a stiletto-heel-wearing vixen.

Imogen was holding her breath and fancied all the parade participants were doing the same, waiting to see if this would be the moment when life emulated art. Would Niall Heneghan finally see Nuala, whom everybody knew was in love with the widowed pharmacist, properly?

Her breath huffed out disappointedly, hearing him ask Nuala whether she'd remembered to put yesterday's shop order through before they closed for the day.

She turned her attention to Carmel's Colleens instead. They were chattering excitedly amongst themselves in between practising their fancy footwork.

Sweet Jaysus, Imogen thought. Could they not have invested in decent sports bras for the support? It was eyewatering. And, whoever gave Carmel a whistle had unleashed a curly-wigged monster.

Rita Quigley had a roll of Sellotape and was tearing pieces off with her bare teeth to stick bits of green tinsel back onto the trailer on which the new entrants from Emerald Bay's school were all sitting cross-legged with novelty green sunglasses on. They were dressed in green-and-white striped onesies, each with either an orange or green balloon. They looked like miniature prisoner escapees.

Imogen loitered, waiting for Lorcan while Carmel and her whistle began to move the parade participants onto the road. She supposed if Lorcan were a no-show, she'd have to walk down Main Street tossing out her sweets.

Nev.

His name sounded as clearly in her head as though she'd spoken it out loud, bringing her up short. This was the first opportunity she'd had to think about him properly since opening her eyes this morning. Last night, sniffing in the darkness with a tissue bunched under her nose, their relationship had played over in her head like scenes from a film. The good, the bad and the ugly. She'd heard her family trooping upstairs and going through their bedtime rituals, and all the while, her hand rested on Napoleon. The Persian didn't seem bothered that Shannon had abandoned him for her American paramour in Room 5, and she was grateful for the company. She'd kept her phone switched off, even though she knew Nev would be preoccupied looking after Deb the Diva. Besides, even if he did try to call her, there was nothing more to say.

She pictured his daughters' smug exchange when they figured out their father was all theirs again. The usual churning she felt when thinking about the gruesome threesome had been replaced by overwhelming relief. They were no longer her problem.

Imogen's last conscious thought before slipping into sleep was whether she'd regret her insistence that Nev did not come to Emerald Bay in the morning. There'd been no time to switch her phone back on and check whether he'd left messages trying to change her mind before she left. Her phone was still sitting on the bedside table because there was no room for it on her person. Did she care whether he'd rung, one way or the other? Aside from a slight bruising to the ego, should he not try to talk her around at least once? The answer was no.

She wasn't second-guessing her decision, because she'd made the right call. It was finished between them.

A rumbling noise sounded, pulling her back to the here and now. If she thought her morning couldn't get any worse, she was wrong. Lorcan McGrath had just pulled up looking like he'd emerged from a cave after six months' hibernation as he perched atop a belching beast from the previous century.

Why couldn't he have ridden his John Deere into town? she thought, stalking over, and as she attempted and failed to gracefully climb aboard the old steam traction engine, she wondered why he couldn't have showered for the occasion.

Lorcan gave her a blackened tooth grin, and she gripped the side of the seat as Carmel Brady gave a piercing whistle. A blast of tinny Riverdance music blared out of the loudspeakers on Dermot Molloy's van, and as Carmel's Colleens began to jig, they were off.

39

Imogen was amazed to find she was enjoying herself. All thoughts of Nev and relationships ending were swept away because the happy atmosphere of villagers lining Main Street waving miniature Irish flags was contagious. The excitement on the children's faces as she pelted them with sweets made her light-up inside. She was also breathing through her mouth, which helped where Lachlan was concerned. As for Emerald Bay's bachelor farmer, he was in his element on the old machine, huffing and puffing along. It put her in mind of an old children's story 'The Little Engine that Could' with the *I think I can* mantra.

'Imogen, smile,' Hannah shouted out from the sidelines. She was holding her phone up, as were Grace and Ava, loving every minute of freezing their sister on film for all time.

Imogen's finger twitched, but she'd spied a photographer from the *Kilticaneel Star* in the crowd, and she had no wish to be splayed across the front page under the heading *When Leprechauns Turn Feral*. So instead, she aimed and fired three times, scoring a triple bull's eye as the sweets bounced off her sister's heads.

'Don't forget your dear old dad, Imogen!' Liam waved out, receiving a jab from Nora, who was now beaming proudly at her daughter despite her earlier horror at Imogen's outfit. A star attraction in the parade.

A little way ahead, Imogen saw Ryan, and her smile widened as she locked eyes with him, and before she knew what she was doing, she was half standing on her seat, waving over vigorously. Cinderella in her carriage. But then, hearing a child shout, 'I can see that leprechaun lady's knickers, Mam!' She sat down and got back to her sweet-flinging.

The parade was over too soon, but there was more fun to come. Mr Whippy was rumoured to have rolled into the village and could be found in the park. The stalls would be set up there now, including the Great Emerald Bay Bake-Off tent, and the church committee had organised games like sack races and an egg-and-spoon race for the younger children.

First things first, though, there was Mass to be attended.

Lorcan dropped Imogen back where he'd picked her up earlier, keeping the old traction engine running the whole time because he said if it stopped, it wouldn't start again.

'Would you happen to have any female friends in Dublin city who might be interested in a simpler life with an eligible farmer, Imogen?' Lorcan enquired overtop of the steam engine.

'Er, no. Sorry, Lorcan, no one springs to mind, but I'll keep an ear open for you.' Imogen was eager for the off. 'Thanks for the ride.'

'Well, if you think of someone, be sure to mention I can offer a cottage, twenty hectares of land and a flock of Scottish blackfaces.'

'I will, Lorcan. I'll be seeing you now.' Imogen scrambled off the machinery, thinking he could also offer onion breath and a permanent manure odour.

He doffed his cap at her and rumbled on his way.

Imogen kept a wary eye out for bees as she strode toward

the Shamrock, eager to get out of her leprechaun get-up. Her dad was manning the bar, where a few locals were already setting up camp for the day. He had green tinsel draped around his neck, worn like a scarf he'd tossed over his shoulder, and the buttons strained on the green shirt reserved for the seventeenth of March. The pub had been decorated with green and white balloons, and a Happy St Patrick's Day banner was draped above the bar. 'Any sweets left in that basket of yours?' he asked hopefully as he poured a pint of Guinness.

'No.' She held out the basket to show him they were all gone. 'Dad, did you know Dermot Molloy's apprentice was after getting stung this morning out by the beer garden? Twice on the arm. You need to do something about those hives.'

Liam frowned and, turning off the tap, placed the Guinness on the settling tray. He'd top it up after two minutes. 'I'll think on it, Imogen.'

It would have to do, Imogen thought. 'I'm going to get changed, then go and check out the craic in the park. Sure, it's gorgeous out now the sun's shining. I wonder how the cake judging is going?' She was curious to meet Freya's Oisin and wouldn't mind a 99 ice-cream cone herself. Her mouth watered at the thought of the creamy treat with its mini Flake chocolate bar.

'All will be revealed tonight, Imogen. And if you know what's good for you, you'll get yourself changed and off to the Mass, not the park.'

Father Seamus had the Feast of St Patrick Mass celebrating Ireland's patron saint down to forty-five minutes and not a second longer. So by the time the villagers emerged blinking in the sunlight, there was enough time to duck home, put the dinner on and nip back to the park where the rest of the day's festivities were underway.

Carmel's Colleens were doing an impromptu performance in the park when Imogen reached the grassy area where people milled about the various tents.

'Doesn't Lorna's hair look bonny?' Mrs Rae, Father Seamus's housekeeper, watching the Colleens Riverdance display, said to Imogen as she paused alongside her.

Imogen checked out Lorna McCready, whose curls bobbed up and down along with everything else.

'She's after telling me she didn't even need the big curly wig thanks to the lovely perm Nessie's after doing for her,' Mrs Rae added, patting her hair wishfully.

Imogen fancied she could feel the ground shaking beneath her feet as she made her way to where Shannon was loitering by Freya's stall, showcasing some of her jewellery and art from the gallery. She didn't recognise a man chatting to the photographer from the *Kilticaneel Star* and gesturing to the paintings on display. But, given that he wasn't wearing green like the rest, she should pinch him. It was tradition, after all.

There was no sign of James, and she zeroed in on her sister, helping herself to a tuft of the candyfloss Shannon was stuffing down.

'Get your own,' Shannon said, hugging the bag to her chest. Then she had a change of heart and held the bag of pink spun sugar out to her.

Imogen eyed her suspiciously.

'G'won, help yourself.' Shannon shook the bag.

'Are you feeling sorry for me because Nev's not coming?'

'No.'

Shannon always got two pink spots on her cheeks when she fibbed, which were visible beneath the shamrocks painted on each of them. Imogen decided to milk her sister's goodwill, nonetheless. She pulled a tuft out and enjoyed the sweetness of the sugar crystalising on her tongue. 'I've broken things off with him.'

'Nan said. Are you OK?'

'Surprisingly so.'

'Here she is, Emerald Bay's Ms Leprechaun. Great job, Imogen.' James appeared with a pottle of hot chips doused in sauce. He had matching shamrocks on his cheeks and was wearing a green sweater that Imogen suspected belonged to their dad because of how big it was on him. 'I've sent the video of the parade through to my mom and Maeve. They'll love it.'

'It was fun,' Imogen said, surprised to hear herself say so. 'And it was for a good cause.' She made them laugh by relaying Lorcan's vital statistics as she asked James to keep an ear to the ground once he returned home in case he heard of any woman who might be looking for a lifestyle change in rural Ireland.

James offered her a chip, and she took one, blowing on it. 'Don't let Nan catch you with those or the candy floss, because she'll go mad if she thinks you're spoiling your appetite.'

Shannon nodded that this was the case as she took the last tuft from the bag. 'Remember, it's early dinner,' she said, making short work of the sweet treat. 'We're all expected to be seated around the table for five o'clock before things get going in the pub later. It's tradition.'

'I like the Kelly family traditions. Especially when they involve your mam and nan's cooking,' James replied.

With their arms linked, Grace and Ava wandered past. They waved over but were clearly on a mission to check out the cupcakes with green icing the church committee ladies were selling. Hannah was doing a walkabout handing out Feed the World with Bees pamphlets.

'Is that your fella then?' Imogen leaned past Shannon to speak to Freya, who was making puppy dog eyes at the long-haired, sensitive-looking soul she'd thought about pinching. She decided he was good-looking if you liked the arty sort, wincing as she caught snippets of his conversation. He was banding about phrases like 'hidden pain' and 'unleashing joy' as he described his painting style. She added pretentious arty sort to her appraisal.

'Yes, that's Oisin.'

She might as well have said, 'Yes, that's God,' Imogen thought, seeing Shannon roll her eyes.

He looked over, hearing his name, and Freya gave him a dreamy smile. Imogen held her hand up in a hi. Then said, 'Well, I'm off to get a 99.' She left them chatting and paused to admire the cakes inside the tent with the chalkboard sign outside it: Great Emerald Bay Bake-Off.

Dermot Molloy, Sergeant Badger and Father Seamus were sampling the offerings and looked to be in seventh heaven. It wouldn't be an easy job, Imogen thought, wondering how on earth they'd decide on a winner. And not wanting to be in their shoes if it wasn't Kitty Kelly!

40

Liam rang the bell usually reserved for last orders and then shouted over the hubbub in the shoulder-to-shoulder bar, 'C'mon, you lot. Quieten down now. Sergeant Badger's about to announce the winner of this year's Great Emerald Bay Bake-Off, with all proceeds going to the O'Malley family.'

The publican's announcement set off a round of clapping, foot stamping and whistling. Liam waited until it died down before setting off a fresh round by adding that the auction for dinner with Emerald Bay's very own eligible bachelor builder would be held after that.

Ryan raised his glass to acknowledge the cheer that went up, and Imogen, clearing the tables that were filling up again as fast as she carted the glasses away, craned her neck for a glimpse. She'd not had a chance to talk to him, surrounded as he was by his sisters behaving like bodyguards, along with Posh and Becks.

Liam signalled that it was over to Sergeant Badger now, and the Gardai officer standing at the bar cleared his throat. He was flanked by Dermot Molloy, holding the silver and bronze rosettes, while Father Seamus clasped the small trophy cup destined for the winner's mantel.

There was strength in numbers, Imogen thought, pausing to listen. Then, standing on her toes, she sought out Kitty Kelly, knowing she'd be on tenterhooks waiting to hear who'd won.

Kitty was standing alongside her rival, Eileen Carroll. Catching her eye, Imogen mouthed, 'Good luck, Nan.' She'd tried a sliver of her lemon cake when the judging was completed, and she might be biased, but it was divine. Seeing Kitty and Eileen eye each other like it was pistols drawn at dawn as the third-place winner was announced made her smile. Whoever didn't take home a rosette or the trophy would sulk for a week, and then they'd clink teacups with the winner and begin putting the world to rights over tea in the Silver Spoon.

Carmel Brady pushed her way to the bar to accept bronze for her chocolate Guinness cake. Imogen thought the tears and the thank-you speech was a little reminiscent of Gwyneth Paltrow at the Oscars and wished she'd get on with it. But at last, with her rosette pinned to her cardigan, she rejoined her family and friends.

The tension ramped as Sergeant Badger said, 'And second place is awarded to Francesca Andretti for her melt in the mouth Pan di Spagna.'

The Leslies' housekeeper looked unimpressed as she accepted her silver rosette and declined to make a speech.

Then Dermot Molloy did a drum roll with his hands on the bar top. Imogen held her breath, waiting for the announcement as the judges stood in line like the Three Stooges, and Sergeant Badger said, 'First off, we'd like to say the standard of baking we sampled today was world-class.'

Father Seamus nodded, saying, 'It was. It was a tough call picking a winner.'

Dermot added, 'And, after much deliberation and taste testing, we've come to a unanimous verdict.'

'Not guilty!' one of the Nolan brothers shouted out. Laughter rippled through the pub.

Sergeant Badger looked toward Eileen and Kitty. 'This year, we have a tie. The winners of the Great Emerald Bay Bake-Off are Eileen Carroll for her outstanding sweet-and-tart apple cake and Kitty Kelly's zesty lemon cake.'

The two women tripped over themselves trying to reach the trophy first. A skirmish ensued, with Sergeant Badger having a quiet word which resulted in Kitty and Eileen each holding one of the trophy's handles and raising it aloft together.

Imogen began breathing again. Once they'd worked through the fine points of time-sharing the trophy, Eileen and her nan would be grand. No doubt they'd be swapping recipes before the evening was done, she thought as she carried the glasses she'd collected to the bar.

'Congratulations, Nan, Eileen!' she shouted over to where they were preening at all the pats on the back.

Once the glasses were stacked in the dishwasher, deciding she wanted a decent view of Ryan's auction, she wedged in beside Shannon and James, who'd bagged a prime spot at the table closest to the business end of the pub.

Cathal Gallagher stepped up as the auctioneer, and Ryan joined him, looking uncomfortable. However, as the catcalls began, he struck a few body-building poses in good humour to much cheering and ballyhooing. He'd dressed for the occasion in a flannel shirt and worn-in jeans slinging his tool belt around his hips for good measure.

Imogen, realising she was grinning like an idiot, tried to temper her smile as Cathal kicked things off.

'How much is an evening spent with such a fine specimen of man worth, ladies and gents? Come on now, don't be shy. And we're talking a three-course meal courtesy of the Wild Swan in Kilticaneel, who've sponsored Ryan O'Malley's fundraising effort for his family. Young Thom, a birthday present for your gran, perhaps? Or Trena, you were still single, last I heard.'

Trena went red and giggled loudly as her friends all nudged her, batting their false lashes, saying things like, 'I wouldn't say no if I weren't with Pat,' and 'I wouldn't kick him out of bed.'

Imogen felt her hackles rise. He wasn't a piece of meat!

Ryan was taking the ribbing in good form, egging the girls on by blowing a kiss in their direction.

'Who's going to get the bidding underway? Do I hear ten euros?'

Imogen looked about and saw a hand shoot up at the back of the pub, but she couldn't see who it belonged to. Then 'Fifteen' was called.

'Thom, you'll be your gran's favourite. Fifteen euros, do I hear twenty?'

A woman's voice called out, 'Twenty-five.'

'Twenty-five, do I hear thirty euros?'

Imogen was in danger of whiplash as the bidding suddenly took off, thanks to another woman joining the mix. There was something familiar about her and, leaning over to Shannon, she asked, 'Who's your woman there with the caterpillar eyebrows, displaying all the skin?'

'That's Orla. Remember her from school? She was always in trouble for rolling her skirt up at the waist to make it shorter.'

Obvious Orla! Of course, Imogen thought as the bidding reached two hundred euros. She could hardly believe it.

Orla and Trena were pushing the price up, because the next thing Cathal announced was, 'Three hundred euros! Ladies and gents, do I have three hundred and five?'

Shannon squealed. 'This is so exciting!'

A hush had fallen over the pub as they waited to see if Trena would outbid Orla.

Trena's friends had their phones out and were busy checking their bank balances to see if they could loan her any cash, but after a moment's conflab, Trena shook her head. 'I'm out.'

'Going once,' Cathal called, clapping his hands as the bids slowed, then stopped, leaving Orla in the lead. 'Last chance for a candlelit evening in the company of this beefcake you see here before you.'

Imogen's hand shot up. The only person who didn't look surprised was Kitty Kelly, who gave an approving nod.

Orla narrowed her eyes as past rivalries were remembered, and she upped the ante.

'Imo, are you sure you know what you're doing?' Shannon whispered.

'Three hundred and fifty,' Orla raised her hand.

Imogen raised her hand. 'Three hundred and sixty.'

Ryan's head spun from Orla to Imogen as the bids continued to rise, and you could have heard a pin drop in the pub.

Imogen was in the lead when the bidding hit five hundred euros, and Orla's sister said something in her ear. She must have been the voice of common sense because Orla, at last, lowered her hand.

The hammer came down with Imogen having just donated five hundred euros to the O'Malley family.

'You watch this space, Eileen. It's an investment Imogen's after making. An investment in her future, so it is,' Kitty said to Eileen as she joined in the clapping.

The adrenaline surge that had seen Imogen's hand continually rise was ebbing away, and she was overheating. 'I'm heading outside for some air.'

'I'm not surprised.' Shannon shook her head.

Imogen weaved her way out of the pub, receiving slaps on the back as she made for the back door.

The beer garden was nearly as noisy as the pub, but she found a quiet corner to gather her thoughts. It was an expensive meal she would be having at the Wild Swan. The food had better have improved since the last time she dined there, she thought, enjoying dusk's nippiness after the pub's stuffiness.

She avoided asking herself what had driven her on. The thought of Ryan spending an evening entertaining Orla, Trena, or anyone with romantic notions, had turned her into a woman possessed. It was a lucky escape she'd had at five hundred euros, because she would have kept going. But still, five hundred euros – it was a holiday, for feck's sake!

A hammer and a village, Fran the tea-leaf reader's words, swam about her head. It dawned on her then that the hammer signified Ryan. It was so obvious. He was a builder and a hammer was one of the tools of his trade. The hammer had just come down on her final bid too. As for the village, well, he belonged here in their small village of Emerald Bay. Had the leaves foreseen that she did too, with him?

41

Imogen didn't know how long she'd been standing in the Shamrock's beer garden. She was too lost in thought to hear the back door to the pub open over the shouts of laughter and chatter from the smattering of outside tables.

'I'm flattered you bid so much, but I won't hold you to it.'

Imogen whirled around at the sound of Ryan's voice. The air outside might have cooled pleasantly with the advent of the evening, but internally, she was a furnace. It crossed Imogen's mind that this was what her mam harped on about, although her body heat had nothing to do with a hot flash. In facing up to her simmering attraction toward Ryan, she'd fanned the slow-burning flicker into flames and didn't know what to do about it. All her usual bravado vanished in his presence now, and even though there was so much she wanted, no, that wasn't right, needed to say to him, the words alluded her. Instead, she gave a light shrug and said, 'Don't be silly. No one was twisting my arm. I bid, and I won. It's for a good cause. But you owe me a thank you for rescuing you from Obvious Orla.'

'Obvious Orla.' Ryan's face creased. 'First time I've heard

that. And thank you.' His black eyes pinned her searchingly, 'What are you smiling at?'

Jaysus, she was at it again. She must look a right eejit with her face breaking into an uncontrollable goofy grin whenever she thought about him, let alone stood this close to him. How would he react if she reached out and pulled him to her? If she were to snake her arms around the back of his neck and tilt her head, her lips ripe, ready— Stop it, Imogen!

Mirth shone back at her, and for one panicked moment, she wondered if he could read her mind. Then she remembered his question and desperately tried to straighten her features. 'Oh, nothing.'

'Well, I hope "nothing" continues to make you smile because I like how your eyes crinkle at the corners when you do.'

'You do?'

'Yeah, I do.' There was a softening in his expression.

Imogen's intake of breath was sharp, and she felt unsteady on her feet because she'd seen that look on his face before. The afternoon she'd confided in him down at the bay when he'd been about to kiss her. This time it would happen, and giddy anticipation welled up inside her.

The back door opening saw their heads jerk back and eyes blink slowly as though drugged.

'Allo, allo, what's going on here, then?' A tipsy Cathal Gallagher staggered out of the pub for a sly smoke, putting on his best Policeman Plod voice.

'Have you gone AWOL from the Bus Stop then, Cathal?' Imogen enquired, trying to smother her irritation at the corner shop owner's interruption.

Cathal swayed as he fished a packet of matches out of his pocket. 'Shush, don't be telling Brenda where I am now.'

Ryan took hold of her arm, pulling her away as Cathal

struck a match. 'Do you think your mam and dad could spare you for an hour?' he asked.

Imogen nodded, her skin goosey at his touch. She had four sisters who could help with clearing the tables. 'Why?'

He let her arm go and stuck his hand in his pocket to produce his keys, jingling them. 'I've somewhere I want to take you.'

'Where? The cashpoint? I'm good for it, you know.'

His broad shoulders shook as he replied, 'No. C'mon. You'll see when we get there.'

Intrigued, Imogen followed him across the lawn to his Hilux, clambering into the passenger seat and groaning as Bon Jovi blared out when he started the engine.

'Sorry,' Ryan's teeth gleamed white against the outdoorsy bronze of his skin and, turning the music down, he pulled out of the car park.

Main Street was deserted, with Emerald's Bay population squeezed into the Shamrock Inn. The green and orange bunting fluttered as they passed under it and headed away from the village.

Imogen sneaked a sidelong glance at Ryan. He was very focused on getting to wherever they were going, and they rode along in silence while she fidgeted in the seat next to him, unsure where to put herself. But finally, an understanding of where he was taking her dawned as he slowed, and then they bumped off the road into the area where she'd parked a week ago. Her mind swirled over all that had happened in the last seven days.

'You should have swung by your house to pick up Lulu,' Imogen said, thinking the little dog would have loved a seaside outing.

Ryan stilled the engine, looking at her in a way that made her tingle. 'Next time. Tonight, I don't want any wet-dog inter-ruptions. Shall we?' He had one hand on the handle, and

Imogen nodded, opening her door. A delicious shiver coursed through her at his choice of words. Curiosity jostled with anticipation as she climbed down from the Hilux.

The heat that had suffused her body disappeared as a stiff breeze whipped up from the ocean, and she wrapped her arms around herself, wishing he'd told her they were coming to the bay because she'd have grabbed a sweater. Ryan, noticing her stance, dropped an arm around her shoulder, and she let her arms fall to her sides, suddenly very glad she hadn't brought a warm top. He steered her toward the path, and she hoped his gesture was more than just chivalrous as feeling his body rubbing along next to hers as they kept pace, she trembled. It was so hard to concentrate on putting one foot in front of the other when she wanted him to stop and kiss her.

The coastal path was deserted, as was the bay, and their feet left prints in the damp sand. Neither of them said a word as they made for the rocks, seeking out the same flattish one they'd sat on the previous weekend.

Ryan was seemingly reluctant to move his arm away from Imogen's shoulder, and they laughed at the awkwardness of sitting down. The sea continued to roll in and out, shushing up pebbles and shells hypnotically as he said, 'There's something I've wanted to do since you punched me in the nose when we were kids.'

'Oh?' Imogen twisted around. She was facing him now, all her senses on high alert as she raised her eyes to his, wanting to read where this was headed.

He traced a finger down the side of her face, his touch melting her, and she felt the soft blonde hairs on her arm rise as he trapped her with his dark gaze. He cupped her chin gently with his hand tilting her face towards him.

'This.' He bent his head, holding her gaze as his lips sought hers.

The sea faded into insignificance, as did the distant seagull cries. Nothing mattered except Ryan and the feel of his lips soft, warm, insistent, and so perfectly right pressing against hers.

This felt like her very first kiss.

This kiss was a new beginning, and her hands reached out to clutch his shirt, the fabric bunching in them as she pulled him into her greedily. She could feel the heat of his chest and the beat of his heart through the flannelette material next to hers. His scent was both salty and musky. They were one, and she didn't want this ever to stop.

This was a kiss that proved him right.

She wasn't a city girl.

She was where she belonged.

Home.

A LETTER FROM MICHELLE VERNAL

Dear reader,

I want to say a huge thank you for choosing to read *New Beginnings in the Little Irish Village*. If you did enjoy it, and want to keep up to date with all my latest releases, just sign up at the following link. Your email address will never be shared and you can unsubscribe at any time.

www.bookouture.com/michelle-vernal

I love being transported to Ireland's Wild Atlantic Way when I write about the Kelly family, and I have a firm picture in my head of the village, the bay and the fishing harbour, along with the big house on the hill. With their lives and loves, the Kelly family come alive for me, as do the village's various characters, and I think we all know a Mrs Tattersall! I so enjoyed Imogen and Ryan's love story, and I firmly believe we all need happy endings like theirs.

Hmm, which sister's story will be next?

Years ago, I discovered and devoured Maeve Binchy's books. She made me feel I was there with her story characters, curled up in a cosy chat. That's how I hope the Kelly family stories make you feel.

I hope you loved *New Beginnings in the Little Irish Village*, and if you did, I would be very grateful if you could write a review. I'd love to hear what you think, and it makes such a difference helping new readers to discover one of my books for the first time.

I love hearing from my readers – you can get in touch on my Facebook page, through Twitter, Goodreads or my website.

Thanks,

Michelle Vernal

www.michellevernalbooks.com

 facebook.com/michellevernalnovelist
twitter.com/MichelleVernal

ACKNOWLEDGEMENTS

I was super lucky to meet my wonderful editor, Natasha Harding, in person last December at the Bookouture offices. It was a dream come true to visit their London office, be shown around and be taken for lunch to hash over plans for 2023. Natasha is always so positive and enthusiastic about my stories and has a knack for spotting what's needed to lift them to the next level. I am super fortunate to have her input.

I am also incredibly grateful to my fabulous publisher, Bookouture, and to have such a brilliant team on my side. You all work tirelessly to send the best possible complete book package in its different formats out into the world. Thank you to every one of you for your positivity, creativity and enthusiasm for the books.

Thank you, Kim, Noelle and Jess, for your tireless work promoting my stories.

Also, a big thank you to team Vernal. Paul, you are so supportive and work so hard. I love you and our boys, always and forever.

Printed in Great Britain
by Amazon